PRAISE FOR

D1539389

"The first of Martin's Mercenar... k-
ing a story filled with a large cas ...re
and heated love scenes. Martin showcases her talent for storytelling
as this fast-paced tale moves from one adventure to another at lightning speed ... readers longing for a good old-fashioned adventure
with empowered women will find much to enjoy."

—*RT Book Reviews*

"Appealing ... a solid thread of teamwork and family, provided by
the strong supporting cast of Ariana's fellow spies underlies the
romance between Ariana and Connor, creating a community that
will surely thrive as the series continues."

—*Publishers Weekly*

"Highlanders and spies come together to make the perfect match in
this Historical Romance read. *Highland Spy* by Madeline Martin sup-
plied a kick ass heroine and a troubled hero all in one page turning
adventure. Emphasis on kick ass... All in all, it was a fun story full of
intrigue, backstabbing, secret missions, and most important: a kitten."

—LampshadeReader

PRAISE FOR THE HIGHLANDER SERIES

"Readers will greatly admire Martin's ability to capture their attention with the combined allure of romance and the swift-moving
elements of suspense."

—*Publishers Weekly* on *Possession of a Highlander*

"Martin's Highlander series is filled with interesting characters and
is an enjoyable read."

—*RT Book Reviews*

"*Deception of a Highlander* is enchanting, adventurous and down-right
breathtaking!"

—Literary Junkie Extraordinaire

"An awesome story by a new author and one I looked forward to
reading again. A must read!"

—My Book Addiction Reviews on *Deception of a Highlander*

HIGHLAND
Ruse

MERCENARY MAIDENS - BOOK TWO

MADELINE
MARTIN

DIVERSIONBOOKS

Also by Madeline Martin

The Highlander Series
Deception of a Highlander
Possession of a Highlander
Enchantment of a Highlander

The Mercenary Maidens Series
Highland Spy
Highland Ruse

Diversion Books
A Division of Diversion Publishing Corp.
443 Park Avenue South, Suite 1008
New York, New York 10016
www.DiversionBooks.com

For more information, email info@diversionbooks.com

First Diversion Books edition November 2017
Print ISBN: 978-1-63576-157-3
eBook ISBN: 978-1-63576-156-6

LSIDB/1709

To my very own Mr. Awesome, John Somar,
who is everything a real hero should be.
Thank you for all your patience and kindness and love—you are
the final piece that makes this family completely whole.
I love you, and I love our wonderful life together.

Prologue

Delilah Canterbury had risen above her station. In fact, she'd just risen above every flat, mediocre note of her existence.

She sauntered down the wood-paneled hall toward the king's private room, following the same path she'd left that very morning. Her heart tapped against her ribs in an excited beat, impatient for everything to unfold.

Her victory.

The heavy silk of her dress rustled in the silence like an eager whisper. The gown had been costly enough to have fed her family for a month. Not that her parents had purchased it. They'd never be able to afford something so fine. Her aunt had called it a gift—one Delilah would reimburse as soon as she was able.

Perhaps the time to do so could be soon.

Delilah ducked her head and allowed herself a giddy smile behind her curtain of light brown hair before she knocked on the large wooden door.

Voices sounded on the other side, male voices—ones that determined which wars were fought, who became titled, who became wealthy. Her foot bounced silent and anxious against the thick carpet.

The door swung open to reveal a group of men bustling about the lavish room beyond. The king's personal chambers.

She knew exactly how they looked. The gold-threaded tapestries, the thick, velvet cushions, the massive bed.

A man stared at her with bored disinterest. Between the curls of his black wig and the crowding of his neck ruff, his face was barely more than a pair of squinty eyes over the stump of his bulbous nose.

"I'd like to see the king." Delilah hoped her tone came across as more sweet and flirtatious than the breathy-excited she felt.

The man's gaze swept down her once, then returned to her face. It had been a quick but thorough assessment, and his disapproval was tangible enough to heat her cheeks. She would ensure he showed her the respect she deserved when she'd spoken to James.

James.

How many people were actually allowed to address him so informally?

The man turned away and approached the king. James lifted his head, and his dark eyes found hers. She cast her gaze away, demure despite the warmth tingling up her spine.

When she'd first come to court, her mother had told her she'd never be anything more than a lady's maid, a poor relation given a job to assuage the cost of a mouth to feed back home. The discouragement hadn't dampened Delilah's anticipation to arrive at Hampton Court Palace. Not one bit. She'd always known she'd be something more—something great.

And now she would become the king's mistress.

She, the eighth child of fifteen. She, who'd not been married off like her other sisters. She, who had spent her entire life perfectly in the middle, perfectly ignored.

Delilah's mind raced with images of her and James, wearing the most luxurious clothing on an extraordinarily costly boat on the Thames. They laughed in the sunshine together and placed their heads against one another's as they read books, and—

"His Majesty will see you."

Her attention snapped from her dreams. But rather than flit away, the dreams curled deep in her heart where they stayed happy and safe.

The remaining few men in the room exited when she entered.

The idea of them clearing out—for her—made her blood run through her veins. She lifted her head a notch and regarded James with a coy grin.

They were alone.

The breath squeezed from her chest.

She bowed low in front of James and let her gaze lift to him before she rose. Last night he'd liked that. He'd caught her chin with his thumb and forefinger and whispered how eager he'd been to see her alone.

Now, however, James appeared unaffected.

He stared down at her over the slope of his nose, his mouth set in a hard line. He wore his ornate black hat atop a fine wig, but she'd seen him without both, when his hair was downy copper beneath her fingertips.

"I bid you good day, Your Majesty." Delilah rose and tucked her hands behind her back to tease him with the strain of her breasts against her bodice. "You needn't have cleared out the room on my account."

James tilted his head. "I thought it the best course in preserving your pride."

Delilah's confidence stumbled for the briefest of moments. "That was kind of you, Sire, but entirely unnecessary—"

"Yes, well, I'm a kind sovereign." His cold gaze did not reflect any such kindness. The subtle spice of his exotic perfume wafted toward her and brought back memories of the sweaty, frantic mash of their bodies.

It hadn't been entirely unpleasant, and she heard it got better over time. Such knowledge was heartening. Even now, the private place he'd claimed throbbed with the dull aching reminder of what she'd done.

What she'd given him.

"You were especially kind last night." Her cheeks flamed hot as the embers in the hearth, and the words felt foreign on her tongue. She offered him a pretty smile, the one she practiced in the mirror regularly.

James regarded her a moment before glancing away. "I was also especially libidinous last night, and you filled the role I needed quite well. It need not be repeated; however, I do appreciate your having consented."

Delilah stared at him dumbly. Her heart crumpled in her chest, but her mind refused to accept what her ears had heard.

Surely he hadn't meant...

"Is there something else?" Irritation played over his apathetic features. "Did you expect coin?"

He might as well have slapped her. "No, of course not. I came willingly. I thought..." Her body was on fire, and her throat clogged with the threat of tears. She would not cry. Not in front of him. "I thought you wanted me." Speaking was difficult around the tightness in her throat, but she forced the words out. "You said I was lovely."

A betraying tear rolled down her cheek before she could blink it away.

"Of course you're lovely." James gave an exasperated sigh. No, not James—the king. He was the king to her again. And he was staring at her as though he thought her daft. "Do you think I'd be with a homely woman?"

Delilah swallowed the sob trying to claw free from her throat.

The king touched her cheek. His palm was cold as ice and dry as parchment. "If anyone admonishes you for your absence the prior night, send them to me. I'll ensure you receive no punishment." There was a tether of patience to his tone. He clearly thought he was being kind.

He patted her head as if she were a child being placated. "Take a moment to settle yourself, then return to your duties."

His hand slipped from her hair, and he walked away. "I truly am sorry, Diane." He offered his apology like an afterthought and the door clicked closed behind him.

Delilah stared at the door through the cobweb of hair he'd inadvertently pulled over her face. The knot in her throat was unbearable now, burning, aching, tearing at her to give in to the pressure. "It's Delilah." Her voice croaked out into the quiet room and melted into the lush upholstery as if her words had never been spoken, had never existed.

As if she had never existed.

Delilah wrapped her arms around herself, but it did not ease the chill clutching at her heart and slithering into her gut.

All she'd wanted was to stand out, for once. To mean something. To be someone.

But she'd sacrificed too much.

Oh God, what had she done?

She'd offered up the one bit of treasure on her person, the only thing she might somehow manage to use in scraping a marriage at court. Without her maidenhead or a dowry to speak of, no man would want her. Especially when the king would not step forward to declare her his castoff.

She winced at the word "castoff."

But that's what she was now, wasn't she?

She gave in to the drawing squeeze at her heart. Her folded arms pushed to her stomach where a white-hot pain burned and curled into it, embracing it.

"You're not going to cry, are you?"

The feminine voice broke through Delilah's thoughts and shattered the intimately private moment with a bolt of fear.

A woman materialized from the shadows. Her pale blonde hair was pulled back from her face in a number of braids, and she wore a plain blue dress which made her pale eyes appear all the more so, like chips of ice. A bit of silky black ribbon had been tied around the woman's throat in a delicate bow—her only adornment.

Delilah had not seen her at court before.

The woman was disquieting in the masculine way she stood with her feet braced apart and her shoulders squared, overly confident and comfortable in her own obvious power.

And while it made Delilah suddenly sticky hot with shame over her grief, the tension in her throat abated. "I thought I was alone."

"Aren't you glad you're not?" the woman asked.

Delilah gave a choked laugh, a bubble of hysteria finally breaking the turbulent surface. "So that you could witness the single most humiliating moment of my life?"

Her throat clenched like a fist.

Perhaps she was going to cry. And she did wish she'd been alone. Never had she craved the small closet space she slept in more than now. True, she shared the cramped quarters with three other servants, but they would all be working, like she should be. She wanted the caress of silence on her ears and the freedom to loose her tears into the thin pillow on her bed.

"He's not worth it," the woman said.

"He's *the king*," Delilah countered.

"He's *a man*. And he's left you in a position no different than any other man would." The woman shrugged, as if this were some minor notion, as if it were not a life-crushing event.

Another emotion crept over Delilah's sorrow. It stiffened the slump of her back and shot energy through her slack limbs. Rage.

"You don't know," she hissed. "You don't know everything I've lost. And who are you, sneaking around the king's quarters? Are you a thief?"

"Sylvi." The woman inclined her head in the lazy, bowing way men were wont to do when acknowledging one another. "And he knows I'm here, but not to the same purpose as you." One blonde eyebrow lifted sardonically. "He just didn't know I stayed."

"And why did you?" Delilah asked through clenched teeth.

Sylvi approached her and Delilah stiffened. "Because I saw the look on his face when you arrived, and I saw all the hopes and dreams on yours and knew they were about to be crushed."

And so she'd stayed to watch. Like the men who enjoyed bear-baiting and dogs tearing apart exotic animals for sport.

Disgust roiled through Delilah and she turned from Sylvi, set on quitting the king's quarters for the quiet sanctity of her own room.

"I can help," Sylvi said.

Delilah kept walking, away from the woman who was too confident for her own good, away from the awful memories the room held.

Sylvi appeared beside her. "You don't have to be ruined, Delilah. Your life is not over."

The woman was close enough now that the delicate scent of leather prickled Delilah's awareness over the floral notes of her own perfume.

"Leave court," Sylvi said. "Come with me to Scotland. I'll teach you everything you need to know to be powerful. No one will care about your past, of what you have or don't. There is no judgment." The bow on her neck was decidedly out of place, a note of femininity on a woman who appeared anything but.

Had someone suggested earlier in the week that Delilah leave court, she would have called them mad. Coming to court had always been her dream, from the first moment she'd heard of the velvets and silks and balls and rich food—all a far cry better than the squat house she'd been crammed into with her overlarge family.

But now the idea of leaving court held appeal. To never see the king again, or worry who might whisper in the wake of her departure, or wonder if her aunt might discover her indiscretions—for surely Delilah would be sent back home in shame.

And she was not welcome at home. Another mouth to feed. Another body to clothe. Another person to scour coin from already bare coffers.

No, she had nowhere else to go.

"What would you teach me?" she asked. As if she had a choice.

Sylvi's gaze narrowed. "To fight, to defend yourself, to be strong enough on your own. I'll teach you to become a spy."

Spy.

The word jolted through Delilah. Her, a spy. It sounded dangerous.

Her heart thrummed with a renewed vigor.

It sounded…exciting.

It wasn't a boring life, married to a base noble's youngest sons like her sisters, nor was it a position on a boat like most of her brothers had assumed, and it wasn't living on the scraps of food her family was able to manage.

She would learn to fight and would possess the same self-assurance as the woman in front of her.

Sylvi was right—Delilah's life was not over.

It was about to truly begin.

Chapter One

CUMBRIA, ENGLAND
JUNE 1607

There were two coaches in front of the remote inn, one for a noble lady and one for her imposter.

Delilah being the imposter.

There were similarities between the women, of course, or Delilah would never have been hired. They had matching curvy, petite figures presently clad in maroon traveling dresses, and the same shade of honey brown hair. At a rapid glance, one might assume them to be the same woman.

But the gems on Lady Elizabeth's gown were genuine, hard and glinting.

And those on Delilah's were paste—a shoddy comparison when placed next to the stunning original.

Like Delilah herself.

A paste decoy of a fine woman.

Lady Elizabeth glanced around the common room of the inn with an element of uncertainty. The light of dawn had only just begun to press against the dingy windows, and the soft tallow candles steeped the air with fetid, greasy smoke.

They were just within England, hanging on the border of Scotland—the perfect location to trade routes with Lady Elizabeth prior to her journey into Scotland for her wedding to Laird MacKenzie.

Elizabeth's dark brown gaze met Delilah's. "You look very similar to me." Lady Elizabeth had a dainty, almost songlike voice. Her cheeks tinged pink, and her gaze flicked to Sylvi before darting back to Delilah.

Sylvi watched the noble woman with an unflinching stare, her arms crossed over her narrow chest and her stance strong and stolid like that of a soldier. She seldom wore dresses anymore, opting instead for leather trews and a black leine. Her multitude of braids had been twisted back into a splayed mass of blonde, which hung down her back like the feathers of a commander's helmet.

Still though, she'd kept the black ribbon tied at her neck. Only now Delilah knew the reason for the uncharacteristic feminine adornment.

Many men found themselves intimidated by Sylvi's appearance. The subtle glances Lady Elizabeth slid toward Sylvi indicated the noble woman was absolutely terrified.

Delilah stepped forward in an effort to put the other woman at ease. "We do look indeed similar. I am glad to aid you in ensuring your safe travels to meet your betrothed."

A delicate smile teased the corners of Lady Elizabeth's mouth. "I do appreciate the risk you take on my behalf."

Delilah nodded. For truly she was putting herself at risk. It was not every day she allowed herself to be led into a potential trap where she might be kidnapped.

Dangerous, yes, but Delilah could not quell the skip of excitement in her veins. Finally, after five long years of combat training and weapons mastery, after countless plots uncovered and thwarted, and many successful assignments, she was being given the opportunity to operate entirely on her own.

Without Sylvi there to ensure all went according to plan.

The hard set of Sylvi's face indicated how she felt about being excluded from the mission.

There was far more for Delilah to think on now than Sylvi's attitude toward the circumstances. Like ensuring Lady Elizabeth made it safely to Edirdovar Castle, and the man who sought her harm was brought to justice.

Lady Elizabeth pulled a velvet sachet from a bag at her waist.

"This is from my father. He said you are to receive only half now and half upon the notification not only of my safe delivery, but also my successful marriage."

She thrust it toward Delilah, and the muffled clink of coins sounded within. Delilah took the small bag and hefted its considerable weight toward Sylvi, who caught it midair with a deft snatch.

"My father also has several requests he'd like known," Lady Elizabeth said. "He does not want Laird MacKenzie to be aware of any of this."

Sylvi stepped toward the door. "We've already been informed of his wishes."

"He wants them reiterated regardless." Lady Elizabeth's voice took on a more authoritative tone. "He does not trust the Scottish, but does not want my marriage to be compromised. Laird MacKenzie is not to know of this."

Delilah's stomach twisted for the woman. Clearly her father thought little of the man she intended to marry, but was still sending her. Not that Delilah's own father would have done any different had she been fortunate enough to secure an advantageous marriage.

Gilded though Lady Elizabeth's life might be, she spent it in a cage and was being passed from one jailor to another.

All the refinement in the world was not worth such captivity.

"Your final destination will be Killearnan," Elizabeth continued. "If you are attacked, try to keep the assailant alive and bring him with you. However, do not do so quickly. I will need at least two and a half months to ensure my arrival and safe marriage to Laird MacKenzie before we can announce any traitors. Again, my father does not wish Laird MacKenzie to know of these plans until after the marriage."

Of course. By then he couldn't reject Lady Elizabeth in sheer spite of her father. Though Delilah had never met the man personally, she found him deplorable.

Lady Elizabeth pursed her lips.

"Is that all?" Sylvi asked.

Lady Elizabeth's chest swelled with a deep breath. "There's one more thing. My father says…" Her proud demeanor faltered slightly. "He says to remind you the servants he sent to travel with you are… expendable." The final word left her lips as though it were sour.

Sylvi snorted. "Of course." Without another word, she turned from the room and left, doubtless to ensure Liv was fully prepared to assume the role of lady's maid for Lady Elizabeth on her alternate route.

Delilah shifted to follow Sylvi when Lady Elizabeth darted forward. Her delicate hand curled like a vise around Delilah's arm.

"I have another request," Lady Elizabeth said in a breathy voice. "From me."

Her cheeks were bright and her dark gaze dropped to where she still gripped Delilah. She released the captive arm with a gasp.

"I'm sorry," she whispered and tried to smooth the wrinkled silk with trembling fingers.

Delilah lowered her arm. "Your request?"

"I don't agree with my father." The words tumbled from her mouth in a frantic whisper. "Please try to ensure the people traveling with your coach remain unharmed, especially Leasa. She is—"

"It's time." The words were followed by the jangle of a multitude of bracelets. Isabel peeked her head through the doorway, her red hair veiled beneath a scarf and her eyes lined with thick kohl.

"Thank you, Isabel."

Delilah gave a single nod to Lady Elizabeth, whose look of quiet relief warmed her. It was good to protect a woman who cared for more than just herself, who thought of those below her.

Within minutes, Lady Elizabeth was placed in her coach with Liv, one of the other spies in Sylvi's retinue. Liv wore the simple gown of a lady's maid, and her gleaming copper hair was plaited into a smooth braid. Liv's petite gray cat, whom she insisted on bringing wherever she went, lay curled contentedly in Lady Elizabeth's lap.

Lady Elizabeth would be safe.

Delilah climbed into her own coach beside a woman with brown hair. The maid was comely enough, save for an extraordinarily strong jaw, which made her appear more handsome than beautiful.

A nervous smile flitted across the woman's features. "I'm Leasa."

"And I'm Lady Elizabeth," Delilah said gently. The less the maid knew of her, the better. She knew only that the real Lady Elizabeth traveled a different route. She knew not of Delilah's skills or ultimate intentions.

"Oh, yes, of course." The maid's gaze dropped away with a shy dip of her head.

The cabin smelled of freshly cut lumber with an acrid hint of lacquer. The coach had recently been constructed, no doubt for this purpose.

Delilah settled herself on the velvet cushion and shifted to ease the squeezing tension of her over-laced bodice. While it might be beautiful, it would be uncomfortable for travel.

Leasa pressed her lips together and turned toward the open window where the sun was beginning to break between the trees in a ball of golden light. Just beyond the forest, the curved stone wall rose and fell with the swelling hills, like the limp body of a snake laid out over the lush land.

Leasa's shoulders shook slightly, and she gave a wet snuffle.

Expendable.

Delilah knew how very painful being expendable could be.

Without warning, the coach lurched forward. Delilah braced her feet against the narrow bench opposite her to keep from shooting forward while Leasa tucked herself deeper into the thin cushions. A whimpering sob emerged from her throat.

Delilah slid her bodice dagger from where it had been sheathed flush against the busk of her bodice. The blade was narrow and sharp, as perfectly concealed as it was lethal. It was also one of the many Delilah had on her person, all courtesy of Percy, who also created all the potions and ingenious accessories which kept them all safe.

Before she could allow herself to regret the action, she held the dagger toward Leasa's balled up fists.

The maid turned a watery brown gaze on Delilah and sniffed. "What's that for?"

"You." Delilah offered with a smile. "We'll be fine."

While she couldn't promise to care for the woman without going into detail, she could at least offer the comfort of reassurance and self-protection.

A tiny smile crept over Leasa's face in return, and she accepted the dagger with the pinch of her fingers, holding it as though it might bite.

"Thank you." She placed the blade held awkwardly in her lap, but the sobs ceased and the two fell into companionable silence.

Delilah let her body rock in time with the coach and gazed out to where the forest sped by on the opposite side of the window. The long stone wall was all but obscured by the close trees.

Soon they would be in Scotland, and then the real anticipation would begin.

Would one of Laird MacKenzie's enemies truly seek to harm them?

Would they be attacked with the intent to murder, or would they be held for ransom?

What if the assailants attempted to rape them?

Delilah threaded her hand into her pocket, past the large hole where it had never been sewn together, and to the dagger she had strapped to her thigh. She curled her fingers around the hilt to remind herself of its presence.

There would be no murder and no rape. Not on her guard. And if someone tried to abduct them, they would find themselves in quite the opposite situation, with her leading them captive to Inverness.

They would be safe.

All they had to do was wait.

• • •

Kaid MacLeod had been waiting for a moment of weakness. He'd been vigilant, unrelenting.

And he'd been rewarded.

Seumas MacKenzie had a weakness.

The setting sun cast a red pallor on the mud-spattered road, turning puddles to blood.

Elizabeth Seymour was supposed to have been on this trail the previous day. Certainly there'd been enough talk near Kenmore about her impending visit these last several weeks. He'd have to be deaf and blind to miss the rumors of the lady's intended path of travel.

Being so far from all the gossip now would allow him enough distance to take a different trail, to lose anyone following them, and get her to Ardvreck Castle undetected.

Only the coach was late.

At the very latest, it should have graced the path by noon. But it was significantly past noon, and still the coach had not shown, despite the recent bout of good weather.

His stomach tightened against the unease of her delay.

"I dinna think she's coming tonight." Donnan appeared beside Kaid with a stealth most found unsettling. "Tomorrow, perhaps." He rubbed the back of his neck and gave an exaggerated grimace. "This business of kidnapping lasses—it's no' sitting with me verra well."

Kaid let his gaze wander back to the stillness of the puddles. "If I had to choose between seeing more of our clan slaughtered or kidnapping an English noble's brat, I'll take my chances with the brat."

A hollow clattering sounded in the distance. Kaid's body went taut with anticipation. His fist curled around the hilt of his blade until the fine leather wrapping burned against his palm.

But though his body was still, his heart galloped into a frenzy.

"We'll no' hurt her." Though he'd said it as a statement, Kaid knew Donnan was asking for confirmation.

The world began to sway around Kaid, and the request rankled. "MacKenzie's men killed our children and raped our women, and ye're worried about a single lass?"

He forced his gaze forward once more, focused on the puddles.

Not a good idea, not when they were so much like blood.

Sweat prickled at his brow and palms.

No. Not now.

"We're no' MacKenzie." Donnan's voice sounded distant. "And with all the coin spent around the last few villages in preparation for Lady Elizabeth's arrival, she's obviously loved."

Kaid's throat pinched tight, and his breath became so difficult to draw that his lips tingled. "She's obviously well valued," Kaid corrected. "There's a difference."

Though he couldn't see the coach yet, its rattling became easy to discern. Donnan straightened and drew his sword.

With a quick nod, Donnan darted across the narrow path and disappeared into the forest on the opposite side.

The hollow wooden clattering grew louder, closer. Close enough for Kaid to make out the sucking steps of the horses.

Images flashed in his head in rapid succession, mingling with the white spots in his vision.

His people lying dead in the mud, staring at nothing, blood covering their bodies, the ground, their faces.

His hands.

Kaid's mouth filled with saliva, and the world spun around him. Blood everywhere.

Not now.

He clenched his teeth and blinked as hard as his lids would allow. He was stronger than this, damn it.

This woman was MacKenzie's only weakness, the one chink in his armor—the only way to defeat him without sacrificing more MacLeod lives.

Kaid let the air hiss through his teeth, shoved out with the force of his raw determination.

Bold yellow livery showed like a challenge through the layer of leaves. He focused on them until his vision cleared enough to count.

Six. There were six of them. He needed them out of the way so he could get to her.

This woman wasn't just MacKenzie's betrothed. She was the bartering tool to negotiate peace with MacKenzie and quite possibly the one thing he needed to get back into his clan's good graces, to be accepted into the fold again. To have a sense of belonging once more.

Kaid's footing was sure against the wet forest floor, and for that, he was grateful. The weakness had passed.

He let the heavy coach jostle past them before he leapt from the bush and caught the rear soldier by the throat while Donnan tackled the one on the left. Both were knocked unconscious before they hit the ground. The two guards heading the front of the coach wheeled around to face them and charged.

The powerful chest of the guard's brown horse blocked Kaid's view, but he did not move from his position. Not until Donnan had taken on one man, leaving only one remaining.

Kaid waited until the last possible second before he swung to the side and propelled his weight from a tree root. The guard tried to twist around, but Kaid was faster. He locked his arm around the man's neck and pulled. His body tensed with resistance, but it did not last under the pressure Kaid applied to his throat.

The man's horse continued into the depths of the forest. With any luck, villagers would stumble upon the treasure and put the beast to good use.

Kaid eased the man to the muddy floor and pulled the length of rope from his waist to bind their captives by their ankles and wrists. A quick glance over Kaid's shoulder confirmed Donnan did likewise.

Not that Kaid was against killing, but the guards were merely doing a job. Unlike the thieves they usually hunted.

He left Donnan to complete the task of binding the guards together and approached the stationary coach. The coachman sat in the hard, wood seat and stared wide-eyed. A man not even worth the fight.

Kaid nodded toward Donnan. "Have him tie ye up and ye'll stay safe. Try to run and we'll kill ye."

The man nodded and slid from the coach, obediently making his way toward Donnan.

A woman's high-pitched whisper sounded from inside the coach. "Are they going to kill us?"

Kaid's gut gave an uneasy wrench. He didn't like this business of kidnapping women either, but he had little choice. MacKenzie needed to be stopped, and if this were the only way, so be it. Besides, he had no intention of injuring anyone.

Kaid stalked toward the coach, hand on his blade in case a guard had been stationed within. A sob sounded from the coach, and Donnan frowned where he knelt beside the man he was tying up.

Donnan had been instructed to knot the rope loose enough for the men to eventually wriggle free. The location Kaid had chosen was at least two days' walk on foot to the next village. Plenty of time for them to disappear and have no one on their tail.

He grasped the flimsy handle of the coach door and pulled. It opened at the slightest pressure, and a scream pierced the cramped space, pulling his attention to the brunette who stared at him in horror. She glanced at the woman who sat opposite her before turning to him once more. Her mouth fell open so wide, her back teeth were visible, and she let loose another shriek.

The other woman, the one dressed in fine velvet and jewels, gaped at him. While her face remained smooth, her body was pressed hard against the noble, velvet cushion she sat upon. The lass looked as had been described: light brown hair and brown eyes.

A red and gold crest stood out proudly above the window emblazoned with a set of gilded wings. The unmistakable Seymour crest.

This...this was the woman he sought. The one who would be his leverage over MacKenzie.

The key to his clan's freedom.

Chapter Two

It had finally happened—they were under attack. After almost a month and a half in the coach, and all that time spent looking over her shoulder. After Delilah had finally assumed there was a strong likelihood they would arrive safely and without incident.

Her heart pounded hard and steady, thrumming in her ears like the smooth beat of a drum.

She wasn't scared. Not of this Highlander with his long, black hair and grizzled jaw. Though she did wish for nothing more than her hand wrapped around the hilt of a sword. But then, ladies did not carry swords.

Already she assumed the guards were dead. She'd heard the scuffle outside, the low groans as men went down.

Nausea churned in her stomach.

There'd been nothing she could do to save them, those men she'd come to know these past weeks. Their humor and dreams, the families waiting for them back in Cumbria.

Their attacker stared at her with a blue gaze so brilliant, his eyes nearly glowed. He never turned from her, not even as Leasa continued her skull-piercing cries of panic.

If Delilah hadn't received her training, would she have screamed thus?

"Sit beside yer maid," he said. His voice was surprisingly kind for a man who had just murdered several innocent men.

Delilah lifted her chin to incline her head a haughty inch, the way her noble breeding dictated. Not that it was worth the dirt on a pauper's feet.

His gaze narrowed, not with anger, or even irritation. He had expected her to decline.

Leasa sucked in a deep lungful of air, but before she could scream again, Delilah caught the woman's hand. Leasa's palm was sweaty, her pulse ticking wildly beneath Delilah's thumb. The poor maid was frightened, an emotion Delilah herself had not felt in quite some time.

The Highlander's gaze fell to their clasped hands. He had surprisingly long eyelashes for a man.

"I willna hurt ye so long as ye do as I say," he said.

Delilah gave a stiff nod and kept her eyes wide. If he knew she was completely unafraid, everything could be ruined.

She would allow him to think her fearful, but not cowed.

There had been too many times in her life where she'd wilted beneath her emotions. She was stronger now.

No man would ever see her so weak again.

Leasa's hand squeezed into a death grip around Delilah's, and her breathless sobs filled the cabin. Delilah's heart clenched for the young woman, and for her own role in Leasa's misery. The maid had not been prepared for such risk and violence.

Delilah shifted to the seat beside her maid. "We will do as you say." She kept her voice smooth. Perhaps she ought to have made it tremble, but she wanted to ease Leasa's fear with her own strength, a difficult balance to strike.

The man stepped into the coach, setting it creaking and swaying. He eased himself into the seat she had occupied and closed the narrow door.

Leasa leapt and gave a little shriek.

Delilah angled herself slightly in front of Leasa. While there'd been no stopping the massacre of the guards, she could at least prevent the young maid from being injured.

But the Highlander did not attack them. He sat across from them, his large frame filling the seat where Delilah had only occupied half. He rested his elbows on his legs. The scent of leather and outdoors filled the confined cabin.

"I'll take yer food." He held out a large hand toward her.

Calluses showed rough on his palm at the base of his fingers and smudges of ink showed on his thumb and forefinger, but his nails were trimmed and clean.

He was no rogue highwayman.

"Please," he offered.

No rogue highwayman indeed.

With a look toward Leasa to warn her silently to comply, Delilah lifted the bag of food they kept in the cabin. He could have it if he liked. They had more with the rest of their bags behind the coach, having stopped just the day before.

Delilah hefted the rough linen and thrust it toward the Highlander. He gave a subtle nod of thanks before accepting it and immediately rummaging through it.

He pulled a wrapped parcel out, sniffed it and set it aside before doing the same with two other items.

"What are you doing?" she asked, trying to adopt the indignant countenance of a courtier.

He sniffed another parcel before dropping it back in the bag. "Taking out the meat."

An edge of unease scraped up her spine. Was he mad? "Whatever for?"

The Highlander opened the door, tied the bag off and tossed it into the road. "Wolves and other predators would smell it."

Without further explanation, he smacked the top of the ceiling with his palm and the coach jumped forward.

The sudden lurch shoved Delilah back into her seat, but she immediately righted herself. "Why would you—?"

Movement outside the window caught her attention. Her guards and the coach driver were all tied together, their arms and legs bound in front of them and placed back-to-back with their legs jutting out like the spokes of a wheel.

They jostled and writhed against their bonds.

Alive.

The bag of food had landed in a patch of grass not far from them.

Delilah's gaze cut to the Highlander. "They're alive."

The Highlander nodded. "Aye. They willna be getting out of those ropes any time soon, but nor will they die there either. The food will last them until they find a village." His vivid blue gaze shifted from the window to her. "Long enough for us to be far enough away that they willna be able to find ye."

. . .

Kaid had not expected Elizabeth Seymour to be so beautiful.

The sun spilled over her face and turned her skin to golden-lit cream, and her almond-shaped brown eyes gazed up at him, large and long-lashed, like those of a doe.

She stared at him with a defiance he ought to find maddening. It burned deep in her gaze, simmering above the fear.

A spike of disbelief shoved through his gut.

He was really doing this, kidnapping an innocent woman who had done nothing more than find herself unfortunately betrothed to MacKenzie, as if that were not its own special punishment.

The image of MacKenzie touching this delicate woman flashed through his mind and brought with it a flood of fiery anger. MacKenzie did not deserve a woman so fair. Certainly he should never be allowed to possess something so fragile as the dainty Elizabeth Seymour. He would break her and take joy in having done so.

"Why are you doing this?" She asked.

He wanted to look away, to keep from having to face her accusation, her betrayal, her fear.

His hand curled into a fist until the muscles of his forearm burned. He had to remember his people.

She was his leverage to obtain his father's sword stolen in battle when he fell. She was the means to barter for an agreement which could lead to peace—a way to retaliate without losing men.

Images brushed at his memory, images of the massacre they'd suffered, but he quickly shoved them aside lest they overwhelm him again. He couldn't appear weak in front of the women.

"Ye dinna need to ask questions." His reply came out sharp. Her brow flinched, but she said nothing.

The maid whimpered again. The sound left Kaid wincing, but he did not blame the lass.

He blamed himself.

"How could I not ask questions?" Lady Seymour said in an equally sharp tone. "You've bound my men and stolen our coach with us still inside. If your intent is not harm, what is it then?"

It was a bold question for one in such a dire situation as hers, yet she demanded answers with the authority of a queen.

Aside from her exquisite beauty, she was no different than he'd imagined. She wore the air of entitlement around her like a fine sable mantle and seemed to expect the world to bow at her feet, all because she'd been born to great wealth.

He could tell she'd never known the pain of loss, the horror of seeing those she loved slaughtered, nor how difficult it was to win back the trust of men who sought answers.

There'd been a time where he had never known such things himself.

"You'll find out in time," he said. "All ye need to know now is that I mean ye no harm."

She folded her arms over her chest. The simple act pushed her ample bosom against the lush red fabric of her bodice.

"What are we to do for food?" she asked.

"We'll make do." He leaned back in his seat, careful to avoid the parcels of salted meat beside him. When they'd finished what remained of the food stores he'd kept, he'd hunt and Donnan could head into a nearby village.

"Where are we—"

"Enough questions." He gave her a level look.

Silence fell between them, long enough even for the maid's whimpers to stop.

The side-to-side sway of the coach lulled him, tempting him toward sleep.

The groggy sensation was unwelcome, not because the women might seek to flee—he knew he'd wake before they even touched the handle of the door—but because of the horrors which sleep brought.

He dipped in and out of his fight with sleep when the hushing of whispers broke through his fogged mind. He opened his eyes and found Lady Elizabeth's hard stare fixed directly on him.

"We have needs which must be met." She arched one well-groomed eyebrow, as if daring him to challenge her.

He did not need to ask which needs she'd referred to and had already anticipated such interruptions. It was one of the many reasons he'd chosen to bring the maid as well.

He rapped his knuckles against the roof of the cabin three times, as he and Donnan had discussed prior, and the coach rolled to an easy stop.

Kaid opened the door and stepped out. Donnan hopped from the driver's perch and curiously glanced into the cabin where the women were easing from their seats.

"At least that noise stopped, eh?" Donnan winked at him.

By "that noise" Kaid knew Donnan referred to the maid's crying. And though they'd been responsible for her keening wails, Kaid too was grateful for the quiet.

Lady Elizabeth emerged at the mouth of the coach, and before Kaid could even realize what he'd done, his hand shot out to aid her down the single stair.

She accepted the offer with the nonchalance of entitlement, and he suddenly realized she had expected his help. Not that he should be surprised by her reaction. Doubtless it'd been how she'd lived her entire life.

She arched her back slightly, a discreet stretch after having been in the coach so long. It did not escape his notice the way the rounded tops of her bosom swelled against her bodice.

Again.

While he might not appreciate English ideals, he found the cut of the gowns appealing.

Kaid's thought was echoed in the lift of Donnan's brows.

In fact, all of Lady Elizabeth was rather bonny now that Kaid could see her standing rather than sitting in a fluff of skirts. She was shorter than he'd initially thought. Her head scarce came to his chest. While the cone of her skirts concealed her hips and everything below, the narrowness of her waist was entirely visible.

Unaware of his assessment, Lady Elizabeth turned toward the coach and beckoned the woman still huddled within. "Come, Leasa."

The wheels creaked, and the cabin rocked. "Coming, my lady."

No sooner had the maid spoken than she appeared in the doorway and stumbled out of the coach in a graceless splaying of arms.

Kaid and Donnan both stepped forward to help her, but she managed to catch her own balance.

Her cheeks flushed to a deeper red, and she lowered her face to hide her embarrassment. She smoothed at her skirts before glancing up at Elizabeth. "Are you ready, my lady?"

Elizabeth stepped toward the forest. "Yes, I—"

"Only one of ye," Kaid said.

The noblewoman stopped and turned slowly, a look of measured patience on her face. "Are you saying my maid will not be able to attend me?"

He crossed his arms over his chest. "I'm saying I dinna trust ye to no' run off and intend to hold one of ye while the other goes."

Her eyes narrowed.

He'd known she wouldn't like it even before he had said it.

Not that kidnapping women should be easy, but this woman was going to make the upcoming days a veritable hell.

Chapter Three

Lady Elizabeth put her hands on her hips, and Kaid knew he was in for a tongue-lashing.

"You expect us to go into the woods," she said. "Alone."

He didn't budge. "Aye."

She opened her mouth to speak, but he cut her off before she could start.

"Or I could let the two of ye go together while I join ye both to ensure no one leaves." He shrugged.

Her mouth opened wider, this time in obvious outrage. "How dare you?"

"Then maybe ye should do as he says," Donnan said with his customary good-natured smile. "One of ye stays while the other goes."

Elizabeth let her gaze slide over to Donnan and then back to Kaid. He could see the indecision warring on her face.

She heaved a great sigh. "Very well. Leasa, you go first."

Leasa cast an anxious look toward Kaid.

"Ye'll be fine," Kaid offered reassuringly.

Still the frightened maid hesitated.

"Ach, ye'll be fine, lass. I give ye my word." Donnan flashed her his ready grin.

As always, his effortless charm worked its magic and Leasa's shoulders relaxed. This would indeed be a long trek if Donnan was to repeat everything Kaid said.

"Thank you." Leasa gave a short nod and made her way off the path at a pace somewhere between a walk and a restrained run.

The conversation ceased with her disappearance, so only Lady Elizabeth's glare filled the space between them. Donnan muttered something about checking the horses and disappeared around the coach.

"Who are you, anyway?" Elizabeth asked.

Kaid looked toward the woods where the maid had disappeared. The lass made enough sound crashing through the brush he didn't have to guess her location. Based on the volume of her screams earlier, he'd know well enough if she required rescuing. "Dinna ye worry about who I am."

"Yes, we've already had this conversation." There was a note of frustration in her voice. "What are we to call you?"

"Ye dinna need to call me anyth—"

"Kaid, where did ye want to set up camp tonight?" Donnan peeked his head around the corner. "I think we're near—" His words dropped, and only then did Kaid realize he was glowering at Donnan.

A triumphant grin showed on Elizabeth's face. "Kaid." She nodded toward Donnan. "And who are you?"

Donnan's uncertainty melted away in an instant, and he bowed low like some damn courtier. "Donnan MacLeod at yer service, my lady."

With a growl, Kaid snapped forward and hauled Donnan against the cart. "We've abducted these women," he reminded his friend in Gaelic. "Ye need to have a care what we tell them. They now know who we are, and ye almost told them exactly where we are. Ye need to speak to me in Gaelic from now on and give them only what they need to know, aye?"

Donnan's face hardened into a look Kaid had only seen perhaps twice in their entire lives. "I guess I'm no' used to kidnapping lasses."

The slight hit its mark. He released Donnan's leine, though he didn't remember having grabbed it in the first place. "I dinna want to do this either," Kaid said, though he knew it didn't matter.

Lady Elizabeth frowned and strode toward them with such

clipped steps, her skirts kicked out in front of her. "What are you saying?"

Irritation drew tight across Kaid's shoulders, and he had to collect the scraps of his patience before answering, "Things we obviously dinna want ye to hear."

Her hand was in the pocket of her large skirts, shifting under the heavy layer of fabric. As if she were seeking something.

He'd never thought to ask them if they were armed. After all, what noblewoman carried weapons on her person? But then, this spitfire might.

He let his gaze wander over her stiff gown. "Do ye have any weapons?"

Her brows lifted. "Of course I do not. And you've still not answer—"

"No needles?" he pressed. "Sewing scissors?" He'd never kidnapped a woman. In fact, he'd never been in a situation where he would need to pursue a woman in this regard. Still, he didn't want to underestimate his foe, no matter how unassuming she seemed.

The hand in her pocket had not moved again.

Her head tilted a fraction of an inch higher, and her gaze remained steady. "I have no sewing items on my person."

She'd been disciplined like all the other girls of the English court to keep her emotions bottled beneath an expressionless exterior. And while she was indeed far calmer than her high-pitched maid, he detected a hint of breathlessness in her words.

The lass hid her fear well.

He stepped toward her, and his foot squished into the thick mud. He *would* draw out the truth.

Her haughtiness slipped for a moment and gave way to a flash of vulnerability that left her mouth soft and the delicate muscles of her neck standing taut against her creamy flesh.

"Do ye have nothing in yer pocket then?" he asked and stepped closer.

This time she did not respond, which was answer enough.

She pulled her hand from her pocket.

He stalked toward her until he was close enough to feel the brush of her heavy skirt against his shin. A delicate floral scent caught his attention, which he recognized from their close quarters inside the coach. Doubtless her perfume, and doubtless expensive.

"What's in yer pocket?" he demanded.

His intent was to intimidate. His closeness, the harshness of his words, his unbreaking stare. And it worked as far as he could tell. Her eyes were wide, as if she wanted to turn away.

But she did not. "You stand too close," she said in a snide tone. "Move away, Kaid."

Her disparaging demeanor caught at his nerves, and his name on her lips left his muscles tight. "I think ye have something." He reached toward her heavy brocade skirt. "Here."

Her hand shot out like a striking snake and connected with his cheek in a ringing slap. His cheek stung where her palm had made contact. Some men he knew would have struck her back. Tempting though it might be, he would never be one of those men.

"Dinna ever hit me again." He let the warning come out low and composed. A threat calmly delivered held more promise than one bellowed in rage.

A thin, high-pitched scream came from the woods. They both turned in time to see Leasa break through the tree line in a wild thrash while pealing out her earsplitting cries.

"Leave her," she shrieked and rushed in their direction.

Her hasty steps were clumsy on the muddy path, and she slipped once. At first she caught herself, but then stepped on her dress and pitched forward into a tangle of skinny legs and flailing arms.

Kaid shared a shocked look with Donnan from his place by the horses.

It was Elizabeth who ran forward to help her maid. She knelt into a thick patch of mud at the girl's side to better aid her to her feet.

Leasa was weeping again. The snuffling, wailing sound carried with it an endless stream of apologies. Elizabeth's voice murmured beneath the sobs, not with chastisement at her clumsy servant, but in soothing tones.

Thick mud caked the front of Elizabeth's skirt, but she did not appear to notice. She asked the maid something, and Leasa offered a shy smile to Elizabeth, who beamed back in return.

Kaid couldn't help but watch the exchange. This was not the entitled noblewoman who challenged him at every turn and had only recently slapped him. This woman in muddy clothes was patient and compassionate.

Her action had been immediate, the kind one does not realize they are doing until it is being done. The kind borne of instinct and displaying a person's true heart.

Guilt squeezed at Kaid's chest like a vise.

Despite the man she'd been sent to marry and the entitlement of her upbringing, she was a good person.

And he was the monster who would see her exploited.

• • •

Delilah waited for the crash outside.

It was her first tactic of many to prolong their arrival at Edirdovar Castle—or wherever it was Kaid sought to take them.

She sat in the jostling coach, awaiting a hearty bang to interrupt the cheerful pitch of Donnan's whistling coming from the driver's seat. Poor Leasa had finally quieted at her side, though she continued to offer stricken apologies periodically regardless of how often Delilah tried to tell her they were unnecessary.

Leasa had a large heart and a brave soul. She'd thought Kaid had meant Delilah harm and sought to intervene, to save Delilah. Her actions had been so heartbreakingly selfless. And if Kaid truly had meant to cause Delilah harm, it would doubtless have been Leasa who would have been injured.

The Highlander was gazing out the window once more. Delilah appreciated that he seemed to be affording them a modicum of privacy.

Her foot jiggled beneath the concealment of her skirts in

anticipation. She'd loosened the luggage ties on the coach prior to climbing back in, but she'd had only a moment to complete the task.

Had she loosened them enough?

A horrifying thought struck her.

What if the luggage *had* come loose and fallen silently onto the trail? She hadn't intended for their items to be lost, only for a diversion to be created, one where she could insist they search for the scattered items to buy at least an hour of time.

After all, several occurrences of stolen hours would add up to a considerable sum.

But if they lost their bags, they lost everything. Aside from just the fine clothing Lord Seymour had provided her with to resemble Elizabeth, she would also have no more of the tonics or specialized gear Percy had crafted.

Percy was one of other women in Sylvi's employ, but she didn't go out on missions like Delilah. Her role was actually more important as she created tools for them to use—poisons, healing teas, tools to open locks and conceal weapons.

Losing her inventions would make accomplishing the assignment difficult. Not impossible, of course, but with Delilah's first solo mission at stake, she did not want difficult.

Leasa turned to Delilah with a slight frown on her lips. "I'm so sorry for—"

A great shudder jolted the coach and something clattered behind them. Donnan's whistled tune cut off abruptly.

Delilah's foot stilled and her heartbeat came a little faster with her victory.

The coach drew to a hard stop which jerked both her and Leasa forward. The maid gave a cry of surprise and grasped Delilah in an iron grip.

But Kaid didn't notice them. He already had his blade unsheathed, his brilliant blue gaze sharp on the forest outside the small window. He leapt from his seat and burst through the door with an agility he hadn't appeared capable of. But he didn't leave the front of the partially open coach door. He stood there like a sentry.

He might be a man who kidnapped women, but he was obviously trying to ensure they were protected.

Donnan appeared at his side. "It's no' an attack. The ties came loose and the lot of their bags scattered all over the trail."

"That's fine," Kaid said with a shrug. "We'll reload and continue on our way."

"I dinna think it'll be as easy as all that," Donnan said, switching to Gaelic, a language Delilah knew well from her training at Kindrochit Castle.

Donnan nodded to the foliage lining the trail. "I think some of them fell into the stream."

Delilah cast a discreet glance to the other side of the window where the road dropped off into a downhill slope and ended in a rushing stream.

Her excitement waned. She'd wanted a distraction, yes, but she hadn't wanted to see her items destroyed.

This needed to be handled, and quickly.

She knocked on the partially open door, letting the obnoxious rapping continue until Kaid slid his gaze toward her with poorly concealed annoyance. "What is going on?" she asked. "What did he say about our bags?"

His chest swelled and relaxed with a sigh before he replied, "It would appear they werena well secured and came loose."

Delilah gave him a shocked frown. "Are they lost?"

He shook his head. "Donnan is gathering them now."

"No." Delilah shoved up from her seat with all the indignation of a noblewoman whose modesty was to be preserved. "I'll not have a man handling my undergarments if any contents were loosed."

Leasa started to rise, but Delilah shook her head. "You've taken a bad tumble, Leasa. Stay here. I can gather my own things."

A shocked expression filled Leasa's face. "My lady, that isn't necessary, I—"

Delilah shook her head to still her maid and pulled open the door. Kaid filled the exit with his large frame, blocking her exit. "Sit down."

She ignored the request and pushed forward, an awkward attempt with him so thoroughly in the way. "I assure you, it is entirely necessary."

He crossed his arms over his chest, and she did likewise.

His eyes narrowed, and she narrowed hers as well.

It was like playing a mirror game with one of her younger siblings back home.

She lifted her chin as high as she dared in the hopes it might give her more height and tried to stretch her back, as if she could make herself taller by sheer will alone.

"Ye're pretty stubborn to be an English woman." He spoke in a wry tone. "Are ye sure ye're no' a Scot?"

"Maybe if I start to kidnap women I would be," she countered. But instead of more verbal parrying, Kaid smirked and stepped back.

He uncrossed his arms and called for Donnan before returning his attention back to her. "Fine, help yerself to a walk through all the mud. I'll have Donnan stay with Leasa so I can ensure ye dinna run away."

Delilah was about to protest, to insist the more affable Scotsman be her guard. But now was not the time to feign an escape attempt. She glanced behind her to where Leasa sat in the coach, watching them. Leasa would be better off with Donnan's carefree company.

Donnan appeared, and Kaid issued a rapid set of orders in Gaelic for him to remain with Leasa at all costs.

With that, Delilah and Kaid set off in stark silence to gather the belongings that Donnan had not yet been able to locate.

When the remaining bags were found, Delilah's fears were realized. The bags had indeed ruptured upon impact with the ground and propelled their contents across the trail and into the running stream.

The refreshing breeze swept against Delilah's skin and made her realize just how stuffy the coach was becoming. It'd already been a compact space with her and Leasa, but Kaid's massive body seemed to leave no room to even breathe properly.

Of course the lack of proper breathing might be due to the incredibly tight corset she'd been laced into.

Rather than wheeze out her air, she held her breath and bent to flick her sark from the forest floor. Kaid had assisted with gathering outer garments and various other items, but had left anything appearing to be an undergarment for her. It was a kindness she could not help but appreciate.

Granted, she hadn't been abducted before, but she would imagine most men in Kaid's position would not be so accommodating.

When they'd collected most of the items from the muddy trail, they made their way down the sloping hill to the rushing stream where countless items had been strewn, some in the mud, some in the water.

Directly beside the stream, Delilah found her steel-boned corset. She lifted the heavy garment with great relief. Save several leaves plastered to the pale brocade silk, the fabric was not wet, which meant the steel had remained dry and would not rust.

While it was heavy, the strategic placement of steel boning on the inside rendered her torso slash-proof. A discomfort she was willing to endure. If only the blasted corset she wore now served any purpose for the extent of its squeezing torture.

Something white caught her eye in the stream, and her heart went heavy. There, almost entirely submerged in the deepest part of the water, was the bag containing their extra food.

Chapter Four

Night was the most dangerous.

Kaid glanced outside where the trees had grown shadowed and the gray light of dusk dampened the summer sky. They would need to stop soon.

While he knew the women would prefer they stop at a village to restore their food supply and have a comfortable place to sleep, Kaid could not risk the exposure.

While there were no villages nearby to threaten discovery, wandering men could be just as dangerous.

The maid had long since fallen asleep on her mistress's shoulder, but Elizabeth had remained awake, her gaze alert. Her hand, he noticed, had continued to hold her maid's, even after the other woman had long since faded into sleep.

The coach rocked hard to the right and then teetered to the left.

Leasa bounced forward and then knocked back, smacking her head on the wooden wall. Her eyes flew open, and she clapped her palm over the injury.

Elizabeth shot him an accusatory glare, as if he had personally rocked the coach.

"We're going off the path to set up camp for the night," Kaid explained.

Elizabeth turned Leasa's face to the side and examined what was most likely a large knot on the woman's scalp. "It would have been nice to have had some form of warning."

The coach swayed and bounced in earnest now, and they all braced themselves in the small cabin, their bodies stiffly jerking and fighting the momentum. Ages seemed to pass before they finally rolled to a stop.

Leasa bolted out of her seat and lurched toward the door with her hand over her mouth.

Kaid jumped up to stop her, but she moved more quickly than he. She stumbled out of the coach, fell to her knees and retched.

"Does yer maid ever actually care for ye?" he asked Elizabeth sardonically.

She threw him a dark look and rose from her seat.

But Donnan beat her to her maid's side. He bent over her and offered a square of linen. The wet sound of her blowing her nose soon followed.

Kaid disembarked from the coach and aided Elizabeth onto the soggy ground. The evening summer air graced his skin with a chilled breeze. Donnan's murmured voice hummed quietly as he spoke to Leasa in gentle tones.

Elizabeth watched the two as well. "That was kind of him to help."

The gentleness with which she spoke and the softness in her brown gaze as she regarded Donnan and Leasa made a flicker of jealousy prickle through Kaid.

He'd received little more than the sharp side of her tongue when he knew she was capable of far more. No sooner had the thought entered his mind, he steeled himself against the absurdity of it. She was his captive.

In the end, she was his bargaining tool to return to MacKenzie for peace. She would be married, and he would never see her again.

"We'll eat after we set up camp." His voice came out gruff with his determination.

If she noticed it, she did not chastise him for it. Perhaps she was as tired as he.

"We have no food," she reminded him. "Our main stores were ruined when our bags fell from the coach."

"We'll make do." Though he tried to sound optimistic, there

wasn't enough food for all of them. The scant amount of meat remaining wouldn't be enough to fill any of them.

He surveyed the area, letting his gaze skim over the tree line, straining his vision against the darkening sky until he saw several puffs of smoke in the distance. A town or a village, far enough away not to be a threat, but close enough that they would arrive by midmorning.

Once he and Donnan had set up camp and Leasa appeared recovered enough to not lose what she ate, Kaid distributed the remaining food.

Elizabeth accepted the meager hunk of salted ham with a quiet note of thanks. It wasn't until they began to eat that she regarded him with a shrewd glint in her eye. "Where's your food?"

"We already ate," Donnan answered.

She nodded to Kaid. "He didn't. Only you did."

Donnan slid a questioning gaze to Kaid, who offered a nonchalant shrug in reply.

In truth, he'd given Donnan his quarter of the share and hadn't expected the women to notice he hadn't given himself one. Apparently Lady Elizabeth was more observant than he'd given her credit for.

"What will you eat?" Her voice was gentle.

Kaid shrugged off her question. "A warrior isna worth his weight if he canna take a bit of hunger for a night."

She tore her piece of ham and held out half to him. The meat was a deep, roasted pink, charred along the sides. Its briny scent made his mouth water.

"Take this," she said. "Please."

A part of him, a larger part than he cared to admit, wanted to snatch the hunk of meat from her palm and devour it. But, he reminded himself, Lady Elizabeth was not used to hunger. The piece she had was already too meager to see her sufficiently filled.

"I'm fine," he answered and strode away before she could offer again. Before his resolve could crumble.

When he was far enough away from them, he drew a slender

vial from the pouch at his waist. The clear liquid within rolled against the glass like a fat droplet of rain.

There was only enough left for tonight. Maybe tomorrow as well, if he was conservative with his dose.

His fingers shook at the prospect of having so little remaining.

The women were not the only ones who lost several items when the bags came loose. The bag he'd packed had spilled its contents, and the remaining vials the seer had given him had been lost. He'd looked for his stock with barely contained madness, but to no avail.

This was his last.

Perhaps he ought to try one night without it. To sleep without the blanket of valerian root to pull over his mind.

He clenched his teeth. The images would flood his mind at all attempts to sleep and keep him in wakeful horror. His muscles went tight in anticipation.

The bodies.

The empty stares.

The blood.

He pulled the stopper from the bottle. Carefully. Carefully.

His fingers were clumsy, too large for so tiny a bottle, and shaking with an overwhelming anticipation.

He touched the vial to his lips and let a slight amount of the bitter liquid wet his tongue.

He needed this. The sleep. The escape.

Kaid shoved the stopper into the vial and pushed hard to ensure it was in there deep enough to keep the contents from leaking.

"Why are you doing this?" Lady Elizabeth's voice sounded from behind him.

He slipped the vial into the pouch at his waist before turning to face her. But it was not accusation on her face. It was sincerity.

"You and Donnan both, you seem kind. But you're committing an egregious, heinous crime."

His soul chilled at her delicate claim, hating the truth behind her words.

She shook her head. "I've been trying to think why you could possibly do this and can come up with no morally sound answer."

A warmth started in the base of his neck and pulsed slowly through his body. The valerian root was beginning to take effect. Soon he would be numb. Soon even the burden of his guilt would be assuaged.

"There are more people at stake in this than Donnan and me." Perhaps it was more than he should have said, but he wanted her to understand, to not judge him so harshly. Not when she was affording him her kindness.

She cast a glance behind her to where Donnan and Leasa were chatting by the glow of the fire. "If you let us go, we won't tell anyone." Her heavily lashed brown eyes searched his. "You're a good man, Kaid. Please don't do this."

Even the numbing blanket of the valerian root could not stop the ache from spiking in his chest. "We need rest," he said. "We have a long day tomorrow."

She studied him for a long moment, her face blank, then finally turned away. For that he was grateful.

He wished he could return the lasses to the road and walk away as if no wrongdoing had ever occurred.

But he was not a man with the luxury of options.

• • •

Delilah's inability to sleep was due more to the discomfort of her mind than that of the thin cushion upon which she tried to sleep.

She envied the men their freedom, under the stars with the cool earth beneath their backs. The walls of the cabin were becoming too familiar, too close, as if they were pressing against her and choking the air from her chest. At least she'd taken off the blasted corset.

The sound of Leasa's even breathing came from the opposite bench. Delilah was glad the other woman slept after the taxing stress of what had transpired since their quiet ride through the forest that afternoon.

Had it truly been only one day when it felt another lifetime ago?

Delilah rolled onto her back to get more comfortable. The coach squeaked and rocked with the simple movement. She suppressed a sigh and tilted her head back on the cushion to stare out through the top of the narrow window where the sky was alight with countless stars.

London never had so many stars. The skies of Scotland seemed vaster and more open. She'd been in the country for over five years and still loved the wildness of it all. For as much as she'd dreamt of London's court as a girl, she truly did not miss it as a woman.

A low groan came from outside.

She froze and locked her breath in her chest, fearful the simple act might keep her from hearing something important.

The groan came again, louder this time, followed by the incoherent mumbling of a man's deep voice.

Kaid?

The voice cried out.

Was someone hurt?

Delilah sat carefully upright to keep from making the coach move too much. The glow of the firelight momentarily blocked her vision before she made out the shadowed form of a man lying near it on the ground. His head thrashed from side to side and a low growling sound emerged from his throat.

Kaid.

Her heart went tight.

She got to her feet and exited the confining coach.

While she did not intend to demonstrate her skills, she would not allow herself to be surprised either. Nor would she allow any harm to come to Leasa, no matter what it took.

The sweet night air bathed her face, washing away the oppressive suffocation of the coach. She glanced around their camp and noted Donnan's absence.

Kaid's brow puckered and his head shook from side to side once more in a silent no.

Was he asleep?

She crept closer when a raw and anguished cry erupted from the back of his throat.

"Kaid," she whispered.

His brow remained furrowed, his body tense in his slumber.

"Kaid." She spoke louder this time and reached for his shoulder.

He lurched awake like a gunshot and thrust the blade of his dagger to her throat before she had time to register the threat.

Her heart slammed hard in her chest, but she did not back away.

"Kaid, you had a nightmare." She put her hand on his and tried to push the dagger from her throat, but found his arm locked tight.

His blue eyes were pale gray in the firelight. "They're dead." His voice was flat. "They're all dead."

Her heartbeat came harder and faster. Was he referring to Donnan? She cast a quick glance around the clearing, confirming the lanky man was still missing. "Kaid, who's dead?"

"There's so much blood." He sniffed hard and looked away, but not before she caught the gloss of tears in his brilliant gaze. "The men. The women. God, the children." His voice caught.

Chills raked over Delilah's skin. She stared at him, not seeing the things he clearly saw in his mind, but witnessing well enough the horror etched on his face. Never had she seen a man so vulnerable, and it made her wince with the force of his suffering.

Her mind whirled with a million different thoughts, all warring against one another.

To prod for information, or to comfort?

To worry about him, or to worry about herself?

To let him continue, or to stop him?

Delilah pushed at Kaid. "It was a dream." This time the blade shifted from her throat.

His hand sank to the ground, limp, and his gaze drifted toward the dagger. "They're all dead. And I couldna save them."

He dropped his head forward and might have pitched to the dirt had Delilah not caught him.

Perhaps she ought not to have done it, but her arms came around his body, and she rubbed small circles against his back, as she'd done with her younger siblings back in London. "It's a dream," she whispered. "Just a dream."

He smelled of sensual masculine spice, and his body was strong beneath her touch. Hard muscle beneath firm flesh. The observation set her nerves on edge. Hadn't she allowed men to interfere enough with her life?

She eased him off her and settled him as gently as possible to the ground, not an easy feat when his body was so much larger than her own.

In the end, she got him lying on his blanket with one arm awkwardly tucked beneath his body. With a sigh, she leaned over him in an attempt to liberate the trapped limb. After much tugging and grunting, she finally freed it.

Using that very arm, he caught her around the waist and pulled her down and back against him.

Everything in her body went on high alert, tensing for a fight.

But it was not a fight she got.

Kaid held her with the heat of his strong body and nuzzled his face into her hair, tracing the line of her neck with his lips.

Tingles prickled over her flesh and suddenly the night air was too warm.

He was cradling her to him like a lover would.

She lay still, uncertain what to do.

Part of her wanted to leap up and away from him in…what? Fear? Modesty?

But there was another part of her, a shamefully large part, which wanted to relax into his embrace and revel in the affection of his mouth upon her naked skin.

Footsteps sounded beside them, startling her. She'd been so engrossed in her own thoughts, she had failed to hear the person approach.

With a start, she jerked her gaze upward and found someone staring down at her with raised brows.

Donnan.

Chapter Five

Avoiding someone in close quarters was an uncomfortable task.

Kaid tried to keep his gaze from drifting toward Elizabeth on their journey to the nearest village for food.

But it was almost impossible to keep from letting his stare trail up the point of her chin to where a sliver of sunlight glowed against her smooth cheek. Just above the delicate freckle beside her mouth.

He wanted to apologize.

He *should* apologize.

Staring wouldn't make it better, though.

He pulled his gaze toward the window of the coach. Several trees blocked the view of the nearby village where Donnan had ventured to purchase more food. Kaid had waited with the women on the outskirts to avoid being seen, but was now regretting the decision.

The coach was too damn small.

Leasa sewed beside Elizabeth, and the quiet pop of her needle going in and out of the fabric scraped over his raw nerves.

While Elizabeth had maintained her polite civility in addressing him, he knew her memory of the previous night would not fade quickly.

And, damn it, he hadn't even remembered doing any of it.

Donnan had pulled him aside that morning and told him how he'd found Delilah wide-eyed and stiff in Kaid's arms. Apparently he'd had a nightmare, and the lass had tried to help.

He'd rewarded her by holding her captive in his bed.

He clenched his jaw until it felt as though it would seize up.

While he didn't remember having done it, he did remember the dream he'd had, and then the comfort he'd felt.

It made him even more ashamed of his actions, but he could no sooner pull them from his mind than he could pull his heart from his chest.

He could recall the dream with far too much ease—the floral scent of her curling around him like a summer breeze, the softness of her words, a whispered strength in his ear. She was there with him, a beautiful warrior parrying the stab of painful memories.

His gaze drifted back toward her once more.

He wanted to sketch her.

The careful line of her cheekbones, the curve of her lips, those long, velvety lashes.

If only there were a bit of charcoal in his hand and a square of parchment in front of him. He rubbed his thumb over his fingertips to assuage the growing desire. He would draw later, while she slept. Before the contents of the vial worked their magic over his restless mind.

It was then he realized she was staring directly at him, her gaze unflinching. He cleared his throat and looked away.

"Is there something you wish to say?" she asked.

There was—he wanted to apologize to her for having trapped her at his side when she'd meant only to help, and thank her for what she'd done. He wanted to see how much he might have said in his valerian-induced haze.

He hated that he didn't remember.

He glanced toward Leasa whose head was bent over her needlework. Speaking of the compromised position in which he'd placed Elizabeth would hardly be prudent in front of her maid.

"Outside." He indicated the door.

Elizabeth gave a quick nod and leapt up with an eagerness she didn't bother to mask. Perhaps she too was tired of being confined within the coach. After only two days, he felt as though it were squeezing him in a box of stale air. He couldn't imagine having endured it as long as she.

Once outside, they both took a grateful moment to draw in the fresh air. The forest around them was thick and left the breeze heavy with the sharp scent of pine.

"I want to talk about last night," he said.

Dappled sunlight and shadows from the trees above played over her bonny face. "I do too."

"I dinna mean to—"

"I know." Her cheeks flushed red, and she glanced away in a way that could only be described as demure. This woman who had so sharp a tongue, who readily stood up for herself and always had something to say, actually appeared shy.

"You had a nightmare," she said.

She stepped closer and gazed up at him. Light fell over her, showing the depth of rich brown of her eyes, which appeared almost black in the shadows of the coach.

A slight sprinkling of freckles showed across the bridge of her nose, so faint he'd not seen them until now when he was close enough to touch her. They would be so easily accomplished on the page with the barest of touches from his charcoal.

The scent of her floral perfume nudged at the recesses of his mind, and for one fleeting moment, he had the ghost of a memory of her in his arms—warm and sweet, the skin of her neck like silk beneath the brush of his lips.

"What's happened to you?" She grazed his forearm with her fingertips. Her touch was delicate, and the heat of her palm seeped through the linen of his leine. "I think…" She paused and pursed her lips. "I think your dream has something to do with why you're doing this."

He swallowed.

There was so much to tell, so many years of anguish from MacKenzie. And then the idea of giving voice to what he'd seen the day of the massacre. It was too agonizing.

"It isna so easy, my lady." Before he could stop himself, he brushed the pad of his thumb down her cheek, taking care to swipe over the freckle just beside her mouth. Her flushed skin was almost hot beneath his touch.

Elizabeth stepped back abruptly, putting a modest amount of space between them, and darted a glance toward the coach.

Leasa's face jerked back from the window, and the coach gave a little sway.

"I assume what happened last night will not be repeated." Elizabeth's voice took on its usual haughtiness.

Though everything in him wanted to close the distance between them again, to repeat that gentle stroke on her cheek, Kaid held his ground. "Of course, my lady. Forgive me for my indiscretion."

A hearty rustle came from the woods, capturing both their attention. Kaid touched the hilt of his blade and turned toward the sound in time to see two men emerge from the trees.

They were filthy, as though they'd been traveling for some time. Both wore kilts darted through with red and brown wool tartan, and their hair hung lank around their faces.

Kaid cast a quick glance toward Elizabeth. He never should have let her out of the coach. One word from her and these men would know she had been abducted.

Her face belied none of this.

"Good day," Kaid said to the newcomers with a nod.

The taller of the two men nodded back in kind. "Ye having trouble with yer coach?"

Kaid kept his gaze fixed on the two men and hoped Elizabeth wouldn't speak. "Just taking a rest."

The shorter man made a show of looking around the forest. "Where are yer guards?"

The men gave each other a suspicious glance, and Kaid's heart knocked into his ribs.

The taller one stepped forward. "I'll take yer silence to mean it's just the two of ye."

The shorter man followed suit. "The lady is mighty fine for the likes of ye."

Elizabeth edged toward the coach, and Kaid slid his blade from its sheath. The hissing glide of steel was loud in the silence and pulled both of the men's attention toward him.

The taller one swept an axe from his belt and lunged at Kaid, who easily dodged the blow.

Behind them, the shorter man reached out to Elizabeth, grabbed a fistful of her hair, and snapped her toward him.

No.

Kaid's mind swam and his palms went sweaty with anticipation. He would not lose this battle. He could not.

He swung downward, and his blade sliced through the air, glancing off the man's arm.

Brilliant red blossomed against the man's filthy leine, and a coppery scent overwhelmed Kaid's senses.

Blood.

A rush of saliva filled his mouth. He swallowed hard, but the world around him blurred and spun.

He tightened his grip on the hilt of his blade.

He needed to concentrate.

His body acted on instinct, blocking the blow aimed at his head.

He needed to win.

To save Elizabeth.

But the blood. Wet and vivid and violent.

On his blade. Not his hands.

His blade.

A scream rent the air and burst through his narrowing thoughts.

Elizabeth.

• • •

Delilah screamed because it was expected. Her throat ached from the ferocity of the act.

Still the man did not let go of her hair, fool that he was.

Who pulled hair?

She wanted to grab his arm and throw him to the dirt so she

could plunge her blade into his throat while he was still in a state of surprise.

But she had to act like a lady. Frustration niggled at her thoughts. She shoved it away and focused on her situation instead.

Kaid had only one man on him. If he'd so easily taken down her six guards previously and not managed to kill a single one, she knew he could take on the one man and save her when he was done.

Her attacker gave a savage wrench on her hair and sent a fresh wave of pain burning across her scalp. "Where's yer jewelry?" he asked in a grating voice. "And yer coin?"

The grunts and clangs of the battle Kaid fought sounded nearby. They were preoccupied enough that she could allow herself some offense. After all, the hair pulling was getting ridiculous.

Delilah lifted her leg and let her foot come down hard atop his. Surely a lady would have no qualms with stomping on an attacker's toes. The man released her hair long enough for her to stand upright.

"Leave me," she said in a hard voice.

The man snarled at her, revealing a missing front tooth. "I'll take that necklace ye're wearing."

Before she could back away, his clammy fingers caught at the large paste jewel at her neck. One hard jerk and the simple clasp snapped free.

Her hand darted out, and she slapped him, not with the delicate touch of an offended lady, but with all the strength she possessed.

The power of it turned his head and left an angry handprint emblazoned on his cheek. When he turned back to her, his expression burned with rage.

"Ye foolish chit." He pulled a dirk from the top of his boot.

"If you kill me, you won't know where my coin is." She spoke in an arrogant tone she was sure would enrage him.

"I'm sure I'll find it." He jerked forward.

She stepped back in time to avoid the slash of the blade.

Strong arms came around her shoulders, locking her in place. "Get the man," a gruff voice shouted against her ear. The man squeezed her against him. "I'll take care of this pretty alone." The sickly sweet odor of rotting teeth swept over her.

Delilah swallowed against the rise of disgust in her throat. This man had obviously been hiding in the woods in wait for this perfect opportunity. And she'd given it to him.

The odds were no longer as carefully balanced as she'd initially assumed.

The man in front of Delilah ran to join the one already fighting Kaid. The tall man was covered in blood, and the swing of his axe was weak.

He would not survive much longer.

Obviously the man holding her knew this.

"While they're busy…" He said in her ear, and the weight of her skirts was shoved upward.

Summer air bathed her legs and buttocks, and a gasp tore from her throat.

It was one thing to delicately thwart an attack. It was quite another to allow herself to be exposed and possibly raped.

"Get off of me," Delilah growled through clenched teeth.

The rough hair of the man's legs rasped against her naked calves, and he laughed in her ear. "Ye may like it."

She brought her elbow back as hard as could and connected with his ribs. Her skirts fell back into place, and he gave a hard grunt.

She burst from his embrace and spun around, bringing her knee up as she did so, landing it directly into his groin. He pitched forward to the ground.

Delilah put a step of distance between them and cast a quick glance at Kaid. The taller man lay in the mud at his feet while his battle with the shorter one continued.

Their attackers were better fighters than most. Obviously this was not their first raid, and obviously they were usually successful.

How many men had they killed? How many women had they raped?

Delilah's stomach churned.

She stared at the writhing man on the ground. Perhaps she ought to pull the dagger from her pocket.

But ladies did not slit men's throats.

Her attacker cupped his nether region and groaned. He was not going to get up any time soon.

She took another step back to wait for Kaid when the man gripped the back of her heel and pulled. The world swirled around her and she landed hard on her back.

The man moved with the nimbleness of a cat and leapt on top of her. "Ye may be a powerful bitch, but ye missed." He gave a great, huffing laugh and bathed her face with his rotting sweet breath so thick and awful, it clogged in her chest.

He shoved a blade against her throat. "But I find I dinna want to have ye anymore. I want to kill ye."

Her right arm was pinned in place. There was no way she could reach her pocket for her dagger.

She brought her shoulder up hard and shoved him back. It was only an inch, but it was enough time to get her left hand to her busk to grab the hilt of her hidden blade there.

Except it was empty.

Shock.

Confusion.

Horror.

All of it washed over her in rapid succession.

Then she remembered: she'd given it to Leasa to offer her a feeling of protection.

Her act of generosity would be her death.

Delilah wriggled in earnest to free herself, but the man was too heavy, his grasp on her too tight.

He gripped a handful of her hair and yanked her head back, leaving her throat exposed. A metallic taste filled Delilah's mouth and ice ran through her body.

For the first time in as long as she could remember, she was truly afraid.

The man's hand jerked back to strike, a blade gripped in his fist.

She was going to die.

The man's chest punched outward, and he threw his head back in a yowl of agony. He whirled around and brought the dagger with him.

Away from her.

Leasa stood behind him, her face white and her eyes round with horror. The man leapt off Delilah, revealing her busk blade jutting from his back.

He lunged at Leasa before Delilah had time to stand. Her skirts were too voluminous, her bodice too tight.

Leasa screamed.

No.

Delilah floundered against her clothing in her attempt to rise in haste.

Not Leasa.

Chapter Six

Leasa had saved Delilah, and now she would die for her bravery.

The man raised his knife overhead and Leasa cowered from him. Delilah shoved herself up from the ground, but before she could lurch toward the man, something flashed in front of her—the bulk of a body and a glint of steel.

Kaid plunged his sword into their attacker's chest so hard, the tip of the long blade showed through his back.

The attacker's breath choked from his lungs, and his dagger fell with a wet splat into the mud.

Kaid pulled his sword free with a moist sucking sound. For a moment, the man stayed upright on bent knees before finally crumpling to the ground with a long, low exhale.

Delilah stared at the body, wanting to be sure he was dead before she turned her attention from him. Her heart beat so hard and fast, it rendered her breathless.

She'd almost lost her own life. She'd almost lost Leasa.

The man stared into the distance, dull and unfocused with death.

Strong hands gripped her arms. Her body responded by thrusting an arm into her pocket where the dagger lay against her thigh. No sooner had her fingers curled around the hilt than she recognized the face in front of hers as Kaid's. His blue eyes were fixed on her as if he were trying to peer into her soul.

"Elizabeth." The name came out in a hoarse cry.

But not her name.

Elizabeth.

The woman she had been paid to become.

Why then did the name cut into her heart so?

Kaid's gaze ran a wild trail down her body and back to her face. "Are ye hurt?"

Dots of blood peppered his face and stained the front of his shirt. He did not appear injured either, and a wash of gratitude swept over her.

Delilah lifted her head in the haughty manner. "I am uninjured." She swallowed down a squeeze in her throat. "Your investment is still secure."

His brow creased, and she knew the barb hit where intended. "That isna why—Elizabeth, I wanted to ensure ye were safe. I—"

She held up a hand to stop him. Her fingers trembled, much to her surprise and dismay. Quickly, she balled her hand into a fist and snatched it back. "I want to check on Leasa and then change before we resume our journey."

Kaid nodded and stepped away from her. His gaze wandered toward the body at his feet and then to his blood-smeared fingers.

Delilah remembered the nightmare Kaid had had the night before.

They're all dead.

She faltered, wondering if perhaps she ought to be kinder.

But first, Leasa.

She turned to care for the other woman and found Donnan kneeling at her side. His head was bowed over hers, and he spoke quietly to her. Leasa's lower lip quivered, and then he pulled her into his arms. She buried her head into his chest, and her sad sobs filled the air.

Donnan continued to hold her thus, the heavy sack of food on the ground beside him.

Delilah turned back to Kaid, to thank him, to apologize, to be the better person as she should have when he first saved her.

And found him gone.

• • •

The awful encounter would add a serious delay to their journey. Obviously she wasn't responsible for the attack, nor would she have wanted to be, but the time lost was welcome.

She and Leasa both retired to the interior of the coach with the shutters drawn to change into clean garments. Leasa helped her into a yellow dress, something cheerful to lighten the darkness of the mood that had descended upon them all. Leasa shook so terribly, it was a wonder she could even assist Delilah into the gown.

Delilah heard only one sentence uttered between the men from where they conversed outside.

The bodies must be cleared by the time they're done changing.

It'd been spoken in Gaelic by Kaid. Donnan gave a grunt of approval, and Delilah intentionally slowed her pace to ensure the men had the time they needed. Not that she feared dead bodies, but for Leasa's sake, and because she did not wish the men to think their protection had been inadequate.

For certainly they had protected the women.

Never again would Delilah stunt her own abilities for the sake of keeping her secret. It almost cost both women their lives.

Delilah pulled at the final ties on Leasa's gown and squinted in the darkness to knot it securely.

"I want to thank you for saving my life today, Leasa." She turned the woman around to face her, a feat not easily done in such a cramped space with their removed garments billowing around their feet in great puffs of fabric.

"You're my lady," she said. "I'd die to save you."

Delilah embraced her. "You needn't do that ever. I don't want you to be harmed." A tug of guilt pulled at Delilah for what she was about to do.

She hadn't intended to ask now, but the poison had been in the same bag as the yellow gown. The timing was awful, especially when Leasa was recovering from their attack, but it might be the only moment they were completely alone.

She pulled the blue bottle from her pocket where the glass

had grown warm against the heat of her body. "I need you to do something."

Leasa nodded eagerly. "Of course."

"Take this." Delilah dropped her voice to a whisper. "And when we stop to eat, put it into their drinks."

Leasa hesitated before reaching for the poison. "Will it harm them?" she asked in a small voice.

"It will make them ill," Delilah said. "Nothing more. A distraction to ensure we arrive later than Elizabeth."

Percy had said only a few drops would make someone ill for a day, and even more would result in up to a week of nausea, retching, and heavy exhaustion. There wasn't enough in the bottle to kill anyone, so Delilah needn't have a death on her conscience.

Leasa scooped the blue glass bottle from Delilah's palm and tucked it into her own dress for safekeeping. "So long as it will not truly harm them," Leasa said. "They've been kind to us."

"But they have also taken us." Delilah's reminder was not for Leasa alone. She also needed to keep that one glaring thought forefront.

Her mission.

Kaid and Donnan were committing a serious offense and would ultimately need to be brought to justice.

• • •

The blood would never wash out.

Kaid sat once more in the jostling coach, the silence heavier and more uncomfortable than before in light of their recent ordeal.

He continued to stare at the smear of blood on the sleeve of his leine. He'd changed into fresh clothes after they'd disposed of the bodies, but somehow there had still been enough blood on him to leave the stain.

It pulled at his attention like a beacon on a moonless night, and he could not tear his gaze from it.

Nor could he stop the path of his thoughts on their slow

downward spiral. He should have avoided the raw memories, but he curled them into his heart to suffer.

They were his punishment for failure.

"Kaid." Elizabeth's voice interrupted his inner turmoil.

He tried to shove aside the grate of irritation at having his penance interrupted. The sun flickered in through the narrow window of the coach, its brilliant light blinking in and out, like a dagger plunging repeatedly into Kaid's skull.

If only his head did not ache.

He lifted his attention to Elizabeth and found her gaze fixed on him, her brow creased with concern. She was lovely, even when worried.

"Is everything well with you?" she asked.

He wanted to bark a mirthless laugh into the stuffy cabin and burst from its confines in an eruption of rage and sorrow.

Nothing was well with him. Not when so many of his people had been massacred, not when the remaining ones were so displeased, not when he had blood smeared on his clothing to remind him of even more misdeeds. More death.

Nothing would ever be well with him again.

"My head aches fiercely," he offered finally. It was best not to admit the truth. Lady Elizabeth was a noble woman who had been horrified by the day's events. He would not prod her pain any further with his own suffering.

"Were you injured?" She sat a little straighter in her observation, her face anxious.

Her concern was a momentary balm for the blazing anguish in his soul.

"Nay, lass. Dinna worry yerself. The headaches just come from time to time." And they had. Ever since the attack. When sleeplessness had begun to plague him.

The valerian root.

He held the remnants in the pouch at his waist.

His heart raced, and something warm and hungry tingled at the base of his neck.

He swallowed.

Not now.

He must wait until the evening. After what had transpired the previous night, and after everything the women had already gone through, he would not allow himself to sleep in front of them lest he frighten them by having another night terror.

The desire for the vial permeated his thoughts. How he longed to feel the slick glass against his fingertips, to hear the gentle pop of its stopper. He even ached for the bitter taste on his tongue, for what it brought was beautiful and calming and eased him into the velvet nothing of sleep.

He might have nightmares while under the blanket of slumber, but he did not remember them in the morning. For those few hours, he was numb of mind and body. Blissfully, perfectly numb.

"Can I help with anything?" Elizabeth was speaking again.

Kaid clenched his jaw against the consuming weakness of his own desire and shook his head.

She sat forward and took his hand in hers. Her fingers were smooth and delicate, her skin a comforting warmth. "You can talk to me."

Her gaze was soft, her bonny face open and honest, and for one brief moment, he wished he could speak to her. To share the horror of everything he'd witnessed and see if somehow she could pull him from the hell of his own mind.

He nodded his appreciation, and she sat back with a pensive expression lining her brow.

He glanced down, and his gaze found the blood smear.

The vial.

He wanted it. He *needed* it.

So much so, he did not notice the coach roll to a stop and hardly acknowledged the women leaving the cabin.

It was not until he heard voices outside that his attention finally caught.

"I'm worried about Kaid." Elizabeth spoke quietly, as if she did not want him to hear. "Did something happen to him during the fight?"

"No' this one," Donnan answered quietly in return. "He wasna injured."

Silence, and then Elizabeth said, "On another attack, then?"

"Aye," Donnan said. "Our village was invaded no' long ago. Many were slain."

Kaid's breathing had become hard and ragged and seemed to pulse around him from all sides of the coach.

"He'd tried to help them," Donnan said. "But he was hit in the head. When he finally woke, everyone was—"

"Enough!" The word exploded from Kaid, and he jumped to his feet. The coach rocked with the sudden movement, and the voices abruptly stopped.

He yanked open the door with such rage, it almost tore from its paltry hinges. His muscles burned, and he leapt to the ground.

Both Elizabeth and Donnan regarded him with shocked expressions.

"Go with yer maid," he told Elizabeth. "And heaven help ye if ye decide today is when ye run off."

Elizabeth hesitated, as if she intended to say something, then thought better of it and turned toward the forest.

Kaid grabbed Donnan by the shirt and hauled him up against the coach. "Have ye lost yer damn mind?"

Donnan broke Kaid's hold and shoved him back. "Have ye?" Donnan's usually carefree expression was hard. "Isna it bad enough we've taken these women? Then we exposed them to violence no lass should bear witness to, and now ye act like a man possessed when she asks after ye because she's worried?" Donnan dragged a hand through his hair, as he'd done the few times Kaid had seen him vexed. "Hell, Kaid, *I'm* worried about ye."

Kaid glanced toward the tree line to confirm the women had not yet returned. "Ye needn't worry about me."

Donnan's anger eased from his face. "Let's let them go. We can leave them at the next town, and we can go back to Ardvreck. There are other options—"

"There are no other options," Kaid replied in a low growl.

The women emerged from the forest, their expressions somber. Kaid swallowed the remainder of his temper. Donnan was right about one thing: the lasses didn't need anything else to encourage their fear.

But he'd be damned if he let them go. Not when they were his only salvation.

Not when Lady Elizabeth made him finally feel something other than hurt.

Chapter Seven

Anger was oftentimes a mask for deep hurt.

Delilah knew the fit of it well. She'd experienced such rage herself when she first left London and joined the other women in Scotland. She'd given up her life for the mistake of one night with a man who had suffered no consequences.

But Kaid's aching went deeper than a lover scorned.

It stole his thoughts and colored every decision he made.

Including abducting her.

He sat across from her in the bouncing coach, his gaze focused on the smear of blood on the sleeve of his leine. It was a scant thing, really. Little more than the tip of her pinky and long since faded from brilliant crimson to a dull and flaking maroon, but it seemed to be enough to capture his thoughts.

Leasa stared at the empty seat beside Kaid, fixed on her own demons.

The silence of the coach was stifling.

Leasa cupped something in her lap.

The little blue bottle.

Delilah's heartbeat quickened.

She'd been so sure when she'd handed it to Leasa. But now…

The ache in Delilah's chest was poignant, indicative of her empathy for the unknown horror Kaid had faced, what had so obviously shattered him. Now was not the time to poison him.

Perhaps later.

She tried to catch Leasa's eye, but the maid continued to look forward.

In an attempt to break Leasa's plaintive gaze at nothing, Delilah shifted in her seat and gave a delicate cough.

But it was Kaid who looked up. "Are ye well, lass?"

Perhaps Delilah could have lied, easily passed off her own comfort with a dismissive wave of her hand. But she wasn't fine. She had to speak to Leasa to keep her from poisoning the men. Kaid needed his heart to be well before they so altered the state of his health.

"I need to get out of this coach," Delilah conceded. She longed for one of the fans from court, or perhaps even the shaded coolness of a garden. To be out of the awfulness of the fashionable corset and into something more serviceable.

"I wouldna mind a pause myself." He rapped on the top of the coach three times, and they drew to a slow stop. Rocks ground against one another beneath the wheels in gritty pops and snaps.

Delilah waited until Kaid was climbing from the coach before she grabbed Leasa's hand and shook her head. Leasa nodded slowly in reply, and Delilah's anxiety eased into relief.

Leasa understood.

Delilah accepted Kaid's ready assistance and climbed from the coach into scenery so lovely it gave her pause. Sunlight danced atop a loch in flecks of gold, and the world around it was green and alive with lush trees and hills. The sky stretched endless and high overhead, leaving her feeling small in the most humbling of ways.

She tilted her head back and took it all in, the chill of a breeze on her face, the fresh air in her chest, the liberation from the tight, stale box.

"It's beautiful," Delilah breathed.

"They dinna have this in London." A slight smile touched the corner of Kaid's mouth. It was closer to a smile than she anticipated seeing on him anytime soon, and it lightened her heart.

Donnan hopped down from the driver's seat with the food bag in his hand and a wide grin on his face. "I could go for an early midday meal."

She caught the faint scent of spiced meat and freshly baked bread. Her mouth watered in anticipation.

The food, the entire reason they'd stopped when they did, had been unwanted after the attack. Now she felt as though she could devour the entire sack on her own and said as much.

Donnan laughed and swung the food behind his back. "Then ye'll no' get any at all." He peered playfully toward the coach. "Where's Leasa?"

Her head poked tentatively from the door.

"Come join us, Leasa. It's lovely," Delilah said.

Leasa tucked her lower lip into her mouth and shrank back inside slightly. "I thought you—"

Donnan swept into the coach and emerged with Leasa in his arms along with the bag of food. "I've the finest seat for ye."

She gave a shrill cry, but the smile on her face showed it was all in good fun. Delilah couldn't help the laugh bubbling up from her throat. A quick glance at Kaid showed a true, genuine smile on his lips.

Donnan set Leasa on the grass by the water's edge, far enough away to ensure she would not get wet, and then plopped down beside her. "See? The finest seat in the land." He winked. "By me."

Kaid appeared at Delilah's side and held out the crook of his arm to her like a courtier. "My lady," he offered with a formal bow.

"How could a lady refuse?" Delilah asked and slipped her hand to his arm. His sleeves were pulled up, and her fingertips brushed his naked forearm. The sprinkling of dark hair was far less coarse than it appeared, and it was all she could do to keep from giving into the temptation to stroke his skin.

Kaid formally showed her to her place on the ground then sank down beside her. They supped on their midday meal in a bubble of light and happiness, the morning a shoved-aside memory for the moment.

It was as perfect a day as Delilah had ever had.

All until she rose from where she sat and someone gripped her hard around the wrist.

"My lady," Leasa hissed, her eyes wide with horror.

Delilah's heart skipped a beat. She scanned the area and found nothing amiss. Kaid had gone to the coach to tuck away the rest of the food, and Donnan had disappeared for a moment into the forest.

"What is it?" Delilah asked.

Leasa's face crumpled. "I don't remember which flask I put the drops in."

Delilah's blood went cold. "The drops?"

"The poison you told me to use." Leasa looked genuinely confused and held up the blue bottle.

It was empty.

Delilah shook her head. "No, I told you in the coach not to use it."

Leasa's mouth fell open. "I thought..." The color bled from her face. "I thought you'd wanted me to stay in the coach."

Suddenly it made sense, the reason why Leasa had not been as eager to leave the enclosed compartment. Frustration clambered through Delilah, but she quickly held it back.

It had been an honest mistake.

"Think on which flask you used," Delilah said.

Tears shone bright in Leasa's eyes. "They both look the same. I don't know, and we all shared them."

"What are you saying?" Delilah asked, knowing full well what was being said.

Leasa's head dropped forward. "I think we've all been poisoned."

• • •

The day had been better than any Kaid had experienced since the massacre.

He'd even laughed.

It was hard not to when Donnan flirted with Leasa like a consummate courtier and Elizabeth kept staring at him with that quiet smile on her face.

He felt a grin touch his lips at the very thought. Happiness made a light come to life in her expression, and her laugh had been throaty and genuine.

Today, she was not a spoiled nobleman's daughter—she was a woman like any other, sitting on the ground and sharing food and drink with friends.

Kaid settled the bag of food against the packs of clothing and other goods Elizabeth had brought with her for her new life with MacKenzie.

His good humor wilted away.

Much as he did not want to think on it at the moment, she *was* an English nobleman's daughter. She was to marry MacKenzie, and she was the only leverage Kaid had against him.

Kaid would do well to keep such thoughts forefront in his mind.

Agony knifed through his gut. Kaid leaned into the sudden ache with a stifled grunt.

He waited for a moment until it passed before straightening, only to have it happen again. This cramp was far more vicious and made his mouth water with the need to be sick.

A cry came from where he'd left the women. He shoved himself upright and ran toward the shoreline. Both women were doubled over with their arms folded against their stomachs.

Donnan staggered out of the trees with one hand pressed to his stomach, the other holding his blade. His eyes lit on Kaid, and he let his sword dip to the ground where the tip dragged as he continued to march forward.

"All of us?" Donnan asked in a ragged voice. His face was pale and sweat gleamed on his brow.

Kaid nodded.

Leasa gave a squeal of discomfort and toppled to the ground. Elizabeth stepped toward her, but it was Donnan who straightened and lifted her into his arms. "I knew I shouldna have trusted that venison merchant." He carried Leasa toward the carriage with a limping gait.

Elizabeth looked just as wan as her maid. Still, she remained upright, though the waves around her face were now plastered against her brow and cheeks.

Kaid moved to her side and took her arm. She faltered. "I can…" Breath wheezed from her. "I'm fine." She shook her head.

She looked anything but fine.

A fresh blade of anguish lanced through Kaid, but he was able to resist giving in to it this time. Elizabeth might be playing at being strong, but she seemed about to collapse.

She gave a choked gasp and tugged at the front of her bodice. "So tight."

She took another step, stumbled, and started to tilt.

Kaid caught her before any part of her had a chance to touch the grassy bank of the loch. His body clenched around another cramp, but he did not let his grip on her loosen. "I've got ye, lass."

She pursed her lips, and she turned her face into his chest. She was suffering from another attack as well, and took it better than he had assumed any noblewoman ever could.

"Not the coach." Her breath came fast and short between her words. "Please."

Truth be told, he didn't know if he could have lifted her into the coach even if she wanted to be there. He set her as gently as he could in the shade of the coach. Leasa and Donnan were already there, both still, both unnervingly pale.

Kaid knew he should stay awake, perhaps go get a healer, make his way to the village for help.

Everything screamed in agony. His guts, his bones, his head, even his flesh.

He lay on his stomach, where the pressure of the ground against his body eased the cramping and the moist, cool earth pressed to his hot skin.

His eyes closed, though he willed them not to. Awake was pain, but it was necessary. Sleep was comfortable, a reprieve.

He lifted his brows in an effort to also drag his eyelids upward. The world blurred against his squinted vision, greens and golds and blues, all shooting into his brain like splinters of cathedral glass, and he clamped his eyes shut against it.

He should stay awake.

It was his last thought before the bliss of sleep slipped him away from his discomfort.

He did not stay asleep though, and woke in snatches of time.

The groan of someone nearby.

Then sleep.

The fading of the warm sun against his face.

Darkness.

Then sleep.

A rasping voice calling for water.

Water.

He swallowed at the thought and found his mouth so dry, his throat near stuck against itself. His tongue was thick, and the burn of thirst was almost as great as the spasms left behind by the bad venison.

The voice called for water again and again until finally he dragged himself from the welcoming clutches of slumber.

The sky was lit with the glow of a thousand stars. He crawled toward the flask. He wasn't aware he was doing it until he noticed the rocks scraping and rolling beneath his abdomen.

Elizabeth pushed a clumsy hand toward him and knocked the flask from his grasp. It tumbled from his loose hold and landed with a splat. The ale glugged out from it in great, jerking gushes.

Elizabeth stammered out an apology, then licked her lips.

Though she didn't say it, she was thirsty. They all were.

Kaid staggered to his feet and stumbled over slanted earth to where the loch licked the shore. He all but fell into it in his clumsy attempt to fill the flask. The water undulated like a pool of ink with bits of moonlight shattered over its surface.

He let it wash over his lips, bathing them in the cool wetness, and then he drank. Gulp after greedy gulp of icy water slaked the thirst burning in his throat.

His eyes closed a moment.

Just a moment.

Comfortable darkness beckoned him and then a severe jag of hurt sliced through him, pulling him from the threat of sleep and launching him toward his goal. He shuffled those several feet back to camp with his back hunched and the flask of water cradled to his clenching stomach as if it were treasure.

For surely it was.

Elizabeth's face was relaxed in her slumber. She looked so peaceful, angelic almost. He didn't want to wake her.

Droplets of water dribbled from the top of the flask and fell toward her like loosed diamonds.

She blinked. "Water." Her voice cracked in a dry whisper.

He passed her the flask, and she drank with a savage thirst like a warrior just off the battlefield.

Were he not so damn sick, he might crack a smile at it.

But it was not only Elizabeth who needed water. Leasa and Donnan echoed her pleas. As soon as Elizabeth had drunk her fill, he brought the flask to Leasa and then to Donnan, knowing he would want the lass to drink before him.

The horses whinnied in the distance, but Kaid took comfort in knowing they'd been tethered with stays long enough to reach both loch and grass.

At long last, with a body cowed beneath the knifing agony, Kaid settled on the ground near Elizabeth so he could be near enough to protect her.

He pulled the vial from the pouch at his waist. How it had not become lost in the laborious task of procuring water, he did not know, but was grateful.

His fingers shook.

This would be the last dose until they could return to Ardvreck Castle.

The last.

The words echoed ominously in his mind, reminding him again and again of the horror he would soon face without its aid.

He unstoppered the bottle and tossed the remaining contents into his mouth.

It was bitter and beautiful at all once.

His eyes fluttered closed and he waited for relief.

And it came, for a while, before he woke with such illness as he had never experienced. Agony knifed through his insides and everything whirled around him, too fast and too chaotic for him to hold on. His body shivered and clenched. Sweat blanketed his skin and did nothing but set the chill even deeper into his aching bones.

He shut out everything and kept his face pressed into the cold, wet ground, waiting for the pain to stop.

Chapter Eight

The sun was high overhead when Delilah finally woke, but she immediately clamped her eyes shut against the offending brilliance.

Her head felt as though it'd been stuffed with wads of wet wool. She swallowed and found her mouth felt much the same.

She tried to speak, but her tongue was uncooperative. An unintelligible garble rasped from her mouth.

Water.

She wanted water.

Fresh and crisp, cold and refreshingly wet.

Her saliva thickened in her mouth at the very thought.

Something pressed to her lips.

"Drink, my lady." Leasa's voice.

Delilah squinted to see Leasa's head blocking out the sun, her face shadowed by the glow surrounding her.

The muscles of Delilah's throat relaxed, and she drew in the water with large, eager gulps.

She didn't stop until her stomach sloshed with her fill, or at least as much as the corset would allow her to consume. How she longed for the more forgiving leather garments she wore under a leine while practicing with Sylvi and the other women.

A breeze brushed her face, and her loosed hair tickled her skin. Delilah swallowed once more before trusting herself to speak. "Were you not ill as well?"

"I was, my lady, and am feeling much better now." Leasa assisted Delilah into a sitting position. Though they moved slowly, lightheadedness threatened to pull her to the ground once more.

Sunlight slashed over the pathetic remnants of their camp. A bit of scorched earth and ash stood where a fire had once been, and the grass lay flattened nearby, no doubt where Leasa and Donnan had lain, but that was not what made her cry out.

Kaid lay beside her, as pale and unmoving as death.

"Donnan says he's alive," Leasa said. There were smudges under her eyes, so deep in color, the skin looked bruised. Her lips were puckered with dryness, and she'd lost the high color in her cheeks. "Donnan's gathering wood for the fire now. I guess they trust us finally." She gave a weak smile.

Kaid's head rolled to the side and he groaned. The sound, no matter how tortured, eased the clench of Delilah's heart.

He *was* alive.

And she cared of his survival for all the wrong reasons.

She should be glad to see him living so that she might bring him to justice, not because he'd earned her admiration or because she thought of his well-being more than she ought to.

"We should care for him," Leasa said in a quiet tone. "He's helped us, even when he was sick."

Memories floated back to Delilah—the ravenous, overwhelming thirst, crying out with need for water. And Kaid being there with soothing words and much-needed relief.

"You should try to eat, my lady." Leasa pushed a chunk of bread into Delilah's hands. "It will make you feel better."

Delilah's stomach wrenched at the very thought of food, but she knew what Leasa said was true.

An hour later, Delilah was glad she'd listened. The swirling of her stomach had finally settled and the floating feel in her head had dissipated. She and Leasa had even bathed in the loch. The icy water had been a special kind of sweet heaven as it threaded through her hair and swept away the sweat and grit of illness.

She'd even ensured Leasa left her corset slightly less tight in the dress she changed into, the simplest of all the gowns she'd been given. Tiny pink flowers were embroidered at the sleeves and hem, but those were the only adornments on the russet-colored linen.

Although she had rejoined the world of the living, Kaid had still not improved. If anything, he seemed to worsen. He'd been sick several times and had grown paler.

"Ye dinna have to care for him, Lady Elizabeth," Donnan said. "Ye'll ruin yer fine gown."

Delilah shook her head. "He aided us when we were all unwell. I won't leave him now."

Donnan shook his head with a smirk. "We took ye to hold for ransom."

The admission lanced through her, but she kept her face impassive. "I would like to believe you have good reason for what you're doing."

He opened his mouth, and she thought for a brief moment he would offer her the explanation she so desperately sought. But he gave her a smile instead. "Ye're a kind lass."

Heat crept into Delilah's cheeks. She was not kind.

It was her fault Kaid was so ill. It was her fault they'd all been ill.

He lay beside her, his face slick with sweat. Why had he had such a violent reaction to the poison? If he'd been well enough to care for them all in the beginning, what had caused it to worsen?

It was then she noticed one of his hands was fisted and realized it had remained thus since she'd been at his side.

With great care, she unfurled his clenched fingers, noticing again that his thumb and forefinger were both smudged with black. Once she straightened his fingers, a small vial rolled free.

She lifted it from where it fell to the ground and pulled the stopper free. Kaid murmured something unintelligible.

Delilah lifted the empty vial to her nose and sniffed. The pungent odor assaulted her nostrils and she jerked her head back.

Valerian root.

She knew the scent well enough from Percy's workshop. Though she'd smelled it only once, it was awful enough to have seared into her memory. She wished Percy were here now, with her knowledge of herbs and tinctures.

Kaid mumbled once more.

Delilah lifted the wineskin to his lips. "Do you need water?"

He turned his head away from it and said something she couldn't understand. His lips moved again, and she leaned closer to hear.

"They're all dead." Kaid's voice was thick and rasping in his throat, but the words were unmistakable. "They're all dead."

The phrase chilled through her. It was the same one he'd said when he had the nightmare.

Perhaps this might be part of why he had abducted them. He had refused to give her a sufficient answer, and his rage at Donnan's tale of the deaths, all of it seemed too coincidental. Regardless of the awfulness of the crime Kaid had committed, she refused to believe in her heart that he'd done it purely for selfish reasons.

This might not be about coin at all, or anything so tangible. It had to be about something bigger than her, bigger than him, bigger even than the risk of getting caught.

This was the reason they'd been abducted. She didn't know why specifically, but she knew with great certainty it was.

She did know something in the valerian root was causing him to give into the torture of his own mind. While she didn't have the same knowledge of herbs and healing as Percy, she knew well the best way to be free of something was to purge it from your system.

Delilah held the flask to Kaid's lips and tipped water into his mouth until he swallowed. The more he drank, the more he would need to purge.

Sure enough, within a few minutes, the water came back up, and she repeated the process.

She would ensure he came out of this, and she would not leave his side until he was recovered.

• • •

Kaid woke to darkness.

No, not darkness. Stars winked overhead, countless dots of white against the velvet of a midnight sky. The gentle lapping of water broke into his awareness, as did the awareness of someone lying close to him and the subtle weight of a hand on his chest.

He lowered his gaze and found Elizabeth curled against him, her arm slung over him with the easy comfort of a lover.

The warmth of her body seemed to burn against him, and the delicate scent of her floral perfume held him like an embrace.

He didn't know how she'd come to lie so intimately against him, but he was grateful. Part of him wanted to touch her, to stroke her hair, to brush his fingers over her cheek which he knew to be impossibly soft, to pull her against him and revel in her closeness.

But a wary part of him worried touching her would break a fragile spell and replace the relaxed beauty at his side with the spoiled noblewoman.

It was more than just Elizabeth, though. He was more aware of everything. The sigh of the wind against his cheeks, the blaze of the fire against his back, the delicate slosh of waves from the loch, even the burning hunger in his empty stomach—everything was sharper. As if the fog in his mind had lifted.

He lay there for a while, giving in to the quiet of his body, and reveling in the world of feeling more than he'd felt in far too long.

Elizabeth shifted at his side and sat up. Their shared heat immediately chilled. While the night was not a cold one by any means, he missed the warmth of her against him.

Her eyes settled on him, and she gave him the most beautiful smile he'd ever seen. It was filled with a tender kindness and affection—and meant only for him.

"You're awake," she said.

He tried to prop himself on his arm to look at her, but his muscles felt liquid with weakness. Elizabeth put a hand on his shoulder and eased him back. "Don't sit up yet. You've been several days without food."

The clarity he'd experienced only moments ago faded and left him disoriented.

How had he not eaten for several days?

"You've been very ill," she offered in explanation. Her touch lingered on his shoulder, comforting.

"We all were." The words burned as they rasped from his throat.

Elizabeth drew her hand from him and lifted a bag of food. "We all recovered quickly. I think you—" Her lips pursed, and she stopped herself. "Here." She held out a chunk of bread. "It will help you feel better."

He took it from her. "Ye think I what?"

Her gaze slipped away, and he knew something was wrong.

Elizabeth seldom turned her gaze from anyone.

The yeasty scent of the bread pulled at him. He took a bite while waiting for her to reply. The crust was hard and flaky, the inside pliant and moist. His mouth watered, and a hunger unlike anything he'd known before slammed into him.

"I think you were most affected because of the valerian root you were taking. You had more nightmares. I think it's the valerian that's causing those as well."

She offered him a flask of ale, and he washed down the bread lodged in his throat. It all mingled in his stomach like a comforting balm.

Already he was beginning to feel better.

Elizabeth held the empty vial toward him. He pushed himself onto his arm and sat up to reach for it.

She pulled it back with a frown.

"Kaid, I think this is what is causing your nightmares. And I believe something happened to you, to Donnan, to people you loved. I think it has to do with why you took us." She was speaking faster now, like the words had been swarming in her head and she finally had a chance to say them. "Please tell me."

Her eyes implored him, and her fingers closed over the empty vial.

The world spun around Kaid for a brief moment before settling into place once more. A breeze swept through the surrounding forest and sent the leaves chattering amongst themselves.

She was right. He needed to tell her.

The sound of hoofbeats came in a muted clopping, the kind made on wet forest earth. Kaid turned and found Donnan on the back of a horse with Leasa in front of him holding another bag of food clasped in her hands.

They'd expected to stay several more days.

For him.

Donnan grinned at him. "Glad ye could finally join us. We've missed yer charm."

"If I werena so intent on eating this bread, I'd knock ye for that," Kaid said with a grunt.

Donnan laughed and slid from the horse. "Aye, that charm."

He helped Leasa from the horse.

"Are you feeling better?" she asked.

Physically, he hadn't felt better in ages. But deep inside the hurt of an old wound had ripped fresh.

Donnan's grin wilted.

"We need to tell them," Kaid said. He shifted his gaze to Elizabeth and found her watching him with a terse expression.

Donnan led Leasa over and motioned for her to sit beside Elizabeth. "I think we should have told them from the beginning," he said.

Kaid nodded. Donnan had indeed said as much, and deep down Kaid had known it as well.

The time had finally come to tell the women why he had taken them, and why he would hold them for ransom.

Chapter Nine

Telling the story would be like reliving the nightmare. Kaid knew this before he even began.

His gaze drifted toward the wavering surface of the loch, where the moon was mirrored in a grotesque image of itself, smeared and swollen.

He let his mind slip back to a place it constantly flicked away from, that fateful gray morning in December. The wind had been so bitter and ruthless, breathing left his throat and chest raw. Spirals of smoke from controlled fires puffed throughout the outlying village near Ardvreck Castle where Kaid had stood guard with several other MacLeod warriors.

"It happened half a year ago." He did not recognize the hollowness of his own voice. "Our alliance with the MacKenzies had always been a fickle one, which often broke down in minor battles. But never had we suspected an attack to be on so great a scale."

The invasion had started with a woman's single scream. High and shrill in the thin air, and quickly cut short.

A woman. Not a man, or an armed warrior who could have defended himself—an unarmed woman from the village.

"When they came, it was not entirely unexpected," Kaid continued. "We'd had several MacKenzies come from time to time and lay minor attacks on the castle. Laird MacKenzie must have sent every one of his men that day. But the attack did not come to the castle. It was on the village."

The MacKenzies streamed from the surrounding woods in a tidal wave of men, their roars deafening, even from where Kaid stood. He didn't hesitate, nor did the men around him. Blood charged through his veins, his confidence overflowing with the surety of power and training.

Together, they ran from the castle, trusting several remaining warriors to stand guard while they lashed against the enemy to offer protection.

"They were simple villagers. Unarmed." His words came out strained and hoarse.

Kaid paused and took a deep drink from the flask of ale at his side and wished it were whisky or wine, preferably valerian—anything to dull the memories. The very ones he would need to let wash over him and, for once, not fight.

He did not look at the women or Donnan and instead kept his focus on the loch. He could not bear to see the emotions etched on their faces as his were so indelibly etched on his heart.

Chaos.

The world was in chaos.

Fire licked at thatch roofs and spiraled acrid smoke, choking the men's throats and stinging their eyes. All around them were armed men and the cries of their defenseless victims.

Kaid tore through them with all the speed he could muster. His forearm went numb with the repetitive clang of his weapon against others. Mud and gore splashed his face and clothing. Still he did not stop.

Still it was not enough.

"We tried to fight as hard as we could, but there were too many men attacking." Defeat pulled at Kaid's heart as it had that fateful morning. "The village was too twisted with alleys and homes for the villagers to hide."

He took another swallow of the ale, but it did little to ease the rawness, as if he were experiencing the smoke of the fires again, the harshness of his war cry rasping through his throat once more. "My da saw us losing the fight and came out to help the villagers. He fought valiantly, but his men were cut down, and he too fell. The MacKenzies took his body, and they took his blade."

The great and powerful Laird MacLeod was carelessly dragged through the mud like a carcass whose meat had gone bad. His face was slack, and his jaw hung open. Blue eyes bulged, but stared at nothing while bits of mud flew at his face and speckled his teeth.

Kaid glanced but for a brief moment at the high offense before returning his attention to the fight once more. He would mourn his father later. He would get his father's sword back later.

Now was for his people, for he was the new laird.

"I tried to fight as many as I could." Kaid let the memories sweep over him. "But there were too many. And then I saw a cluster of children, banded together inside a ring of women who fought with whatever tools they could grab." It had all been so insufficient—shears, a dirk, a large hook, whatever their men had not taken to defend themselves. "The MacKenzies found them…"

He let his voice trail off and could not put to words what he witnessed. Certainly no lady should ever hear the horrors he'd had to see.

The children's cries came clear and high over the death grunts and screams. Kaid pulled his blade free from the man he'd just slain and tried to run toward them, only to be thwarted by another MacKenzie warrior.

The women around their bairns lashed out, mothers willing to die for their children, but they were no match for the axes, broadswords, and arrows.

Three fell before he was free. Their defeat rang out in the keening cries of their children. Kaid's muscles burned with the determination, but he moved too slowly.

An ache blossomed at his temple and everything blurred to a narrow white dot.

Kaid settled his palm over his head, as if he could still feel the thin trickle of blood. "I was struck on the head before I could get to them. When I awoke…"

He focused on the surrounding forest, the rustle of trees against one another in the moonlight, the gray clouds in a dark sky, the twinkle of stars scattering the sky above. Anything other than what wanted to rise to the forefront of his memory.

He could not let himself see that again.

Not ever.

"My people want vengeance," he said in a resigned voice. "But I know it will only bring more bloodshed."

Finally he let his gaze shift to Elizabeth, who watched him with a puckered brow and an intent stare. "I took ye to hopefully negotiate with MacKenzie, to get my da's sword back, and to encourage peace between our people."

Donnan covered Leasa's hand with his own, and their fingers intertwined.

"Why?" Elizabeth whispered. "Why would anyone do something so dreadful as killing mothers? Children?"

It was then he remembered the man he spoke of was the very one to whom she was betrothed. MacKenzie would be her husband.

"There's been a long-standing feud between our clans," Donnan answered for him.

"But what could possibly start something so violent?" she asked.

Donnan's gaze met Kaid's in the delicate glow of the moon and he knew he must confess the final bit of information he'd held back. "Marriage."

Elizabeth frowned, obviously not understanding the history such a single word encompassed.

"The late Laird MacKenzie's bride fell ill on the road home while she was pregnant. Too far from Edirdovar, she instead came to Ardvreck Castle for aid," Kaid answered, dreading the story even as it fell from his lips. "After she delivered a son, her illness worsened and she died. Rumor has it, she hadna yet been wed, and Laird MacKenzie's babe was a bastard. A previous, legitimate marriage to the old laird had yielded a daughter, but no one has seen or heard of the wee Torra MacKenzie in years. In her absence, the boy rumored to be a bastard succeeded his father as Laird MacKenzie—the current laird.

"The MacKenzies claimed we'd poisoned the young mother and held to that accusation for years. The day we were attacked was the verra day my father was to remarry. It was why they invaded the village—they must have heard she'd insisted on sleeping there the night before her wedding."

"Did they kill her?" Elizabeth's mouth was a tight line.

Kaid swallowed. "Aye."

She looked down at where her fingers were loosely clasped in her lap. "And then there's me."

"Aye." Kaid's voice came out like scraped gravel, as low as he felt. "The next bride in a history of blood and vengeance."

• • •

The real Elizabeth was in danger, whether she made it to Killearnan or not.

Delilah now understood any bride of a MacKenzie or a MacLeod held a death sentence.

When Elizabeth made it safely to MacKenzie and the MacLeods all knew they'd been duped, would one of Kaid's men try to kill the real Elizabeth? Would the feud continue?

Only now did she realize the true impact of what she'd done in replacing Elizabeth. What might have been the civil, peaceful end of a feud could now perpetuate a war.

Delilah knew Kaid was waiting for her to respond, but her tongue was thick and immobile in her mouth.

Elizabeth.

Delilah's heart constricted for the poor girl. Elizabeth, who obeyed a father wedding her to a man he didn't trust, whose betrothed ordered the slaughter of innocent, unarmed people.

It all settled on Delilah's shoulders with such unbearable weight, there was a part of her, the deep-down, selfish part, which wished she had not asked.

Had she never known any of this, she could easily have continued. She could have ensured Elizabeth was safely delivered, and walked away feeling confident the girl would be safe.

Her assignment did not change with the new knowledge. Elizabeth's father would not alter his decision. Sylvi would not relax her orders.

And if Delilah did not do as instructed, she would fail. On her first true task on her own.

Failure.

A word she'd too long known.

"Elizabeth?" Kaid's voice was gentle.

She met his gaze, this man who had suffered, and to whom she was lying and would ultimately betray.

"I'm sorry." It was all she could muster, uttered in a choked cry.

What was she sorry for? Her heart grew heavy as she counted the reasons.

What he'd seen.

How she'd lied.

How she would continue to lie and do whatever she had to.

Her face went hot and her nose tingled with the threat of tears. She wanted to stop them, but her throat was too tight around the uncomfortable lump settled there.

"Excuse me," she said in a croaked voice and rose from the ground. Her knees were stiff from sitting for so long.

Leasa began to rise too, but Delilah shook her head. "I just…" She swallowed the desire to give in to her sobs. "I just need to be alone for a moment."

To gather herself.

To breathe.

To stop feeling so blasted much.

Leasa sank back down beside Donnan, who gave her a gentle nod of understanding.

Delilah walked toward the woods with as much control as she could muster. She waited until the wet scent of the forest greeted her and the press of clustered tree trunks caught at her full skirts. She managed at least that long before she braced herself against the nearest tree and gave in to the dam trembling for release in the back of her throat.

Her free hand came to rest over her wet face, as if she could hide her sorrow even from herself, and kept her sobs as muffled as was possible.

She did not want anyone to see her weakness.

And she was weak.

For she felt too much for Elizabeth, the woman destined for a life of misery regardless of how the situation ended.

She felt too much for Sylvi and the other women who were counting on her to accomplish this mission. They had saved her from a life of shame and degradation. She owed them everything, and they expected much. Rightfully so.

She felt too much for Donnan and Kaid.

Her heart flinched. She especially felt too much for Kaid, with his beautiful eyes and tortured soul.

Why, why, *why* had she pressed Kaid for answers?

Never once had she considered the repercussion of truly knowing the situation.

A footstep sounded behind her, and her hand went into her pocket where the dagger lay against her thigh.

"It's just me." Kaid's comforting voice eased her grip from the hilt of her blade. "I worried about ye. I dinna—I shouldna have said everything I did."

Delilah did not turn around. Surely her face would give away her tears, even if they had already begun to dry. "I asked you to." She spoke in a whisper to ensure the thickness of her emotion couldn't be detected.

"Aye, and I know ye needed to find out." He paused, and she realized he was trying to carefully construct what he said. "I dinna want to hurt ye. I've no' ever wanted to hurt ye. Or Leasa."

He stepped closer. She could sense his body near her back. He had a pleasant, spicy scent that mingled with those of the damp forest.

Something deep inside her longed to lean back against the solid wall of his chest.

But she was not the only one in need of comfort.

Kaid's face earlier had told the tale his words did not elaborate upon.

He hadn't looked at them when he spoke, perhaps to keep her

from seeing the evidence of tears. The things he'd witnessed had been horrifying, evidenced by the catch in his voice and the brilliance of his haunted stare.

Her heart ached.

"I'm sorry." His voice was in her ear and the warmth of his breath stirred the delicate hairs at her neck.

A pleasant shiver prickled over her skin.

"I know." Though she whispered, she knew he would hear her.

He was not the only one inclined to apologize despite needing to finish what he'd started.

Before she could stop herself, she eased back the slightest bit, her body seeking the comfort and strength of his. She didn't allow herself to touch him, but she sensed how much closer that minor shift brought them. Her heartbeat pounded a little faster.

"I dinna ever want to hurt ye." Kaid's burr sounded against her ear. She turned toward the timbre of his voice and the heat of his mouth. A thrum of longing began to pulse low in her stomach.

They stayed poised thus for the lifetime of a moment.

Something brushed against the sensitive dip where her neck met her shoulders, so gentle she almost did not discern its whisper over her skin.

But she did, and the sensation sent her heart into wild gallops.

She leaned her head to expose her neck, welcoming the touch.

His fingers swept down her neck, cold against her blazing skin. She gave in and sank into the pleasure of his touch.

For she wanted so much more.

Chapter Ten

Kaid's breathing came faster, filling the silence in the forest.

His fingertips still tingled with the effect of caressing Elizabeth, the silky warmth of her skin. His body was chilled from having washed in the loch while he waited for her to return. Doubtless his fingers had been cold.

Elizabeth had not turned away, though.

He stared down at the exposed curve of her neck, the slender muscles straining against her skin, the sweet slope of her collarbone.

Her eyes were closed, her lips parted, as if she wanted his kiss.

But she was his enemy's bride to be. She was the salvation of his people. She was a maiden.

Everything in Kaid wanted to caress her again, to let the pads of his fingers sweep down her neck, the same as his bit of charcoal did against the lines he drew when he knew she would not see.

He'd drawn her neck countless times, the same as her face, the sweet shape of her mouth, the complexities of her expressions. She was exquisite.

And now she was directly in front of him with her body leaned toward him.

His hovering fingers came down once more onto her smooth skin at the nape of her neck and traced a careful line upward to the thick light brown hair that reminded him so of honey's sweet golden hue.

A gasp whispered through her lips. Her skin rose with tiny prickling bumps.

Her reaction only spurred him toward what he desired.

To kiss her. To taste her.

Before he could pull himself from her, he leaned forward and let his lips brush against the skin where her neck and shoulders met.

She was warm and supple and wholly perfect.

It was a small kiss, a tease of what he wanted to do, and it was his intention to do no more.

Then the pull of her floral perfume intoxicated him with the promise of her sweetness, the heat of her skin lured him toward everything hot when the loch had left him so damn cold.

He did not straighten away from her. No, he let his lips drift up her slender neck. His stubbled chin brushed the bit of her exposed back beneath the line of her gown, and she gave a little strangled sound somewhere between a cry and a moan.

Longing surged through his body and left him ravenous for her.

He wanted his hands on her, his mouth on her, his body on her. But he held back.

Only his mouth.

Only her neck.

Only a taste.

He carefully traced the line of her neck with the tip of his tongue. Her skin was sweet and salty, leaving him wanting more.

"Kaid." His name was so quiet a whisper on her lips, he almost hadn't heard it.

He paused, thinking she might stop him to point out how wildly inappropriate his actions were. His body pounded with desire, and his blood poured through his veins like liquid fire.

He waited for her protests.

They did not come.

He licked her delicate neck once more, a languid tease of his tongue against her naked flesh.

This time she moaned and leaned further back, until her back pressed against him.

"Yes." There was something pleading in her tone.

He caught her slender waist and held her to him, scraping his teeth against her skin, letting his kiss deepen with sucks and bites.

His cock strained with need. He ran his lips up her neck and caught the lobe of her ear in his mouth.

She whimpered and arched her back, pressing into the part of him which wanted her so desperately.

He wanted to spin her around, so he could gaze at her in those precious moments before kissing her lush mouth.

But those stares, those kisses were not for him.

She was MacKenzie's.

Even as Kaid reminded himself of this, he continued kissing the length of her slender neck, tormenting himself with what he could never have and yet could not stop wanting.

Elizabeth reached behind her and gripped his arms, as if she needed them to stay on her feet. The curves of her body beneath her dress rolled back into him, and her breath came in delicate pants.

"Kiss me," she gasped. "Please, Kaid. Kiss me."

He almost groaned with the need to fulfill her request.

She was MacKenzie's.

His frustration came out in a rasping growl in her ear.

Elizabeth inhaled sharply and tried to crane her face upward, toward him. "Please, Kaid." She writhed in his arms. Hungry, desperate, in need.

He understood those emotions too well. They were the same as his, for he wanted nothing more than to kiss her—not as the woman he'd abducted, nor as the future wife of his enemy, but as the woman for whom his affections ran deeper than they ever should have.

• • •

Delilah was on fire.

Desire singed her body and left her skin alight with a sensitivity that would almost hurt, had it not felt so wonderfully good. It tingled through her veins and pulsed in a place she'd once vowed to never let a man touch her again.

She wanted to be touched there now.

But not just by any man.

She wanted Kaid, with his long, tapered fingers, graceful, capable, strong.

What he could do with those fingers…

His mouth moved down her neck in a maddening tease with no culmination in sight. The rasp of his stubbled jaw against the tender skin of her neck sent a fresh wave of excitement through her body.

She wanted his mouth on hers. The affections he placed where she could not see tormented her.

His lips were sultry and possessive on her neck.

But she wanted him on her mouth.

A cry of frustration sounded from her throat, and she tried to turn.

He tightened his grip on her waist and nuzzled his face against hers, tempting her with the sweet warmth of his breath across her mouth.

She licked her lips, as if she could capture the sensation and encourage it into something more, but he nudged her face forward once more with his own.

He'd dragged her to the brink of helpless insanity.

She couldn't think—all she could do was *feel*.

The crazed thrum between her legs, blazing and insistent, made her heart feel as if it were going to part with her chest and kept any air from entering her lungs.

"Please." Rage at her unmet desires made the word sound harsh.

He stopped. Finally.

Delilah panted and his hold on her waist relaxed. It was all she needed. She spun around and faced him.

He stared down at her, his chest heaving. His hair hung in damp waves around his face, and his eyes seemed mystical in the dusky early evening light.

She drew in a deep breath to ask him once more to kiss her when he caught her by the back of the neck and drew his face to hers.

Then finally, *finally*, the soft heat of his mouth closed over hers.

She was mistaken to assume their lips meeting would douse the fire within. It only served to intensify it.

Delilah gave in to his hungry draw, letting him devour her in sucking kisses and nips. His unshaven chin chafed against her face, but the sensation only heightened her pleasure.

His back was powerful beneath her restless palms, his body hot despite the leine separating them, and the glorious muscles there glided with his every move.

He groaned and stepped forward, compelling her backward. She went without hesitation.

She wanted this.

She wanted him.

The rough bark of a tree snagged the back of her dress. Kaid pressed the hardness of his body over her, and she moaned her desires like a wanton.

In the back of her mind, she knew this was not how a lady acted.

In the front of her mind, she knew she wanted this.

Suddenly Kaid shoved away from her.

She immediately felt his absence. The air was too cool without his heat, her mouth too lonely without the play of his lips, her soul too empty without the strength of his body.

He stood an arm's length away. "I can't."

She nodded in a vigorous, overly understanding gesture.

"I can't," he repeated.

But he did not leave.

A baser part of her demanded she beg for him to continue, to ignore the feud, the impending marriage, all of it.

"We should go back." Her voice was as pathetically weak as her reply.

He motioned for her to lead the way. She stepped past him and tried not to meet his gaze lest she give in to the pull, which knew exactly what it was she truly wanted.

His hand settled on her lower back for a brief, fluttering moment before it fell away.

When they emerged from the trees, the camp lay as they had

left it—the coach idle and empty, the horses tethered near the loch, the fire with its waning flames.

So much had transpired between her and Kaid, and still so much more had the possibility of happening. Facing something so familiar, so mundane, left her mind spinning.

She did not want normal when she'd sampled such passion. She wanted Kaid.

Leasa was immediately at her side, cupping Delilah's elbow. "Are you all right?"

Delilah nodded. For what else could she do?

There was no more talk—not of what Kaid had confessed, nor any questions about what had happened in the forest. Exhaustion weighed on everyone, and within minutes, the camp had settled in for the night.

Delilah spent it all in a fit of sleepless tossing and turning on the thin cushioned seat, back in the blasted coach.

Kaid refused to hear her requests to sleep outside beneath the stars.

Where he was.

He'd insisted the women sleep once more in the relative safety of the coach. And so she lay in the squeeze of the dark box and waited for the cries of his nightmares to sound.

But they did not come.

Though she'd been eager for an excuse to be near him once more, her heart was lighter with knowing he'd been liberated from his hurt. At least for this one night.

And shouldn't one of them be without torment?

For she was not.

Memories of the feel of his body, his mouth, his tongue—mercy, his teeth, on her. Every time she closed her eyes, she remembered his touch, and her heart would catch fire.

A sick realization crashed through her midway through her sleepless night and made the crawl of time even more unbearable.

Despite all the passion, all the earnest desire, it was not her Kaid wanted—it was Elizabeth.

Chapter Eleven

Kaid wanted Elizabeth with more longing than he'd ever possessed.

The desire ate at him and left him circling the same thoughts over and over. Did he want her solely for herself, for her beauty and the kindness that shone through her initial haughty display—or did he simply want his enemy's betrothed?

He tried not to let the rocking coach lull him toward the sleep that had eluded him the previous night. But it had not been the horrors at Ardvreck which had kept him awake—it had been the force of his desire.

He had not slept. Instead he had sketched.

Elizabeth stared at him again. He could feel the touch of her gaze as surely as he'd felt the stroke of her tongue on his the prior evening. He balled his hands into fists to hide the blackened evidence of charcoal smudged across his fingertips. The remnants had been impossible to wash off.

The same was true for his memories. For everything in his life had been recorded through his drawings, a direct connection from his heart to his hand, as his mother had always said. It had been she who had first encouraged the drawings. For all the years he'd been so silent as a lad, for all the thoughts she knew to be swirling within regardless. She had first placed the charcoal in his fingers and watched his world bloom on the pages before them.

Her death had been difficult for him. He'd been only ten, somewhere between lad and man. The child she bore had died along with her. But the gift she'd seen in him, that she'd encouraged, had thrived within him and kept her alive in his heart.

Leasa sat beside Elizabeth with her sewing hanging limp in her hand and her head laying awkwardly against the wooden wall in slumber.

She hadn't noted the tension between him and Elizabeth, for surely she would have commented on it.

Kaid lifted his gaze and met Elizabeth's. She did not flinch away.

No, she stared back at him, and in her eyes he saw the same desire he felt. It lingered for only a moment before she flicked her gaze from his, like a fire ember singeing bare skin before snuffing out.

He should say something. Apologize. Again. "I shouldna have—"

She put up a hand to stop him from speaking. He wanted to take the slender hand and press his lips to the warmth of her palm.

But she was right.

This did not need to be spoken of, especially not where Leasa might hear.

Thick forest crowded the trail on which they rode and pulled Kaid's thoughts from Elizabeth.

They ought to be past the heavier forest by now. He'd anticipated more of the hilly landscape dotted with scruffy trees and patches of forest and rock. But then they'd lost considerable time while they recovered from being ill.

"How long was I ill?" Kaid asked.

The tension of Elizabeth's shoulders seemed to ease. "I believe it was three days."

"Three?" he repeated with incredulity.

She nodded.

His heart thumped hard against his ribs. "And how long were the rest of ye ill?"

She shook her head with a regretful frown. "I'm not entirely sure. Most likely an entire day."

They'd lost four days to being ill. At least.

That was a lot of time lost, a lot of distance they could have covered.

If Elizabeth delayed for too long, MacKenzie might begin to

worry after her and send a party. He and Donnan were strong fighters, but not enough to fend off an army.

"We're going to need to get rid of the coach." He spoke as the idea came to him.

Elizabeth's lips parted in surprise. "How would we travel?"

"We'll use the horses," he said. "We can cover more ground that way."

"There are only two—you can't expect us to ride with you both," she protested. "All my clothes, my jewels…"

"They dinna matter."

"Not to you, but they matter to me." She made the statement without any emotion, but the words struck him regardless.

His decision was selfish. The entire situation they were in was selfish. He was saving his people at her expense.

Elizabeth seemed to sense his resolve. "Please don't do this," she pleaded. Her gaze flicked to Leasa, whose mouth now gaped open in sleep. Elizabeth leaned closer to him, and the delicate scent of her perfume carried with it more memories than he could shut out.

She spoke in a quiet whisper. "If you care for me at all—"

"I canna care for ye." The statement came out in a harsh whisper. "Ye belong to another man—my enemy."

She straightened and gave him a brittle smile. "You're right. How foolish of me to forget."

He studied her erect posture and tensed muscles of her neck while she stared out the window. Away from him.

Even in this moment, where he understood her anger as well as his inability to do anything other than his mission, he could not help but admire her beauty and the quiet, confident strength she exuded.

Rather than argue the matter further, Kaid rapped upon the top of the coach. It would be best to handle this now before an argument could rise. He held his hands out in anticipation and caught Leasa's sleeping form before she could smack her face into the seat beside him.

"What?" She looked up, her gaze bleary. "Who? Where—" Her brows lifted. "Where are we?"

Elizabeth put a protective arm over the other woman. "We're to change from our coach to the horses."

Leasa's gaze focused and her frown deepened. "Why?"

"Because it's been decided by forces beyond our power."

Kaid did not have to look at Elizabeth to see her hard glare. He felt it, like the pointed edge of a blade poking at his neck.

Before he could listen to any additional arguments, he stepped out of the coach and nodded at Donnan's confused face. "Separate the horses," he said. "It's time."

Donnan winked and disappeared around the front of the coach to do as he was bid. The cheery tune of his whistling joined the clinking of iron hooks and links.

Kaid regarded the rear of the coach where several trunks were strapped atop one another. One had been broken in the fall, and a length of rough rope secured it together. There were also several bags made from thick tapestry. Those would serve better in their travel.

The trunks would have to stay.

And he dreaded telling Elizabeth as much.

She appeared at his side and crossed her arms over her chest. "I take it I can't bring the trunks."

Without waiting for a reply, she stepped forward and loosened the first tie holding the pile of luggage in place. Kaid rushed forward and caught the mass before it could topple onto her head.

Elizabeth's cheeks were red and her brown gaze smoldered. He'd have to be daft to not see she was angry.

"I hope you anticipate allowing me time to sort through my belongings to determine what of my life is worth keeping and what should be cast aside like rubbish." She settled onto the rough trail beside a fallen bag. "And to think I'd already pared my entire life down to these few trunks as it is."

Perhaps he ought to try to explain things from his perspective, but he held his tongue. Best not to encourage her disposition.

The horses would help them travel with more haste. Soon they would be at Ardvreck Castle, and then it would be better if she did not like him, perhaps even easier if she hated him.

Even if, he knew, in the depths of his heart, he could never hate her.

• • •

Finery piled around Delilah in stacks of pricey rubbish.

All the beautiful items she'd ever wanted, all finally within her grasp as she played a woman far above her station, and all being taken from her.

She'd whittled down her belongings to the necessities—the steel-laced bodice, false-bottomed shoes, lock picks for her hair, a jeweled ring with a secret compartment, and all the other wonderful inventions Percy had sent her with.

It was a shame to leave so many beautiful gowns, all tailored specifically for Delilah. All the lush velvets and brilliant silks. They'd made her feel, for at least a moment, like someone better than herself.

Someone who mattered.

She turned from the clothing, which Leasa packed back into the trunks with great care. A futile effort.

Delilah would never see those gowns again.

She took her two meager bags and dropped them at the men's feet. "I refuse to take less than these."

Kaid met her stare head-on. "Ye know why we're doing this."

Donnan hefted the bags with a grunt and gave her a carefree smile despite the weight. "I see ye made good use of the space ye had."

All too soon, the bags were strapped to the horses and Leasa and Delilah sat in front of Donnan and Kaid.

Delilah made a point to not look at the coach where it lay nestled against a cluster of trees. This became harder as they rode away, and all her worldly dreams that had finally been hers disappeared from view.

Likewise, she tried not to notice how Kaid's body swayed against hers, how his legs cradled her own over the horse's large body, how his arm encircled her waist.

Try though she might, the awareness of it left a splash of heat spreading over her cheeks and down her chest. She tried to shift forward, but it only resulted in her wriggling her bottom against him and his arm squeezing her tighter.

They rode thus in silence every day with only Leasa and Donnan's quiet conversation humming in the background along with the thud of the horses' hooves on the ground. Of course they traveled much faster—too fast.

Eventually, the thick forest gave way to rolling green hills dotted with large boulders and small patches of brush. It was beautiful, and it meant they were further north than she had anticipated.

They'd been on the road with Kaid for approximately two weeks, including the time they'd been sick, which put their entire journey at a total time of two months.

Delilah would have to stall for another two weeks to allow Elizabeth time to arrive safely before she could expose Kaid and Donnan.

Her burden had grown heavier with each passing day. It nipped at her patience until her nerves were frayed, and she was so lost in the chasm of her thoughts, she no longer heard Donnan and Leasa's chatter.

Kaid was doing what he had to do.

And she would do likewise.

• • •

One more day of travel and they would arrive at Ardvreck Castle.

Kaid nodded toward the cluster of trees in the valley of several large mountains. It would be decent cover for the night.

"Here," he said to Donnan.

He slid from the horse and tried once more to help Elizabeth from its back. As always, she refused.

They'd all fallen into a routine these last few days. Elizabeth set up camp with him, or rather watched while he did, while Leasa and Donnan gathered the firewood.

The weather was colder—an embrace of home. Kaid's mind was sharp, his heart thumping with all the familiarity of being where he truly belonged. Sleeplessness did not hold as tight a grip on him as it once had. The images still surfaced in his mind, the horror, but there were moments he was able to sleep more than before the valerian root. Apparently his nightmares had ceased, as the women had issued no complaints of them.

All since he'd stopped taking the valerian.

The very thought of the small vial left his jaw clenching with want of it. Even still after he knew the benefits of stopping it. Even now when he was so much more clearheaded. He pushed it from his thoughts and untied the sleeping blankets from the back of the horse.

Elizabeth stood beside the horse, her gaze fixed on the magnificence of the mountain beneath a clear sky.

"Do ye like it?" he asked.

She didn't turn to him. He hadn't expected her to. She'd been cold to him ever since they'd abandoned her items, but he sensed her silence was something far more than anger at her lost items.

"This is my home," he offered.

He should be glad for her indifference.

It was for the best.

"What will you do with us?" she asked, her voice hard. "Lock us in the dungeon while you wait to hear from Laird MacKenzie?"

"Ye'll be guests in my home," he said. The room had been set for her arrival before he'd even departed.

"Regardless of the politeness you've extended, it's quite obvious we are not guests but prisoners." She lifted her chin in the pretentious manner he despised so much.

He frowned at her. "I've tried to explain—"

"That changes nothing." She spun toward him, facing him as if he were an attacker. Her body was tense, her gaze bright with passion, and her cheeks blazing.

Perhaps it was those things, or how the sun spilled over her and turned her hair into curls of gold, but she was more beautiful than he'd ever seen her.

"Elizabeth, I—"

"It's unfair." Tears shone bright in her eyes and twisted at his heart. He'd never seen her cry before. Even that night in the woods, when he'd known she'd probably cried, he hadn't seen her. He knew now how very painful it was to behold.

Especially when he was the culprit.

"All of this is so unfair." The tiny freckle next to her cheek stood out to him as it always had: not as an imperfection, but as the final note of beauty on an already exquisite face.

He stepped closer and opened his arms to her.

She shrugged him off.

"Elizabeth."

"Don't."

But he couldn't stop himself. He stepped forward again, toward her.

This time her hand flew toward his face, but he caught her wrist. "Dinna hit me," he warned.

"Let me go," she gritted out through her teeth.

Her other hand came at his face, but he caught that one too. He held her for a moment, her arms pinned.

And then he kissed her.

Chapter Twelve

Kaid should not have kissed Lady Elizabeth Seymour.

Every warning within him told him what he already knew—how the hard press of his lips to hers would reignite the passion between them.

He'd spent the last several days trying not to think of her sweet taste, her throaty moan, her perfect beauty, her cheeks flushed with passion.

But he did kiss her, and now desire licked through his body like a flame across tinder.

He caught her bottom lip between his teeth and sucked.

Elizabeth gasped, but did not jerk away.

He still pinned her arms, keeping her at his mercy and yet not forcing her into anything, as was evidenced by her lean into him.

Her face tilted up. "Please," she whispered against his lips.

Last time he had denied her and left days of regret stretching between them.

This time he would not make the same mistake.

He swept his tongue against the tip of hers, and tingles of pleasure danced across his skin.

Her moan vibrated against his mouth.

Desire tightened through him, demanding more.

She pulled at her trapped hands. He felt the tug and resisted at first. Holding her wrists grounded him, tethered his passion, keeping it from spiraling out of control.

She wrenched once more, and this time he let them slide free from his grip.

Her hands found his chest, his back, his stomach.

He groaned at her exploration and gripped the nape of her neck, leaning her face slightly back to deepen their kiss. Their panting breaths tangled, as did their tongues and their desperate limbs—entwined passion with something deep and primal.

His cock raged with the need for release. Elizabeth's body stretched against him, and the pressure of her hips to his sent pleasure tightening through him.

His touch roamed her body, seeing with his hands what he could not with his eyes. Though she was strapped into the thick layers of corsets and skirts and gown, he knew her to be beautiful beneath. The slender waist, the curve of her bottom no amount of petticoats could hide, the fullness of her breasts heaving atop her bodice.

He kissed a trail down her neck and flicked his tongue across the top of her bosom. The flesh was firm and sweet, and he wanted nothing more than to yank down the bodice to reveal the pink of her nipples.

Elizabeth's knees gave. It was the slightest of staggers, but enough that he feared for her staying upright. Together they eased to the ground, their hands and mouths still greedy in exploration.

He slipped his fingers under her skirt, desperate to discover if her calves were as shapely as he thought them to be.

Her skin was smooth beneath his touch.

Like a starving man at a feast, a taste was not enough. Everything fled his mind but the need for more, more, more.

His caress crept higher, over her slender left thigh which eased aside at his stroking encouragement. Her hips arched against him, and he knew she would be wet with desire long before he touched her.

The knowledge should have satisfied him well enough. And perhaps, had he not spent the last several days trying to ignore his longing for her, it would have.

But the ache in his cock, the fog of want in his brain, it was all too overwhelming to deny.

Almost trembling with the force of his need, he caressed the juncture between her legs and loosed a groan from the deepest part of him.

She was slick and hot and swollen with need. His fingertip brushed the engorged bud near the top of her sex, and a cry rasped from her throat.

The longing was almost excruciating where it strained with an unbearable, pulsing throb at his loins.

Her hips rocked in time with the roll of his thumb.

Stop.

The voice in the back of his head wasn't loud.

And it was far too easily ignored.

He slipped a finger inside her and let her heat clamp around his digit. Another groan eased from the back of his throat. If only that were his cock, locked in the heavenly squeeze of her.

Stop.

Louder this time. More insistent.

He hesitated.

Responsibility rushed forefront to his mind.

His people.

And then Elizabeth's delicate hand slipped under his kilt and wrapped around his cock.

All thought slipped away like the wisp of smoke from a snuffed candle.

His cock lurched in a pleasure so intense, he had to close his eyes against it.

When he opened them, he found Elizabeth beneath him, her legs parted against the tangle of skirts. "Please," she whispered.

He should have said no. It was on the edge of his mind to do so when her fingers stroked over the length of him again.

Want.

Need.

Now.

He lowered himself to one elbow and eased the heavy fabric

of his kilt aside so the tip of his cock nudged against the sweet wet thatch of downy hair.

His mouth went dry.

He knew he shouldn't be doing this, but knew he had no chance of stopping now.

Especially not when Elizabeth curled her hips against him and whispered the word once more.

Please.

He flexed his hips forward and sheathed himself in the wet heat of Lady Elizabeth Seymour.

And discovered she was no virgin.

• • •

Delilah had never known real love.

But now, as Kaid stared down at her, tingles of pleasure sparkled through her, and every thrust brought a new understanding of how it would truly feel.

Her mind was wild, sensing, savoring, wanting.

His mouth was on hers and his hands gripped her bottom, guiding her as much as he held her steady. Her body was on fire, the blaze stroking with each flex of his hips.

She held onto him with one hand, and to the ground with the other, her fingers absently digging into the soft earth beside her. As if she might tumble off if she let go.

All the while, a simmering friction was building, building, building.

It made her breath come in gasps and a cry gather in the back of her throat. She knew she shouldn't make any sound, but everything in her wanted to.

His mouth moved to her neck, her ear. The scruff of his unshaven chin prickled her neck, a delicious contrast to the heat of his mouth on her ear, the flick of his tongue.

Oh God. It was all too much.

Her body tightened, drawing toward something she knew she wanted.

Euphoria gripped her tight, squeezing and letting go. She felt herself clenching in time with the waves of pleasure, overwhelming her senses and leaving her in a luxurious daze.

Her dagger.

She blinked hard as the thought broke through her bliss.

Her mind still fogged with lust, her body still arching and moving with Kaid, she loosed the dirt in her hand and ran her palm down her right leg where her hidden dagger was strapped to her thigh.

The heavy skirts still lay over it like a shield.

Kaid seemed to swell and grow hotter insider her. A wanted distraction from the thought of her hidden blade. She let herself be pulled into the fog of desire once more.

He watched her, his clear, blue stare a fascinating view into the extent of his pleasure. Seeing his enjoyment while she experienced her own sent another winding tightness through her. A cry slipped from her mouth in anticipation.

He held her face in his hands, all the affection she'd never known shining in his eyes. "Elizabeth."

Delilah stiffened at the sound of the other woman's name, and Kaid gave a hoarse groan of pleasure.

Elizabeth.

Kaid's mouth brushed hers, but she no longer felt the warmth of his kiss.

In fact, everything in her had gone cold.

It wasn't she, Delilah, whom he made love to with such passion, such love—it had been Elizabeth.

Delilah had known better, of course. She'd been fooling him the entire time, after all.

Why, then, did it make her feel so empty inside?

The threat of tears prickled warm and certain, but she snapped the emotion shut inside her.

She would not fall into sadness as she'd done the last time she fancied a man in love with her. She was stronger than that now.

The hollow twinge in her chest grew, and she nurtured it. She wanted the cold nothing, the lack of feeling.

She still had a job to do.

Kaid stared down at the woman he thought her to be with love he didn't know was fake, but this time Delilah did not allow herself to be moved by it.

Elizabeth.

Anger tightened through her. She slipped her fingers between the folds of her skirts, grasped the hilt of her concealed dagger and whipped the blade up toward his neck.

He jerked, the way any warrior might do, then gave a confused little smile, as if he were embarrassed at having darted back from a blade. "What are ye doing?"

"I'm abducting you, Kaid MacLeod," she said in a cold voice. "The same as you tried to do to me."

The confusion was replaced with a furrowed brow.

She shoved him off her and got to her feet. Pleasure thrummed still between her legs, but she refused to acknowledge it. Her skirts swept back into place. Aside from the possibility of grass in her hair, one might never know she'd just been rutting on the ground.

Kaid slowly rose, his arms held defensively in the air. "I dinna understand."

"I'm taking you in to be punished for the crime of abducting a lady with the intent to blackmail." The words should have eased the ache in Delilah's chest. Why, then, did they seem to make it more tender?

"Ye lied to me?" There was something in his gaze. Hurt.

Delilah grit her teeth.

She knew why he'd done what he did. She knew how well he'd treated them, how apologetic he'd been—how awful he felt.

But none of it mattered.

She had to remind herself again and again.

"Kaid." Donnan's voice sounded somewhere behind Delilah.

She spun to find him standing near the horses with Leasa at his side. Even Leasa stared at Delilah as if she'd lost her mind.

"I'm taking you both to Killearnan to face punishment for your crimes." Delilah nodded pointedly at Leasa to indicate it was time.

Leasa nodded back, but the movement was uncertain. She hadn't been given instruction on any of the plan. No doubt she wondered what she ought to do to help.

It would all have been easier, of course, had Delilah told her. But with Leasa's open honesty, not only might she have loosed their secret, the burden would have been too raw for her to bear.

"How do ye intend to get us there if ye dinna know the way?" Donnan asked with a confident grin.

"I know more than you think," Delilah replied in flawless Gaelic.

Kaid straightened and gave her a look that made her blood cool.

As if she were a stranger.

And then he lunged at her.

Chapter Thirteen

Even after Elizabeth's betrayal, Kaid still did not wish to harm her.

He caught her around the waist, intending to pull her to the ground and safely remove the dagger from her hold. She darted back with the reflexes of a cat and easily slid free of his grasp.

He swung his arm toward her in an attempt to catch her again. This time, she didn't evade his attack, but ran into it.

Her body slammed into his with enough force to rock his balance momentarily, but he managed to keep his footing.

This was no minor defense, he realized. She intended to fight him. "Stop this, Elizabeth."

"My name is not Elizabeth." She ground the words out and swung a fist at his face.

She was fast.

Almost fast enough to catch him with her throw, but not quite.

He dipped back and put his arms up in a defensive block as he'd done many times when training at hand-to-hand combat with his men.

The kind of training he'd never done with a woman.

Especially not a woman he had only moments ago lain with.

Not Elizabeth.

Her words registered and tingled down his spine.

Leasa and Donnan stood off to the side, watching in horrified fascination. Leasa, Kaid noted absently, did not appear to be shocked by the admission.

Not-Elizabeth circled him with menace. "If you let me tie you up, we can end this now."

Kaid narrowed his eyes at the challenge. "I dinna think so."

She shrugged, then she charged at him.

He braced himself for the blow, expecting her to throw another punch. But this time it was her foot which propelled toward him and would have slammed into his head had he not ducked as quickly as he did.

"Who are ye then?" he asked. "If no' Elizabeth."

Not-Elizabeth went to punch him. "None of your business."

He ducked, and she slammed her fist into him from the other side. Pain exploded in his ribs beneath her hit, surprising him.

He hadn't expected a woman to hit with such force.

Frustration pulled tight through him.

None of his business?

Had he not spent his days thinking of her, trying to earn her trust? She'd played him for a fool, and he'd danced perfectly into her trap.

He needed to stop this madness and get her bound so he could question who the hell she was and why she'd been sent for him.

Kaid tried to edge behind her to grab her from the back, but she spun around and lashed out at him again.

Damn, but she was fast.

Like a little viper, coiled and striking.

He'd only just blocked a new hit when she stepped forward, looping her leg behind his, and her elbow shot toward his face.

His attempt to avoid being struck worked against him, and he pitched backward to the ground.

Her body settled on him, and she pinned his arms back to the ground. He smirked. No matter how strong a lass she was, he would still be stronger.

He pushed his hands forward and her arms moved back despite the resistance of her fighting it. When enough space edged between them, he flipped her onto her back and trapped her beneath his body.

A memory sped through his conscience—they had been in such a position only minutes before, locked in a passionate tangle.

She hadn't been a virgin.

She wasn't Elizabeth.

Who the hell was she?

The woman thrust her hips up and knocked his weight from her as if it were insignificant.

She landed atop him once more and her elbow flew at his face.

Kaid's world went dark.

• • •

Delilah had not enjoyed defeating Kaid, and enjoyed even less the task of tying his unconscious body to Donnan.

Surprisingly Donnan had put up no argument.

Delilah spooled the rope around the two one final time before securing it with a complex knot Percy had shown her. "I didn't want to do this," she said in a quiet voice.

A ghost of Donnan's usual smile showed on his face. "I dinna want to do any of this from the beginning."

Delilah nodded and stepped back to regard her work, to ensure they could not escape.

The men were bound back-to-back, similar to how her guards had been tied up when Kaid and Donnan had abducted her.

Kaid's head hung limp to the side, but a low groan sounded from his chest.

She wanted to turn away, to keep from witnessing the hurt of seeing them tied and helpless. They'd been so protective and gallant toward her and Leasa, even if their intent was immoral.

"My lady." Leasa's voice pulled at Delilah's attention. She was grateful for the distraction.

Leasa's expression was pinched. "I'd like you to leave me at the next village we pass."

Hurt slapped at Delilah's heart. "You don't agree with what I'm doing."

Leasa stared down at the ground. "I understand why you are doing it. I understand this protects Lady Elizabeth. But I…" Her voice wavered. "I ruin everything. All the time. It's why they sent me with you." She looked up, her gaze desperate and searching. "They were going to send me home, but all this happened, and they sent me with you instead."

Surprise at the admission held Delilah's tongue.

Leasa must have taken the silence for misunderstanding because she looked away and continued, "Because if I died, it wouldn't matter."

"Leasa." Delilah breathed the other woman's name on a hard exhale. "That can't be true."

Leasa's nose had begun to redden. "I overheard the earl speaking to his wife before we departed. They said those words exactly."

Delilah wanted to curl her arms around the maid, to console the rejection she knew too well, but she also knew she couldn't allow her emotions to show in front of the men.

They needed to see her strong, stoic.

"If you come with me," Delilah said, intentionally changing the subject, "you can help me take them to Killearnan, and I can help see you home after if that is what you prefer."

Leasa's mournful gaze drifted up to Delilah once more, now brimming with a sheen of unshed tears. "I can't go home. My family has no money. I would just be another mouth to feed, another unwed daughter to—" She shook her head and wrapped her arms around herself. "I want to try a new life in one of the villages here, a place where no one knows me and I can start over."

Delilah saw far too much of herself in the woman for comfort. Her heart swelled with genuine empathy for the girl who had started her adult life much as Delilah had.

Would she be where Leasa was had Sylvi not approached her so long ago?

"I don't want you to go." Delilah met Leasa's gaze, where all the fractured hurt had risen to the surface, and said the words she herself had longed so badly to hear. "You're important to me."

Leasa choked a sob and dropped her face into her palms. Delilah's throat constricted. She knew the power of what she'd said and the impact of feeling needed, wanted, when no one else had ever cared.

And it was the truth. Leasa *was* important. She was necessary to the mission being completed.

The men be damned. Delilah wrapped her arms around the other woman. "You're strong and you give me a sense of purpose on this mission," she said. "I need you to be at my side, to help show these men the same courtesy in captivity we were afforded. Will you stay with me?"

Leasa nodded against her shoulder and stepped from Delilah's embrace with a brilliant smile. "Thank you."

Delilah returned her smile and Leasa strode toward the men.

Now that Delilah had secured the men and convinced Leasa to stay, another thought burred its way into her mind.

They were three days from Killearnan, which gave Delilah at least a fortnight before Elizabeth was expected.

They'd arrived too soon. But could she keep the men retained for the next two weeks?

Something caught her eye next to Kaid's bag.

A leatherbound book. The cover was peeled back at the corners with only a strip of supple leather holding it closed.

She looked up and found Kaid watching her intently, his body tensing. While she'd never seen him writing in the book, she'd noticed how often his fingertips were black.

"What do you write in here?" Delilah said.

He narrowed his eyes.

Suddenly she found herself not trusting him anymore. The certainty there was something important within tugged at her.

She disregarded the warning in his gaze and stooped to lift the book. The leather was worn smooth on either side of the spine where the book had been held often.

Kaid straightened. "Leave it, Elizabeth."

Hearing him call her the wrong name again turned the dagger in her heart.

"I'm not Elizabeth," she reminded him harshly.

Remorse showed in the defeated anger on his face.

She turned from him then and lifted the top cover.

A drawing sketched in smooth strokes of black showed the side of a castle and people milling about in its shadow. She turned the page and saw a market scene where people bustled with baskets tucked against their hips. The next was of the edge of a loch with the sky stretching long and unending overhead.

She frowned and flipped through several more scenes. They were all drawings.

Her fingers froze on a new page. This scene portrayed the village again, but frozen in a tale of violence. Men ran with swords at the ready toward a woman whose face expressed her terror. In the far right corner, lying on the ground, was a dismembered hand.

Delilah's pulse thumped faster in her veins.

Another image showed a woman held between two men, one with a sword, thrusting it through her stomach.

The smooth strokes from before had given way to frantic streaks of thick, heavy black. A nightmare scratched over a life once beautiful. Each picture was more graphic, more horrific than the last. And yet she could not stop. Not until she got to the one with a child.

An indistinct cry escaped her throat, and the book tumbled from her grasp. Its pages fluttered toward the ground, where it landed face down atop a crumple of pages.

Her heartbeat came too fast, her breath too shallow.

Was this what he'd seen?

Her knees lost their strength and she sank into the dirt, crushed beneath the horror of what Kaid had drawn.

If she'd had any doubt at his story, she would no more. Every awful word of what he'd said—and even what he hadn't—all evidenced themselves in his horrific drawings.

Nausea churned in her stomach. If he had not lied about what he'd witnessed, then surely he was not lying about his purpose.

And if he was being honest about his purpose, the success of her mission would damn his people.

Chapter Fourteen

Delilah had wished she'd never looked at Kaid's book. She wished she'd never heard his story.

But she had, and now she would need to press on regardless.

She reached for the book with a trembling hand and let her fingers part the pages near the back. Her gaze wandered toward the sketch there to find a woman, not being tortured or killed, but up close and drawn with such great affection it made her chest squeeze with jealousy.

The woman was drawn with the same striking quality as the previous work. The smooth strokes were beautifully poetic.

Page after page revealed the woman—different angles, different facial expressions, everything different but the woman herself.

Delilah's fingers barely touched the page to turn to the next. The woman again. Her face turned up, her dark eyes wide and full of emotion.

Delilah's pulse flickered.

On the cheek of the woman, below the side of her mouth was a freckle.

Just like hers.

She leaned forward to examine the drawing. Perhaps it was only a fleck of charcoal. She blew at the drawing gently, but the mark remained. She scraped the edge of her fingernail against it and still it remained.

This woman was her.

Her heart swelled. She turned page after page and found new drawings, all of her.

She stopped on one where her head tilted in contemplation and her fingers lingered over her lower lip. Her skin was flawless save for the freckle, every line smooth and perfect.

He'd drawn her beautiful. The way she'd always wished she could be.

She swallowed and turned to him.

He stared at the ground and the muscles of his jaw showed in hard lines against his cheek.

"You drew me." Delilah held up the book, though he hadn't bothered to look up.

He remained silent.

She knelt down beside him. "Kaid."

His gaze rose to hers, displaying the impact of her betrayal—the injury, the offense.

"Why did you draw me?" she asked.

He studied her a moment. "Because ye're beautiful."

Her heartbeat staggered.

He thought her beautiful enough to draw her again and again and again, the way lovers in stories did. The way real men did not.

And yet he had.

She wanted to speak, but found the words thickening in her throat. She swallowed against it. "I'm sorry."

He smirked. "I am too."

A distinct heat welled in her chest and rose into her cheeks. She remembered the touch of his lips to hers, the press of his body cradled between her legs, the tenderness of his stare, as if she'd been the only woman he could ever love.

If only they were different people in a different world.

His stare went hard, reminding her they were not.

"Who are you?" he asked finally.

She shouldn't have replied, but knew herself how hard it was to wait for answers. He'd been considerate with all her questions. She would afford him the same courtesy.

"My name is Delilah."

Donnan chuckled behind Kaid. "I dinna think that could be more fitting."

Kaid tossed an irritated look over his shoulder.

The barb struck her deeper than she should have allowed. Their ire would not keep her from completing her task.

She looked down at the journal still clasped in her grip.

Nor would the pretense of love.

Even the suffering of Kaid's people could not.

"You gave us the courtesy of being captured without being bound. Can I do the same?" she asked. "Will I have your word you will not run off?"

Kaid nodded. "Aye, ye have our word."

She should be skeptical, she knew—but then, they had trusted her and Leasa, hadn't they?

She leveled a hard stare at him. "Then I will bestow upon you the same favor you granted Leasa and me."

From where Leasa stood within earshot, she nodded at Delilah with gratitude. The decision was not made precipitously. If the men decided to escape, Delilah knew she was fast on her feet. She could catch Kaid at the very least. If she'd taken him down once before, she could do so again.

She leaned over Kaid and untied the rope she'd secured only minutes before.

The bulk of it slipped from his large shoulders and tumbled to his side. He shook the remainder of the coil from his torso and stood with a stretch.

They ate their dinner that night in silence. Even Donnan's typical good humor and the light note of his whistled tunes did not grace the cool summer air. It all fell over Delilah like a thick, somber blanket.

After a gloomy supper which seemed to drag on for an extraordinary amount of time, it was finally time to sleep. Delilah had long since thought of how to handle their situation—not only to ensure the men did not escape, but that she would hear if they tried.

The only thing she could determine was to sleep side by side, and so that was what they did.

Leasa slept beside Donnan who slept beside Kaid who slept against Delilah.

And so Delilah lay nestled near the warmth of Kaid's chest and tried to ignore the subtle male scent which triggered too many recollections of their shared pleasure. His breathing came deep and even, stirring the wispy hairs at the back of her neck and sending delicious little chills down her spine.

She squeezed her eyes shut, as if doing so could block out the sensations, the memories, the desire even now beginning to hum through her betraying body.

Suddenly she realized she was not truly afraid of holding them for the next two weeks, she was afraid of herself.

Could she truly spend another fortnight with them and still turn them in, knowing the harshness of the punishment they'd face?

Kaid.

His name in her mind squeezed at a secret place in her heart, a girlish place of hope which had somehow been left untouched by King James.

Kaid was the man who loved her as she'd always wanted to be loved, the man who drew her in the beautiful way she'd never seen herself. No, she reminded herself—the man who loved her when he thought her to be another woman.

Regardless, he did not deserve what awaited him in a criminal's death.

Tears, hot and unexpected, blurred her vision.

Despite everything they'd been through—the passion, the lies and the insanity of how they'd met—could she truly allow herself to be responsible for his death?

Could she, in good conscience, further expose his people to more brutal slayings?

And in the depth of her heart, she did not want to answer.

• • •

Kaid sat on the horse behind Delilah, no different than they'd been the day before.

But it was different. Very much so.

Now he was the captured, or so he let her believe.

His gaze wandered from the road ahead to her glossy brown hair in front of him.

Not that she couldn't best him in a fight. Obviously she could, or he wouldn't be in this position now.

Granted, he'd held back, afraid of injuring her. No man was used to fighting a woman, especially not one with her fighting skills.

Delilah.

What a fitting name for a woman of such beauty and betrayal.

Leasa's easy laugh carried over from the left where she and Donnan rode in their usual jovial exchange of conversation, as if nothing had happened.

A pale boulder nestled between two hills caught his attention. He'd played on that rock as a boy. It lay on the border of his lands.

His men would be patrolling the perimeter. They would be found.

He wasn't sure how much Delilah knew about him—hell, he didn't know anything about her at all—but he wasn't about to risk losing this opportunity to get out of the situation.

He'd given her his word he wouldn't escape, but had said nothing about letting her be captured by his lot.

"Who are ye?" he asked.

Her answer came without preamble or pause. "No one."

It wasn't exactly the kind of distracting conversation he'd hoped for.

"Nobody is no one." He tried to keep the frustration from his tone. "Where do ye come from?"

"England."

"I figured," he answered dryly. "Where in England?"

Delilah was quiet a moment. "A house in the country."

"Did ye have any brothers or sisters?"

She gave a mirthless chuckle. "A few."

Kaid scanned the horizon, picking through foliage for the familiar images of his men. Nothing. "Did ye no' get along with them?"

"I didn't not get along with them."

Kaid frowned. "I dinna understand."

She shifted in her saddle. "I'm done talking about this."

He looked at the open landscape, swollen with the rise and fall of hills velvety with lush grass. They were definitely on his land now. He could not have her notice if she knew the area. And perhaps she did.

Most likely she did.

Delilah might be deceitful, but she was undeniably extraordinary.

"I thought I knew ye as Elizabeth." He lowered his voice to a more intimate level. "I want to know ye as Delilah."

Though he'd spoken the words with a luring intent, he realized he meant them. He wanted to know how she came to live in Scotland, to speak Gaelic, to fight like a man.

Delilah pulled in a quiet breath, but didn't answer for so long, he thought she might not at all. When she finally did, her voice was quiet, somber. "I'm the middle child of fifteen children, the eldest unwed daughter. I was a burden for my family, who could barely afford food, and was sent to work for a rich relative at court in London as many poor relations often do. Suffice it to say, things did not go as planned."

She shifted in her saddle to look back at him with a pointed expression. "I am a far cry from the well-bred noblewoman you assumed me to be."

Her gaze slid past him, and her eyes widened. "Get down."

She jerked low and he instinctively followed. An arrow sailed over their heads, narrowly missing her before it thunked into a tree in front of them.

A warning shot.

Delilah lay low against the horse's strong neck. Her hand slid into her pocket and she withdrew a dagger. The very one she'd pressed to his throat after they'd made love.

Kaid straightened and looked behind him. Two men approached him, Lachlan and Dougal. Grins showed on their faces.

"Mighty fine of ye to bring us a couple lasses," Lachlan said.

Delilah shifted her hold on the hilt of her blade, edging her grip lower with the obvious intend to hurl it toward the men.

"Dinna do that," Kaid cautioned.

Delilah gave him a confused look, but her movements paused.

"Ye couldna handle these lasses," Donnan said from somewhere behind him.

Lachlan stopped next to Kaid's horse and stroked the beast's neck. "We were wondering when ye'd come back." He nodded toward Delilah, who had gone stiff in front of Kaid. "Who is she?"

"MacKenzie's bride-to-be." Kaid knew the words would pour realization over Delilah like a bucket of cold water.

She jerked a hard look at him over her shoulder.

Lachlan gave Kaid a wide grin. "I know what ye're doing." He gave a hearty laugh and patted the horse's neck one final time. "We'll walk with ye to Ardvreck. I canna wait to see the clan's faces when they see this."

Delilah's body tensed in front of him.

Kaid covered the hand holding a dagger with his own. "Ye know fighting wouldna be wise."

She jerked away from him and slipped the dagger back into her pocket. Angry though she appeared, he knew she understood his warning.

"You lied to me," she growled. "I trusted you."

The wind blew over the rolling hills and swept the length of Delilah's hair from where it lay against her back, allowing the slightest bit of her naked neck to come into view.

He wanted to brush her hair aside and let his lips wander over the slender curve of her neck. Giving in to the temptation, however, would probably result in a knife to the gut.

"I gave ye my word I wouldna run off," he said. "I'm no' running off." He pulled his gaze from her lest he give in to his desire.

"Ye were the one who came onto my land and guided me toward my home."

"And will you hold us as prisoners?" she asked in an icy tone.

"Ye'll stay as my guests," he answered. "So long as ye cause no trouble."

"Of course—you have my word." She spoke the last phrase in harsh mockery.

He knew she'd be upset, of course, but not for long. Or at least he hoped it wouldn't be for long. It was part of his plan.

Knowing she was not Elizabeth Seymour had rocked his scheme for peaceful negotiations with MacKenzie, but Kaid had come up with another idea.

To have Delilah help him.

All Kaid had to do was convince Delilah to play Elizabeth for the man to whom it would really matter—Laird MacKenzie.

Chapter Fifteen

Delilah had led herself right into a trap.

Kaid had said she'd be treated as a guest, but would he keep his word when she'd betrayed him once already?

Though she willed it not to, her pulse raced the nearer they drew to the cluster of homes on the outskirts of a great castle in the distance. Hills rose around them and the evening rays of sunlight danced off the water surrounding the castle.

Guest or not, there would be no escape. Obviously he'd known as much when he spoke.

Frustration caught her in its snare.

This was not how her first assignment was supposed to go. She'd acted too hastily and had lost her chance for surprise.

She should have kept with the original plan to delay their arrival and then kidnap him when they were within a day of Elizabeth's arrival.

But there had been two weeks remaining—and too much could have happened in that time.

The village sprawled out in front of them, heavy with the odor of farm animals and peat smoke.

She'd seen those roughhewn structures before, the thatched roofs and laden carts of goods set up where the town center was visible. They'd been in Kaid's book, sketched in jagged lines of thick black and clouded with death.

She half expected to find dark blotches of dried blood in the hard-packed dirt, evidence of past violence. But all that met her gaze was a crowd's curiosity.

Though she was no more noble now than any one of them, her back stiffened of its own accord, shoving strength where weakness wanted to prevail.

She was on display, a prize caught and shown off. Though she wanted nothing more than to fend off the reaction, their stares left her raw with vulnerability.

At first, whispers started with the quiet of tree leaves shushing against one another in the breeze. But as she stopped, as she was helped from her horse and led through the parted masses toward the massive castle, those whispers became a hum, and then a buzz.

Their words came in snatches.

English.

MacKenzie.

Bride.

Death.

She tried to blot it from her mind, but she couldn't stop her ears from listening any more than she could stop her knees from turning to jelly.

"Mama!" A cry cut through the air.

Delilah maintained her composure, but sought out the person who'd spoken as discreetly as possible.

The cry came again, this time in a wail.

Delilah turned toward the sound to find a small girl wrestling against the hold of a woman with long brown hair. The girl jerked backward in a mass of blonde hair and pulled free from the woman's grasp.

The child staggered, almost falling, before she righted herself and ran forward, arms outstretched. "Mama!"

But she didn't head toward any of the women in the village. She ran hard until she smacked into Delilah's legs, and her little arms locked around Delilah's knees in a ferocious hug. "Mama." The word choked from the child on the bubble of a sob.

Delilah stared in surprise at the child. The girl's long blonde hair hung down her back against the rough brown fabric of her homespun dress.

The child lifted her head and met Delilah's gaze with large blue eyes. A gasp tore from the girl's mouth and she jerked back as if she'd been struck.

Delilah stepped away instinctively, worried the girl had somehow been hurt. Perhaps the dagger in her skirts? But no, that wouldn't have—

"I'm sorry." The woman with the long brown hair appeared in front of Delilah, her cheeks flushed. Her English was broken. "Claire," she knelt in front of the girl and switched to Gaelic. "This is not yer ma."

The girl, Claire, looked up at Delilah again. Tears welled in her eyes and left the beautiful blue glossy with such sorrow, it snagged at Delilah's heart like a barb.

"Because my Mama is dead." The girl's voice was flat.

To hear such innocence speak so bluntly of death was more than Delilah could bear.

She had never thought herself a maternal woman. Her older sisters all had been and readily took to the care of the younger children. But now she found her heart aching to pull the girl into her arms and soothe away her pain. A tear ran down Delilah's cheek.

She stepped toward Claire without intending to, but the girl backed away again. "My mama is dead." Her voice was hard with an edge of determination when she spoke this time.

The brown-haired woman offered Delilah an apologetic look and ushered the girl away.

Delilah had not realized the whispers had stopped until the hushed silence exploded into a chaos of voices once more.

Self-loathing simmered like a hot coal in her gut.

She'd let them see her cry. Even if it'd been for a young, orphaned girl and not herself, she'd still cried in front of them.

Someone appeared at her side, strong and sure, and while he did not take her hand or offer her the support of his arm, she sensed his encouragement.

"Enough," Kaid growled at the onlookers. "I'll speak with ye later, but for now, go on about yer business."

The crowd begrudgingly dissipated until Delilah was able to make her way without the burden of being watched.

From a distance, the castle had appeared to float atop the loch like some magical apparition, all smooth stone and block construction. Up close, she could now see a tendril of land extending toward it, blanketed with a layer of toppled grass.

They followed the well-used trail to where a shorter wall stood before the three-story structure behind it.

It was not the largest castle she'd seen, nor the most impressive, but its location was by far the most strategic. It was no wonder MacKenzie had attacked the village rather than the castle. It was far more vulnerable.

Kaid gestured for them to enter the opening in the wall to where a narrow courtyard was visible beyond. "Welcome to Ardvreck Castle."

• • •

Kaid's people were divided on Delilah's appearance—there were those who saw her as a savior, and others as a curse. Then again, they only knew Delilah as Elizabeth, MacKenzie's intended.

Kaid and Donnan made their way to the new part of the castle, where a spare chamber had been readied for their arrival. Hopefully allowing the ladies a bath and a night to rest had eased the offense of their recapture.

"This had better work," Kaid mumbled under his breath.

Donnan gave him a confident grin. "It will."

Kaid did not share his friend's enthusiasm. "It has to," he said somberly.

Truth be told, he didn't know if it could. There were too many opportunities for error in his plan.

First he had to convince Delilah of why she should want to help, then he had to actually ask her and hope to God she said yes. Even if he got her to agree to play Elizabeth Seymour, she would have to find MacKenzie's missing sister.

Laird MacKenzie was only laird regent. His elder sister, Torra, had one day faded from existence, and he had declared himself acting laird in her compromised mental state. There had been no opposition from the people, at least none as far as Kaid remembered. He'd been a boy when it all happened.

No one had heard of Torra since.

If she was alive, if she could be reasoned with, if she could be found and brought to Ardvreck to witness the impact of her brother's destruction—perhaps she could be convinced to restore the truce which had existed before Seumas's mother died at Ardvreck.

But if Torra truly was mad, as MacKenzie claimed, all his efforts might be for naught.

So no, he did not have the same confidence in all of this as did Donnan, but he wished like hell he did.

He opened the door to the chamber and found both women as he'd left them the night before, albeit clean and in different clothing. Leasa perched anxiously on the edge of the massive bed and Delilah stalked back and forth like a caged wildcat.

Leasa's face lit when she saw them, but Delilah's eyes glittered with something shrewd and calculating.

"Leasa, go with Donnan. He'll show ye around." Kaid looked pointedly at Delilah, who had stopped pacing long enough to fold her arms over her chest.

"I'd like to speak with ye," he said. "Alone."

Leasa cast a questioning look toward Delilah, who nodded her assent, and the maid slipped from the room with Donnan.

Delilah didn't move until the door was closed, then she made her way toward Kaid with slow, deliberate steps before stopping directly in front of him.

"Aren't you afraid Elizabeth's innocence will be compromised if you stay in the room alone with me?" Her coquettish tone was both irritating and arousing at the same time.

No doubt she knew exactly what she was doing.

"I think we're well past that." Kaid kept his tone as intimate as she'd made hers.

She tensed and he put up a hand. "I dinna want to injure ye when we fought before. I willna fear as much next time."

"That doesn't frighten me," she said. The edge in her voice did not match the delicate yellow gown she wore or the fine tendrils framing the face he'd spent far too long memorizing.

She was hard and dangerous and so damn beautiful, it was all he could do to keep from reaching out to her.

"It wasna meant to," Kaid said. "I have no intention of hurting ye."

"So abducting helpless noblewomen and holding them captive in your home are where your crimes stop?" She shook her head with what he recognized as helpless frustration.

She was trapped and she knew it.

But he was helplessly frustrated too.

He hadn't wanted this. Hell, he hated being in this situation. But it was the only thing he could possibly do to negotiate peace.

She turned away from him and strode past the large wooden chest at the foot of the bed, toward the heavy green curtains pulled aside from the window. Sunlight streamed over her face, lighting her skin like smooth cream, and his fingers yearned for a bit of charcoal.

"You plan to use me for negotiation still." She stared out at something he could not see. "You told them I was Elizabeth."

"I sent riders to Edirdovar Castle as soon as we arrived."

Delilah shook her head. "And how do you know it was not MacKenzie who hired me?"

"If he wanted me, he'd use my people to get at me—the same as he did my da." It ached him to recall the loss they'd all suffered that fateful day.

Delilah cast her gaze downward and nodded in understanding. "You're right. It was not him who hired me, but I'd prefer not to say who did. It has no importance regarding MacKenzie."

Kaid nodded. He would honor her request—for now.

"You want me to play Elizabeth for MacKenzie," she surmised. "I won't do it. Tell your people I'm Elizabeth, that's fine—it doesn't matter who I am. But I will not go to MacKenzie."

He'd expected as much. She felt betrayed, and he understood. "I was thinking of another way ye could help."

She raised a brow.

"The people's anger toward MacKenzie is more hurtful than helpful," he said. "If ye could show some goodwill toward them, it may ease some of their burden."

Her acquiescence to this part of the plan was vital. She had to be open to seeing what MacKenzie had done. "Please," he said in a low voice.

She stared up at him and a memory blossomed in his mind of the last time she'd looked at him so boldly. When they'd lain together. When he'd sampled everything sweet and wonderful about her.

Before she turned on him.

Her cheeks flushed to a bonny pink and he knew she was remembering too. She turned her bold stare from him, for it was no longer bold and he knew she did not want him to see the thoughts they shared.

"Very well." She lifted her head in a proud manner, the same as she had when he first abducted her. Perhaps in the manner the true Elizabeth Seymour would. "It's far better than sitting in a room and waiting for time to pass."

The pressure in Kaid's chest eased. The first part of his plan had worked.

Now for Delilah to be convinced to truly help.

Chapter Sixteen

Grudging.

Yes, that was the ideal word to describe Delilah's mood as she trudged from the castle to the outlying village. Two massive warriors carefully held a large kettle of savory venison stew, followed by a wheeled cart laden with bread still hot from the oven. Beside them walked Rhona, the aged seer who carried a basket of herbs looped around her forearm.

Delilah hated being captive when she should have had the advantage. Her failure sat in her mind like a pebble in one's shoe. The wind jerked her skirts against her until she felt as though the fine silk were beating her legs. Hair whipped into her face. She irritably shoved aside the offending tresses and pressed onward.

One and a half weeks.

Elizabeth would arrive at Edirdovar Castle in only one and a half weeks. Perhaps there might be a way to still succeed.

The rhythmic squeaking of the cart ceased, and Delilah realized the men had stopped in front of a simple thatched roof house. A small shadow in her peripheral vision darted behind a nearby building, but not before she caught the glimpse of the child's blonde hair.

It was not Delilah who strode toward the door to rap upon its rough surface. Rhona knocked firmly with her gnarled fist and then stepped back, a smile drawn tight across her face.

The door did not open.

The rest of the party waited without complaint while the drag of time scraped over Delilah's fraying patience. She almost suggested they move on when the latch was thrown on the other side and the door creaked open.

A woman stood in the doorway, propped against a makeshift crutch. Her face might have been comely once, but it was difficult to tell with the jagged pink scar running from her right brow to her chin and leaving the eye there milky and sightless. The remaining blue eye sparkled with recognition and she gave a gracious nod. "I wasna sure ye'd make it today with the storm coming in."

"We've got venison today, Agnes," Lachlan, the dark-haired warrior said. "Ye know I couldna let ye miss out on yer favorite."

"Aye, ye wouldna." She gave a reserved smile before moving back with an awkward hop. It was then Delilah realized only one shoe peeked out from beneath the woman's homespun skirt.

The men and Rhona entered the house with a familiarity Delilah tried to mimic. Despite the air of confidence she attempted to portray, she felt very much the stranger in the confines of Agnes's home. Truly it was little more than a room with a pallet by the fire and a simple table and chair at its center. The air within was thick with the smoke of peat.

Rhona swept toward Agnes and immediately pressed at the massive pink scar. "Have ye been putting on the poultice I gave ye?"

The woman winced. "I try, but it is difficult to breathe when I do."

"Ye're no' supposed to put it over yer mouth and nose." Rhona tucked her frizzy white hair behind her ear and regarded the scarred woman with chastisement.

A flush crept over Agnes's face and she flicked an embarrassed glance toward Delilah. "I dinna do it like that."

"Well, then." Rhona pushed aside her bright purple cloak and took several herbs from her basket, setting them on the table beside the bowl of stew and bread. "If ye dinna like the scar, then ye need to use the herbs." Her voice was sweet, but there was something beneath it that made Delilah want to stand protectively in front of Agnes.

"Agnes is still bonny, even with the scar." Lachlan gave her a cheerful wink. "I gave ye an extra bit of venison, but dinna ye go telling the other lasses. I canna have them getting jealous."

Agnes gave a good-natured laugh, and the harshness of the scar on her face lightened to reveal how young she truly was. "Thank ye for coming by today, and every day. I dinna know what I'd do without ye."

Delilah made her way to the door, feeling like an awkward, useless appendage to the party. Agnes stopped her with the gentle grip of her arm.

"Bless ye, my lady." The woman lowered her head with a reverence Delilah did not deserve. "I know ye've no' anything to do with what happened, but we all appreciate ye helping us nonetheless."

Surprise caught at Delilah's tongue and held it in place. In the end, she nodded and squeezed Agnes's hand before exiting the simple home after the others. A little blonde head peeped out from behind the cart.

Little Claire followed them through the course of the day while they delivered food to people in all states of debilitating injuries—from lost limbs to blindness to overall blatant pain. With each new person they visited, Delilah came to appreciate how Kaid insisted his men and Rhona go every day to aid those who were too injured to come to the castle for food.

Each person they visited was kind and grateful, and every one personally offered Delilah their thanks for her assistance.

It should have made her feel good—if she were Elizabeth, the woman they thought her to be. But she was a fraud who'd been asked to go rather than volunteering. The knowledge knotted like rough rope in her stomach as the day wore on. She did not deserve their gratitude.

In the end, she would have to turn in the man who fought so hard for their freedom and safety. She would leave these battered people vulnerable.

Something tight and uncomfortable squeezed around her chest at the very thought. When she looked up, she found Rhona's gaze on her.

"If ye're unwell, ye travel with a healer." Rhona spoke in the same over-sweet tone she used with the villagers.

"I'm well, thank you," Delilah answered. Never had she been more grateful for her knowledge of Gaelic. She'd used it exclusively since her capture. Poor Leasa did not speak any and spent most of her time with Donnan who could translate for her.

A thought occurred to Delilah while she was speaking with the healer.

"What do you know of valerian root?" Delilah asked suddenly.

Rhona's eyes narrowed and seemed to disappear beneath the crinkle of her eyelids. "Why do ye ask?"

"My aunt," Delilah said quickly, realizing Rhona must have given Kaid the vial in the first place. "She took it often and seemed almost plagued by it."

"The English never know how to handle the stuff," she said in a honeyed tone. The brittle smile returned to her face. "I'm a healer. Of course I know a great deal about it."

Delilah had to squelch the temptation to roll her eyes at the woman's condescending patience. "Can it cause nightmares?"

Wind caught at Rhona's long white hair and pulled it in front of her face. She shoved it aside and took a while to see it freed before finally answering. "At times." Rhona's reply came with such restraint, Delilah knew the answer was more likely a definitive yes.

She nodded pensively. "Why then would she have been so eager to take it all the time?"

"Some herbs are like that. They make one reliant upon them. Especially among people who do not know how to properly use them."

The insult grated down Delilah's spine. The trail they were on was a long one, and seemed to curl away from the denser part of the village toward somewhere more remote. Though she did not enjoy speaking with Rhona, the woman was giving her good information—by everything she was *not* saying.

Delilah suddenly wished Percy were there instead. Percy probably knew more about herbs than the seer and would certainly be kinder.

"Why would my aunt take valerian in the first place?" Delilah asked with tethered patience.

Rhona gave a sage nod as she answered, "For pain."

Delilah thought of Kaid. He had no wounds she had seen. Or touched, since she'd touched more of him than she saw. Warmth flushed over her chest. "But she wasn't injured."

Rhona stopped suddenly and Delilah did too. The men carrying the almost empty kettle continued ahead, along with Lachlan.

"No' all pain is of the body, lass." Rhona gave her an appraising look. "Sometimes it comes from in here." She pointed a fleshy finger at Delilah's breast. Toward her heart. "It keeps the sufferer awake all night with hurt they canna endure. The valerian draws them toward sleep, toward forgetting and unfeeling."

The old woman began walking once more, her great purple cape whipping and snapping in the wind, leaving Delilah no choice but to follow.

Was that truly why Kaid took valerian?

Delilah recalled the nightmares, the pictures he'd drawn, the suffering bright in his beautiful blue eyes. And her heart ached for him.

A large stone building came into view, nestled between a trio of swollen hills. Several children played in the soft grass, their voices light and carefree. In front of the door to the building was the brown-haired woman who had apologized for Claire only the day before. And Kaid.

Something stung inside her to see them together, and for the first time, she wondered if he had a lover. If this woman might be his lover.

Before she could wind a maddening story in her mind for the couple in front of her, Kaid looked up and watched their group progress toward him. No, not their group—her.

Her cheeks went hot at the realization.

She shouldn't care. She shouldn't want his notice. But she did.

The understanding hit her like one of Sylvi's blows.

Caring for him was foolish.

And loving him was—

She shook the thought from her mind and strode toward him, toward the man whose heart was both tender and broken.

· · ·

Kaid could not keep from watching Delilah as she approached.

The impending storm swirled wild winds around her, catching at her hair and dress, and yet she walked with the straight-backed pride of a queen. The silk of her yellow gown rippled across her body like sunlight over a loch and gave him teasing impressions of her body beneath.

The little girl who had mistaken Delilah for her mother upon their arrival slipped from behind the large kettle and darted toward the building behind him. Delilah's gaze fixed on the girl for a brief moment, and her lips lifted in a kind smile.

"I see our Claire is still enamored with Lady Elizabeth," the woman beside him said.

He tore his gaze from Delilah and turned toward Aida.

She tucked a lock of brown hair behind her ear and studied Delilah. "I confess, I've no' seen the child so active—no' since her ma died. The lady is special."

Kaid agreed, but didn't say as much.

Delilah came to a stop before them and looked up at the stone building. "What is this place?" she asked. Her yellow gown brought a sensual warmth to her rich brown eyes.

He indicated the children whose arms were outstretched as they turned circles on the velvety grass, their small bodies moving in play with the wind. "It's the orphanage. This is Aida—she cares for the children."

Aida dipped her head in greeting.

"The children can make their way to the keep for meals, of

course," Kaid said. "But with so many lads in their care, there's always a hungry mouth ready to eat."

Aida chuckled. "Aye, that's the truth of it to be sure."

But Delilah did not laugh. She surveyed the yard with a somber gaze. "There are many children here. I assume there are more inside as well."

"There were many slain, and many children were left orphaned." Kaid tried to keep his voice gentle. "There's to be a storm soon. We should make our way back to the keep."

"It isn't so bad," she protested.

A great gust swept over them with enough force to tug her hair free of its binding, sending tendrils of honey locks dancing freely.

"Perhaps it is," she said with a laugh. But still she hesitated and peered behind Kaid, into the keep. "Claire made it inside, correct?"

Aida nodded. "But I'm sure she'll be yer shadow again in the morn. I hope she isna a bother."

"Of course she isn't." Delilah smiled. "I look forward to it."

The large door to the orphanage slammed shut with a bang. Several children shrieked in fear, and Aida immediately turned to see to them.

Kaid touched Delilah's arm to get her attention. "We need to go."

She nodded and waved to Aida before allowing him to lead her back toward the castle where Rhona and the men were already heading.

Delilah did not cower against him from the wind or quicken her pace to escape its wrath. She strode with the same confident gait she always possessed. There was bravery in her that went beyond the pretense of playing someone else. It was genuine.

It made him wonder at what other parts of her were true Delilah, and not the faux Elizabeth.

Knowing Gaelic was a true part of Delilah. She spoke it as well as if she'd been born a Scot and lived as one her entire life. He also knew she allowed his people to know she spoke Gaelic. It was a great act of trust on her part to do so. Pretending to not understand or speak would have been an easy way to glean information. To share it meant she could communicate with his people.

It was the kindness of a considerate woman.

"You're a clever man, Kaid MacLeod." Delilah slid him a sly look.

"Am I?"

She smirked. "Never once did you ask me to abandon my goal to bring you to justice, or try to sway from my path. Instead, you put me to work helping the survivors. You knew they would be grateful, and you knew that would be hard to accept."

"They are good people," Kaid replied.

Her gaze returned to the road ahead, and she was silent for a moment. "They are. And you're a good laird to them."

His people were not all so pleased with him. They would not all agree he was a good laird.

The castle came into view in the distance. Dots of rain flecked from the sky and peppered their faces. "They want a war on MacKenzie," he said.

"Which is why you are a good laird," she replied. "They want to act on brutal impulse and yet you devised a plan to keep everyone safe while securing peace instead of offering blood for blood."

He stopped and waited until she met his gaze. "And that plan has now been compromised."

She gave a sad smile. "By me."

Uncertainty showed for the first time in her expression.

The rain came then, in great fat plops against their heads and amid a chaos of violent winds. Kaid caught Delilah by the arms in a protective motion he knew she did not need.

"To the castle!" he shouted.

Delilah turned to him with a glint in her eye. "I'll race you there."

No sooner had he nodded than she was off like a spooked deer, graceful, powerful, and impossibly fast despite the heavy skirts billowing around her legs.

Together they ran down the path and over the large meadow behind the village. The wet, earthy scent of fresh rain spun through the air around them. The storm whipped and shoved at their hapless forms until their hair and clothing were sodden and clinging to them.

Kaid pushed hard enough to leave his muscles burning with the exertion, yet she still made it to the gates before him.

The guards eyed her with suspicion as she passed, but Kaid shook his head and did not slow until they were both within the castle. Heavy clouds had blotted out the sun and left the main room shrouded by the dark ferocity of the storm.

He closed the door behind them and inadvertently plunged the open stone room into a tomblike silence.

Delilah gave a breathless laugh, her cheeks rosy from the exertion. "I won."

Her voice came out loud in the quiet. She smothered a hand over her mouth and grinned.

Kaid stepped closer to her. "So ye did." He couldn't keep the joy from his face any more than he could stop staring.

Her hair had slipped free of its pins, and the stylish court dress she wore had lost its rigid shape, so the skirts hung limp around her legs. Rainwater glistened against her flesh, beautifully highlighting the curve of her collarbones, her graceful neck, the generous swell of her breasts.

She looked wild and free and altogether too inviting.

"What do I win?" Her eyes searched his with a silent plea he wanted more than anything to answer.

"What is it ye want?" he asked.

She watched him with a playful expression, the same carefree way she'd looked at him when they were traveling. When they'd kissed. When they'd loved.

She may have won the race, but he knew right then and there what he wanted. To find out more about this woman who raced in the rain and didn't fret over her disheveled appearance—who laughed and cared and loved with the most beautiful passion.

He wanted Delilah.

Chapter Seventeen

Delilah knew all too poignantly what she wanted.

To not be in the situation she was in, having to choose between her loyalty to Sylvi and what she knew was right.

To stay in this heady moment of flirtation and forget everything else.

And Kaid.

God, how she wanted Kaid. But more than that, she wanted him to want her. As Delilah, not Elizabeth.

He was staring at her as if he did. The intensity of his gaze left her hot and hungry.

"I want to know what you want." It was a coward's way out, but she couldn't stop the words.

"I want ye." He gave the answer earnestly and without hesitation.

He stared down at her as he had when they'd traveled, as if she were an unreachable woman he wanted.

"You want me," Delilah repeated.

Kaid's fingertips brushed down her cheek and along her jaw. It was all she could do not to tilt her head back against the luxury of his touch.

"I'm enjoying discovering the woman ye are, Delilah." The intimacy behind his silky whisper sent decadent chills down her body.

She loved the sound of her name on his lips. *Her* name, in the gentle burr of his brogue.

"And what kind of woman am I?" she asked in a flirtatious tone.

"Ye're no' the pampered woman ye pretended to be when we

met. Ye had a determination to ye, and I see now that was Delilah and no' Elizabeth." He spoke low enough that they would not be overheard. "Ye're strong, both in spirit and in body. Ye fight like a man, but ye're still delicate like a woman when ye look at me the way ye are now. And for all yer fortitude, yer heart is fragile and genuine."

The threat of tears left Delilah's face blazing. No one had ever seen her in such a way. He saw who she was as he'd seen her physical appearance—a beauty she had never found in herself.

"Delilah." His mouth was now a whisper away from her own. She tilted her face toward his, wanting to feel the familiar touch of his lips on hers. Not wanting to—*needing* to.

His hand slid over her face. His skin was warm despite being wet and in such a cold and dark room. Outside a crack of thunder sounded overhead, followed by the quiet roar of a hearty rain.

But it was not the weather which held her attention, it was Kaid, and how much she needed the escape of his kiss.

"Delilah," he said again. "Ye're exquisite."

Exquisite.

The word coiled around the wounded place deep in her heart, wrapping it in a balm more soothing than she had ever known.

She had but a moment to savor the flattery before his mouth came down on hers, deep and delicious. Droplets of water from the tips of his hair dripped onto her shoulders, cold against the sudden burning heat of her skin.

All the memories she'd kept brushing away tumbled through her mind. The masculine scent of him, the scrape of his whiskered chin against hers as they kissed, the low groan he gave when they'd coupled.

She could lose herself in him again just as easily.

He caught her lower lip between his teeth, nipping it sensually before his tongue brushed hers.

Delilah's body smoldered with a desire so strong, her knees went slack beneath its force.

She wanted him. All of him.

Now.

The rasping sound of a throat being cleared echoed on the stonework around them. They flew apart like lovers caught.

For isn't that what they were?

Rhona's steely gaze met theirs.

"I dinna think ye'll get much for the lass from MacKenzie if ye have her first." Her scolding came out in a singsong tone.

Delilah's cheeks scalded with shame, but Rhona looked right through her toward Kaid. "I've brought ye more of yer sleeping draught."

Rhona strode forward and pushed her gnarled fingers into Kaid's palm, intentionally standing between him and Delilah. A flash of glass showed against his hand.

A vial.

Kaid nodded in thanks. Rhona spoke quietly to Kaid, who nodded again.

She turned to Delilah and sneered at the sodden mess of her gown. "I'll have yer maid come and fetch ye to freshen ye up for supper." Then she quit the room with steps as sharp as the edge to her smile.

Delilah regarded the vial before Kaid pocketed it. She had to tell him what she'd learned of it from Rhona. Her suspicions had been confirmed, and he needed to know what he was doing to himself. "Kaid—"

"I shouldna have kissed ye." He set his jaw. "Especially no' out in the open."

She shook her head. "We thought we were alone."

"Ye're the last chance I have." Something shadowed his eyes. "I canna have people thinking ye've been compromised."

The last chance he had?

She frowned. "What do you mean by—"

"My lady?" Leasa stepped from the darkened hallway, concern evident in the furrow of her brow. "Rhona said you were in a bad way. Are you unwell?"

Delilah suppressed an exasperated sigh. "I'm fine. We were

caught in the storm, and I need to change before supper." She turned back toward Kaid in time to see him slip the valerian root extract into the waist of his kilt. "Kaid, I'd like to continue speaking with you."

"We'll speak later." He nodded toward Leasa. "Go prepare for supper. It will be served soon, and ye dinna want the whole of the clan waiting on ye."

But they did not speak later, not through the food or the ale as it was served, or while they ate, or even during the entertainment afterward when the music played and the whisky flowed.

Later, Delilah lay in bed, her mind as awake as her body. She stared at the shadowed underside of the great canopy bed and listened to the steady, even snores of Leasa sleeping on the pallet on the floor.

Kaid would be alone now.

Memories of his nightmare rushed into her mind. She hated the thought of him poisoning his nights with the valerian root again.

Her mind cycled back to their kiss. Their conversation. Not only what he'd thought about her, but also when he'd said she was their only hope. What did he intend for her to do? Especially when she'd already told him she would not go to MacKenzie as Elizabeth.

She could speak with him now. She knew what room was his. Leasa had mentioned his was near theirs to ensure their protection, but it set the other servants whispering with suspicion.

It wouldn't be proper to see Kaid at such a late hour, alone. It wasn't something Lady Elizabeth would do.

But she wasn't Lady Elizabeth.

Delilah rose from the bed with such care, the bed ropes did not even squeak, and slid a night robe over her bed clothes. After quick confirmation that Leasa still slept, she slipped from the room and headed toward Kaid's.

Impropriety be damned. She would deliver her warning to Kaid, and she would get her answers.

• • •

The vial called to Kaid.

The hour was late and the day had been long. So damn long.

There had been many issues requiring his assistance—disputes which had awaited his arrival, decisions to be made, advice to be given. His head ached with the burden of his responsibilities.

But, no, it wasn't that.

It was coming home to Ardvreck and being reminded of what MacKenzie's attack had done to his people. Though they tried to rally, their spirits were even more broken than their bodies. Many had died, and those who carried on had to work twice as hard to compensate for the loss. The deep lines in their faces bespoke how the extra labor exacted its toll.

At least home brought the relief Rhona afforded him.

He pulled the stopper from the vial. He wanted the bitterness on his tongue, to melt into his body and mind and shroud everything roiling and screaming in a blanket of silence.

A knock sounded at the door.

He clenched his teeth and slid the stopper back into place before bidding the intruder enter.

The door did not swing open as he'd expected. There was a moment of hesitation before the creaking groan of the hinges.

And it was no man who entered his private room, but a woman. Nay, a goddess.

Or so she appeared with her golden brown hair spilling over her shoulders and a cloak of rich red velvet atop a night-rail seemingly made of glowing moonlight.

"Delilah." Her name came out in a low rasp, like a dying man asking for water.

Her gaze swept his large room and lingered for the briefest of moments on his bed. She paused in the doorway before lifting her head and striding toward him with all the confidence of the goddess she appeared to be.

God, how he longed to pull her into his arms and bury his nose in the silken tresses of her hair where he could breathe in the sweet floral spice of her.

"Have you taken the valerian root yet?" she asked.

He blinked.

That was not what he'd expected to hear her say, not when she appeared so brazenly in his room while the rest of the castle slept.

He shook his head and tightened his grip on the glass in his palm.

Delilah's shoulders relaxed. "Please do not take it."

Her words sent a shiver down his back. Not because he feared what she said, but because the idea of possessing the valerian in his grasp and not taking it was almost as agonizing as having Delilah in the privacy of his room and not touching her.

She approached him, and the feminine scent of her perfume caught at his awareness with a far tighter hold than he'd have thought possible. Her hands settled on his fist, delicate and soft.

He wanted them on the rest of him.

"Please don't take it," she repeated. Her pleading look grabbed at his heart. "It's poison to your body. It brings nightmares and sleepless nights and yet makes you want more."

He gritted his teeth. "How do ye know this?"

Even as he prepared to defend the drug, his thoughts searched for the validity of her words. He remembered how he'd been before they all got sick and how renewed he'd felt after.

"Rhona told me, but not because I asked after you. I tricked her into telling me." She frowned. "I know she's one of your people, but I confess I don't trust her."

The aged seer was not actually one of his people. She'd shown up at the castle three years prior, seeking refuge after having been cast from her own clan—an event so painful, she never spoke of it. No one had minded as she'd proved herself to be quite useful in the art of healing.

Of course, divulging this to Delilah would not help his claim. "She doesna trust ye, lass. It's the only reason she acts as she does."

"Please don't take this," Delilah said again. She found the place where his fingers wrapped tight over his palm, sealing the vial safely within, and tried to pry his hand open.

He resisted.

Even if the valerian brought nightmares, they were not with him in the morning. All he ever recalled was the quiet black it welcomed him to, where nights of restless slumber turned into a full block of forgotten everything.

He didn't want to remember. Nor did he want to think. He wanted the nothing. He *craved* the nothing.

She shook her head at him.

Irritation prickled through him at the thought of having to release his precious vial. The prickle quickly turned to an irrational whip of rage which lashed through him.

"And what do ye care if I take this?" he asked. "When ye've seen my people and no' done a thing to help them?"

She straightened as if he'd slapped her. "I spent the day helping them."

"Aye, I told ye to," he countered. "Ye're worried about a vial of liquid when my people will die if ye dinna help us."

Her hands dropped from his. Her expression was wounded, and he knew he'd hit a mark deep within, exactly where he'd intended to strike.

Except now there was a wrench of guilt where his ire had once resided.

"I can't..." she started. She looked hard into the fire and a small muscle worked at her jaw. "It's so much more than me wanting to help."

"Ye canna take me from my own castle to Killearnan," he said. "I know."

"Ye canna fulfill your original purpose for playing Elizabeth with me. But ye can help *us* by playing her again." He wanted to touch her tense shoulders, just a brief graze of his fingertips along the silken heat of her skin. He was close enough to do so.

His hands balled into fists. He would not have her think he was attempting to seduce her into compliance.

The golden glow of the fire flickered across her comely features.

Her expression was impassive and the silence stretching between them was becoming uncomfortably long.

"What would you have me do?" she asked.

"I'd like information ye dinna want to share." He tried not to speak too quickly, to appear too overeager. "Who sent ye, why, what my death meant to them, the details of yer mission."

She tilted her head away from him, as if hearing as much physically hurt her. Worse still, he sensed her wary interest flagging at the demand for information.

She turned back to him. "I told you before, MacKenzie did not hire me—that is all I will share with you."

Kaid nodded and shoved down the fresh rise of questions surging in his mind. Those were things to worry over another time. "Verra well. I need ye to pretend to be Elizabeth Seymour with MacKenzie."

She opened her mouth, and he put a hand up to stop her inevitable protests.

"I want to ransom ye to MacKenzie, but for more than just to get my da's sword or work out peace negotiations. If I do that, he'll agree to peace and then attack without any thought to our deal." A muscle worked in his jaw. "This is something I'm asking ye to do as Delilah. I dinna know that Elizabeth could have done what I'm about to ask for."

Delilah lifted her brow. "Go on."

"Ye remember I told ye MacKenzie had an older sister named Torra? She was the true heir to the MacKenzie lairdship per her father's wishes before his death. Ye need to find her."

She merely notched her chin upward in a way that left her mouth far too temptingly close. "You speak as though Torra will be hard to find."

A palpable sense of relief melted over his shoulders. He understood by her straightened back and her solemn demeanor that she was intrigued. But then she was the same as he—a schemer, a chess player in the game of life. And he respected her all the more for it.

"MacKenzie's sister was deemed mad when her father died," Kaid said. "No one has seen her since."

"Perhaps she is dead."

"If she is, we will have to come up with another plan."

Delilah did not answer, resuming her stare into the popping fire.

"Will ye help?" he asked.

Her chest swelled in a long, deep sigh before she finally turned back to him. "I promise to think on it if you promise to rid yourself of the poison clutched in your hand."

The vial was hot in his palm now. Delilah stared at his fist until he unfurled his fingers and presented the valerian root to her.

He wanted to tell her what he sacrificed, how it was a blanket of comfort she was yanking from his soul, but instead he surrendered it in silence.

She pulled the stopper from the vial and flung the contents into the hearth where the precious droplets hissed and spit. Then she threw the vial and stopper into the fire as well.

He stared into the licking flames, seeking the glossy tube, when Delilah touched his cheek in a tender, distracting caress. His gaze found hers, and he forgot the valerian root. Her lips pressed to his, warm and sweet, before she pulled back, leaving him wanting so much more.

"Good night, Kaid," she said solemnly. Then she turned and left without giving him an answer at all.

Chapter Eighteen

It was a minor victory to keep Kaid from his nightmares.

A far bigger victory awaited Delilah in helping his people.

She pressed her hand to her brow to shield the glare of the sun and watched two boys dash across the lawn near the orphanage. After bringing them the remnants of the noonday meal, Delilah had stayed to assist Aida any way she could. After all, the young woman had her work well laid out for her with so many children.

The air was tinged with the mustiness of sweat and the lushness of a new day after a night of rain. It was a smell which lightened her heart and yet burdened her shoulders all at once.

She could save them.

All of them.

If she played Elizabeth for MacKenzie.

If she turned her back on Sylvi and Liv and Isabel and Percy—the ultimate betrayal.

A boy across the field took up a stick and brandished it like a sword toward a younger boy who was held between two others. The disconcerting scene intruded on Delilah's thoughts and she quickly made her way toward them.

"Take that, ye filthy MacLeod," the older boy bellowed in a nasty growl and plunged the stick toward the younger one's armpit so it seemed to penetrate his chest.

Delilah stopped short in horror.

The younger boy collapsed to the ground in a dramatic death. "Dinna hurt my wife." His head dropped to the side, and he went still.

Aida rushed past Delilah toward the boys and bent at the waist to speak to them. Delilah could not hear what she said, but could tell Aida was not rebuking them for their gruesome display. With a pat on the back for each of them, the boys disbanded in pursuit of other activities.

Aida straightened with the stick in her hand and cast Delilah a woeful, apologetic smile that was altogether too tired for a woman so young. "They dinna know what to make of it all," Aida offered in a sad tone. "They saw more than children ever should."

Delilah nodded silently. Aida patted her shoulder in the same manner as she'd done to the boys, and turned back toward the orphanage.

How could any woman endure such heartbreak daily?

Something warm brushed against Delilah's fingers before sliding against her palm. She found Claire standing beside her, her hand clasping Delilah's.

Claire gave a shy smile. "I'm Claire," she said in a very little voice.

"I'm…" Delilah caught herself. "I'm Elizabeth."

Claire's lips screwed up toward the left side of her cheek, and she studied Delilah with unabashed curiosity. "Are ye an angel?"

Delilah shook her head.

"Ye look like my ma," Claire said in an awestruck whisper. "I thought ye might be her angel since ye said ye werena her."

The girl's voice was so small, so hopeful that it left emotion crowding in Delilah's chest. "I'm sorry to not be. I would very much love to have a daughter like you."

Claire's hand in hers was growing overly hot and sweaty, but Delilah had no intention of breaking the tender hold.

"I think ye'd be a verra good ma," Claire said with a bashful glance at the ground. "Because ye're pretty and ye're nice."

"Is that what makes a good mother, then?" Delilah asked with a laugh.

The girl's lips twisted in thought once more. "I think the nice more so than the pretty," she conceded earnestly.

"Was your mother like that?" Delilah asked.

Claire's fingers tightened and for a moment, Delilah wondered if it'd been wrong to ask such a question.

"Would ye like to hear about her?" The afternoon sun lit Claire's hair like glowing gold. If anyone were the angel, it was she.

"Very much so," Delilah answered.

And the girl talked then—talked and talked and talked, as all little girls do, detailing the way her mother looked, and smelled, and even sang. Every bit of the dead woman was told in an unending speech only a child who truly loved her mother could give.

The two of them walked around and through the orphanage together, hand in sweaty hand, and chatted until the sky began to darken. The onset of evening found them in large, comfortable chairs in front of the fire, where it was warm and snug.

Claire gave a mighty yawn, revealing a missing bottom tooth, where the white flecks of another coming into its place were visible.

"Are you getting sleepy?" Delilah asked.

Claire nodded. "May I sit with ye?" Even as she asked the question, she was already climbing into Delilah's lap.

Delilah had cradled her own young siblings before and now marveled at the ability of all children to comfortably snuggle themselves into a willing lap. Claire's legs lay over Delilah's, and her head rested just under Delilah's chin.

Claire grasped Delilah's arm and pulled it over her shoulders, like one would do with a blanket on a cold night. Delilah smiled and held the girl in her embrace for a long while, even when the child's silky golden hair tickled at her chin.

"My ma protected me when the MacKenzies came," Claire whispered, so quietly, Delilah had almost not heard it. "She stepped in front of me so the men wouldna see me. She was verra brave." Her voice caught, and so did something in Delilah's chest.

Claire's hand blindly found Delilah's and folded around it. "When she died, she told me she loved me, and she…" A slight tremble of the girl's body told Delilah she was crying. "She told me she'd send an angel to protect me because she knew she was going to die."

Her crying was not so silent then. It came in hiccupping sobs that bled hot and wet against Delilah's chest and deep into her soul. She held the child while she wept, and could no sooner stop the tears from silently tracing down her own cheeks than she could stop the shell of her heart from breaking.

• • •

The sky was black with night and still Delilah was missing.

Kaid paced his solar, waiting for Leasa to arrive. Surely she had to know something about her mistress.

If he hadn't been so busy during the day, he'd have kept an eye on Delilah himself. The last damn thing he needed was for her to run off. He needed her for his plan to work.

But it was more than that.

After spending so many weeks with her, seeing her every day, speaking with her every day—the idea of her no longer in his life was incomprehensible and left him feeling...

He grasped at the fragile emotion and pulled it closer to his heart to identify it.

Empty.

Life without Delilah seemed somehow empty.

He stared out into the darkness once more. Would she truly have left? Perhaps that was why she'd given him such a quiet kiss the night before, a final goodbye.

And it was at such damnable timing.

MacKenzie's letter lay on the desk, his acceptance scrawled in a bold script. He would return Kaid's father's sword and allow peace to reign between the two clans.

Not that Kaid trusted that peace.

But if Delilah had left and he had no bride to offer, surely it would be an immediate invitation to war.

A knock sounded at the door, and his heart lurched.

"Enter," he said even as he strode toward the door to pull it open.

Leasa was there, her cheeks rosy and her hair shining. She'd abandoned the silly English gown she'd arrived in for a more comfortable homespun dress one of the MacLeod ladies had provided. The lass had taken well to life in Ardvreck Castle.

She entered the room and Donnan followed.

"Have ye seen Delilah?" Kaid asked in English.

"She's at the orphanage." Leasa cast a hesitant look toward Donnan. "Is something wrong?"

Kaid did not answer. He was already out the door and on his way to the large stone building where the orphans were housed, hoping all the way he'd truly find Delilah there.

Aida opened the door for him when he arrived.

He entered and scanned the large main room where several older children lingered. "Is Elizabeth here?" he asked.

Aida indicated the chairs near the fireplace. "I was wondering when ye'd come for her."

The grip of fear on Kaid's heart relaxed into relief.

He followed Aida toward the large hearth and found Delilah sitting with Claire in her arms. The child was snuggled against her and fast asleep, one thumb tucked in her mouth.

It was the kind of scene which told Kaid what kind of a mother Delilah might make, and for the quickest of moments, he wondered what she might look like cradling their child.

Aida held out her arms. "I'll take her to her bed."

Delilah hesitated and looked down at the child tenderly. "Are you sure?"

"Aye." Aida bent over Delilah and scooped the sleeping Claire into her arms. The girl snuffled and turned her head to the side before falling still once more. "She'll be fine," Aida said in a reassuring whisper.

Delilah nodded and offered a weak smile. She waited until Aida was gone before she looked up at Kaid. She tried to say his name, but it came out in a choked sob.

Kaid was at the chair's side in a single step. He reached toward Delilah, but she stopped him.

She closed her eyes and took a long, slow breath in and out. After a moment, her eyes opened, and she rose with all the elegance she'd ever possessed.

"Let's get ye back to the castle, aye?" Kaid placed a hand at the narrow dip of her lower back and led her toward the door. It was a slight touch, barely enough to allow the delicate heat of her body to tease his fingertips.

She was clearly upset and everything in him wanted to comfort her. He wanted to hold her in his arms and let the breaking of her heart wash against his chest.

But his Delilah was a proud woman.

His Delilah.

He had no right to call her as much, and yet he could no more stop the thought than he could stop his heart from beating.

Delilah allowed him to lead her from the room into the cold night. The wind stirred the trees in a quiet rustle.

"Is everything well with ye?" Kaid asked.

She pressed trembling fingers to her lips. "That poor child. All of them. Those poor children."

She nodded toward the trail in silent indication that they should go on.

Kaid took her hand and guided it to the crook of his arm, the kind of thing an English gentleman might do, true, but it was a comfort he knew she would allow.

They walked in silence all the way back to Ardvreck, the wind chilling their faces and the moon lighting their path.

When the castle gates appeared before them, Delilah stopped and turned to face him, her expression fierce. "I've made my decision." She caught his hands in hers and gave them a hearty squeeze. "I don't care what it costs me, I will help you."

Chapter Nineteen

Delilah found herself in the confidential quiet of Kaid's chamber once more. The spicy scent of him lingered in the air, declaring everything his, from the ornately carved chairs before the fire to the massive bed.

It was the bed which constantly drew her attention.

There was something very intimate about being in a place where a man lived, where he slept.

Her gaze flicked toward the bed.

Where he loved.

She tried not to let her heart wince at the last thought.

"Our plan needs to be a quick one." Her voice seemed almost too loud for the comfortable silence in the room.

Good. She needed the distraction from the thoughts of the innocent kiss she'd bestowed upon him the last time she was here, and how she'd wanted so much more.

But now was not for loving. Now was for war.

For saving the MacLeods from another massacre.

Her gaze shifted from the bed to the shuttered windows where the night loomed black beyond.

Kaid stood close to her. She could sense the nearness of his body against her back.

Delilah forged her resolve into iron before she turned to face him. "It was Lady Elizabeth's father who paid me to stand in her place. He knows nothing of you—only that MacKenzie has enemies who might use Elizabeth as a means to get at him."

She didn't mention Sylvi or Liv, or even the other girls who had not come on the journey—there was no need. Keeping their secrets was the least she could do for them after this incredible betrayal.

"But Lady Elizabeth is still traveling toward MacKenzie," she continued. "We have little more than a week before she arrives at Edirdovar Castle."

Kaid frowned. "It will take two days to reach it from here."

"I know," Delilah replied. "I'd done all the calculations. It's two days for a man on a horse, but I'll be playing a lady who rides in a carriage. The trip will take closer to three days. I'll have to leave in the morning. If I can get there quickly, it will allow more time to find Torra. I want to be gone before the true Elizabeth arrives."

Kaid stiffened and shifted his gaze from her.

"I dinna like it," he said finally. "I thought we'd have more time."

"Time would give us nothing, but a longer wait for everything to be resolved." She was right, of course. She knew as much, and certainly he did as well.

But he stared hard at her with emotion burning bright in the blue of his eyes. "I dinna like that ye have to do this." He stepped toward her, close enough for his body to blot out the heat of the fire and replace it with his own.

"It's your plan." Her voice was softer now, unintentionally so—as if her body was aware of an intimacy her mind had not yet caught.

He brushed his fingertips against her face. She closed her eyes to better revel in the caress. Her lips lifted in a coy smile. "Do you really think I'd let him hurt me?" She opened her eyes and found him staring down at her with a sad expression.

"I dinna want ye there alone. I want to be with ye." He continued cupping her jaw and stepped close enough for her skirts to tickle against his shins.

"You know you cannot." Delilah stared up at him, wanting him to see the truth in her words as she spoke them. "But you can trust me."

"I do trust ye." His thumb stroked against her cheek, and

something desperate showed in his gaze. "But if something happens to ye and I'm no' there to protect ye—"

"Nothing will happen to me." Delilah spoke with confidence. For surely it was easy to don when the chaos of reality lay outside a closed bedroom door.

He stared down at her for a long moment before his mouth came down on hers, hungry and fierce.

Surprise only caught her for a brief moment before she let herself be drowned in the lust she'd been pushing off since their arrival at Ardvreck. She slid her fingers through the silkiness of Kaid's hair. Their kisses were frantic with lips and tongues and teeth.

Her nipples tingled beneath her bodice with each excited brush against his chest, and the place between her legs pounded with a desperate need.

"I want ye." Kaid's admission came out in a groan between eager kisses. He pulled back and his eyes met hers. "I want ye, Delilah."

Delilah.

Joy bubbled around her heart. She could have laughed with the happiness of hearing him say her name. Wanting her.

Not Elizabeth. Her.

He stroked the hair away from her forehead and let his hand glide down the back of her head. "I told ye—ye're exquisite." He came toward her so she had to step backward.

Toward the bed.

Delilah sucked in a gasp.

Kaid edged her back until the hard frame of the bed pushed against her calves. He leaned over her, and she allowed herself to lay back on the pillowed surface of Kaid's bed.

The fur coverlet was soft beneath her palms and it was altogether too easy to imagine herself naked atop it.

Kaid braced himself over her. "Ye're a beautiful woman, Delilah." He kissed her with such tenderness, it almost made her cry out with its teasing, agonizing slowness.

He sucked her bottom lip into his mouth and then drew back

with a playful grin she'd not seen on him before. Something about it warmed low in her stomach.

"So eager, my beautiful warrior?" he said in a velvet voice. "We rushed last time. This is different. We have the night together to love."

He pulled the ribbon of her bodice until the delicate silk bow slipped free. "I want to take my time with ye. To see ye." His gaze drifted down her body, and her cheeks began to burn.

"I want to touch ye." He slid a hand up her skirt and teased the delicate flesh of her inner thighs.

Delilah's legs widened, unbidden.

He ran a fingertip to where her legs met, where the source of her desire thrummed wild and erratic, and she cried out with eager pleasure.

Then, to her great surprise, he lifted the damp fingertip to his lips and grazed it with his tongue.

"I want to taste ye," he said.

Before she could answer, before rational thought even jarred back into her mind, he knelt between her legs and pressed his mouth to her.

A quiet cry left her lips, but she did not pull from his caress.

Not even when he repeated it with his tongue.

He dragged it slowly over the delicate slit, pausing to flick the swollen bud, directly where her body hummed with desire. Everything tightened with a familiar anticipation.

She said his name, and it came out in a strangled moan.

At that one beautiful moment of bliss, nothing mattered but the flat of his tongue against her and the need building.

Her fingers wound through his hair and held him to her while her body trembled. His tongue danced over her once more, and she thought she might go mad with wanting, mad with being so close but not falling over the edge.

He slid a finger inside her while his skillful tongue worked, and her world exploded with tingling pleasure.

He did not stop until her cries subsided and her body relaxed with another kind of languid longing.

She wanted him.

For the last night she was at Ardvreck, before she might possibly never see him again, she wanted him.

Kaid obviously was of the same mind, for he rose from between her legs with a slight smile on his lips and slid off the belt of his plaid. Both fell away, leaving him in only his leine, which he smoothly pulled over his head in one tug.

Delilah's mouth went dry.

She'd felt the muscles beneath his clothing when they'd lain together, even when he'd held her before. But to bear witness to his beauty was another thing entirely.

His shoulders, arms, and chest were carved with muscle and his stomach went flat in tapered bands that seemed to become more pronounced when he breathed. His hips were narrow, his thighs powerful, and...

Delilah, who thought herself long past being a silly girl, warmed with the heat of a blush when her gaze lingered over the length of his hard phallus.

She slid off the bed, and her heavy skirts slipped back over her legs once more. She let her mouth curl into a seductive grin and slipped a finger under the lace of her bodice before slowly pulling it free.

He'd shown himself to her in all his beautiful magnificence.

And now it was her turn.

•••

The undressing of a woman had never been so sensual as Delilah's careful disrobing.

Kaid had had his share of women, of course, but he had enjoyed many without the ceremony of having their clothing slowly stripped away.

Delilah pulled free all the lacings on her bodice and let it hit the ground with a hard thunk. Next came the heavy skirts which rustled like parchment in the quiet room. Then came the heavy corset which eased the rigid stiffness of her frame and left the pink of her nipples visible beneath the thin fabric of her sark.

He took great pleasure in the gradual revealing of flesh, the tease of what was to come. Though he'd had her before, he found himself waiting with strained eagerness for the removal of each item.

She stayed a moment in her sark, watching him before easing the hem over her ankles, her shapely calves, her slender, perfect knees. He didn't know if he'd ever noticed knees being perfect before, but hers were decidedly so.

Higher still revealed the slender gap between her legs. His heart pounded with thundering anticipation. The triangle of dark hair between her legs came next, then the flare of her rounded hips and the narrow indent of her waist.

Kaid folded his arms over his chest to keep from touching her. The last thing he wanted was to interrupt the tantalizing view.

The sark rose high over the expanse of her ribcage and displayed full, lovely breasts. He ran his tongue across the seam of his lips.

Finally, she cast the sark aside, where it whispered to the floor in a graceful heap of fabric.

Delilah was beautiful. Far more so than even his imagination could attempt to supply. Her body was made firm by her ability to fight, lines of lean muscle apparent in the glow of the fire.

Though there was evidence of her true strength, there was still the alluring softness of femininity—the swell of her hips, the roundness of her breasts, the curve of her perfect bottom.

He wanted to trace her body, memorize every luscious contour. He wanted to draw her, to capture her incredible beauty.

But sketching could come later.

He closed the distance between them and skimmed his fingers over her flat stomach. Her nipples hardened and she gave a quiet gasp.

He met her gaze. "Every part of ye is beautiful."

Spots of color showed on her cheeks. "Every part of you is as well."

He almost grinned, but her touch moved to his chest and slowly dragged down his stomach to where his cock strained toward her. His amusement melted into a groan of longing.

Unabashed in that brave way of hers, she let her fingers curl around him before stroking up his length.

"Ye're going to drive me mad, lass." He spoke the words between his teeth.

Her lips slipped into a sly grin. "That's the point."

She lowered herself to the floor, kneeling in front of him so his cock jutted toward her face. Her hand continued to stroke him in slow glides.

She looked up at him and licked her lips.

Her moistened lips parted, and she drew her tongue in a teasing flick over the head of his cock. A grunt jerked from his chest.

She dragged her tongue over him again, tracing the underside of his cock in a slow glide.

He wanted to be inside her mouth, where she would be hot and wet. "Open yer lips," he said through gritted teeth.

She looked up at him and parted her mouth.

He groaned at the whisper of her sweet breath against his fevered skin. "Take me in yer mouth."

She gave him a half-smile and obeyed. Her lips closed around him and her tongue played over his cock.

Sweat prickled on his brow. He wanted to tell her to suck, but couldn't think to form the words.

She eased her lips back over him and then drew him deep once more before repeating the process. His bollocks tightened with the need to release.

But, no, he wanted to feel her body beneath him, squeezing him in her own climax.

He caught the silky weight of a full breast in his palm and teased over the hard nipple with his thumb. Her brows flinched and her muffled whimper hummed against his cock.

Her sensual mouth stroking against his cock, the allure of her beautiful body, the sound of her longing—it was all more than he could bear. Though he'd promised himself he'd take his time with her, the reality was becoming more impossible by the second.

"On the bed." His voice was low and throaty.

Delilah drew him from her lips and eased backwards onto the bed, her fevered gaze fixed on him the entire time. He shadowed her progress until she lay atop the furs and he'd climbed over her.

She moved restlessly beneath him, her hips rolling as they had when they'd lain together before.

He claimed her mouth and let his body come to rest atop her. Her skin was silky, beautiful. He wanted to sink into her, to love her until the light of dawn spilled over their bodies.

She moaned and spread her legs to cradle his hips. His shaft lay against the entrance of her sex. It damn near drove him mad with the power of his want.

He shifted his hips back so the tip of his cock nudged against the juncture between her legs. Delilah arched her hips at the same time he thrust inside her, sheathing so hard, so deep that a cry of pleasure tore from them both.

She clutched him with her thighs and moved with mindless passion. Her nails raked sharp against his back and left him tingling with a delicious sting which only heightened his lust.

She was so tight, squeezing, flexing, moving with him. Their breath tangled with one another and their teeth bumped against lips with the force of their uncontrollable kisses.

Delilah's body tensed under his.

"Yes," he growled. He eased his hips higher and let his body rub against the bud of her sex while he thrust.

She threw her head back and constricted around him, clenching again and again and again until the swelling heat of his own pleasure carried him over with her.

He groaned and buried himself as deep as he could go, reveling in the force of his own climax.

Afterward, he remained where he was for a long moment, holding her to him while letting his heartbeat calm.

When the delirium of passion eased its grip on them both, they stared at one another, lost in a moment of sated happiness.

Delilah was even more beautiful after they'd made love than before, if such a thing were possible. Her hair was a tousled cloud of honey-brown silk beneath her, her eyes were bright, and her lips turned slightly upward in a contented smile.

They stayed there for some time, trailing their fingers idly over each other's bodies. Finally the pull of sleep tugged at Kaid and he curled her in the protection of his arms.

He concentrated on the silkiness of her skin, the comfort of their shared warmth, and tried hard not to think of what tomorrow would bring.

For tomorrow, she would be gone.

• • •

Dawn broke the sky and drew back the dreamy veil love had created.

Delilah didn't want to wake, not when the alternative was to lie in Kaid's embrace.

His arms were around her and his legs twined with hers. Her body was pleasantly warm against him. But it was more than just the bed she did not wish to leave—it was him.

Fight it though she might, wakefulness was coming to her.

Her mind began to race with thoughts for the day, preparations to make, plans for when she arrived at Edirdovar. It would be dangerous.

If she could not convince MacKenzie, or if he found out who she was, it would doubtless be her demise. Every step would have to be carefully trod.

There was so much to prepare to ensure her success.

She would need to pack, to plan, to say goodbye. She would also need to bathe before she left, but there'd be no time for the water to be heated. Surely the servants had risen long ago to prepare the coach for her departure. She would not leave them waiting, especially when there was already so little time to spare.

Kaid nuzzled his prickly jaw against her neck. Tingles of pleasure tickled over her skin.

How she wanted to stay here instead. But the MacLeods needed her. This had to be done.

She knew she should wake Kaid, but feared if she did, leaving would be all the more difficult. Perhaps impossible.

Instead she slipped from his arms into the chill of morning air and silently picked up her discarded clothing. She turned back to where Kaid still slept, his arms over the blanket where she'd been.

Where his love had been fulfilling and beautiful, reality was stark and ugly.

With a heart heavy by her own choices, she turned from the man she wanted and began to ready herself for a journey which might possibly lead to her death.

Chapter Twenty

Kaid had wanted the night to last forever, but the morning had come too soon.

His heart was lead in his chest before he allowed himself to open his eyes. He knew before he even had to look.

Delilah was not there.

He was exhausted from the night they'd spent, tangled in passion, exploring one another, learning everything there was to know about the other's bodies again and again.

He regretted that he had not woken when she had, for it might have been his only chance to say goodbye in private.

He rose from the large bed to ready himself for her departure. It would be a great spectacle, he knew. The clan would be there to see her off, and welcome the prospect of peace once more.

The thought of her leaving clung to him like wet wool.

The man in him did not want her to go, to perform the job he could not perform himself. He was sending a woman to save his people. Not that he didn't think her capable, but she could be injured. And MacKenzie was such a twisted bastard of a man, if she was caught—

His mind jerked from the thought.

The laird in him knew the necessity of Delilah's action. She could breach MacKenzie's defenses where he could not, where no one else could. One woman could save the lives of his people and bring peace.

Kaid dressed in the saffron leine of a laird and pleated his best plaid around his hips before making his way downstairs where the clan would be waiting.

The sky was thick with somber gray clouds, and a nasty wind stirred the air into a chaotic whirl. Heedless of the poor weather, his people clustered around the courtyard. They huddled beneath wraps of plaid, and women pulled their whipping hair from their vision to better see the lady who would save them all.

For Delilah looked regal where she stood. She faced into the wind the same way she faced everything thrown at her— with a quiet, admirable strength. Leasa stood at her side, twisting her fingers together in anxious anticipation.

Kaid nodded toward Donnan who stood behind the ladies. It eased Kaid's fears somewhat to know his friend would be nearby. No one was as quiet as Donnan, as able to blend into scenery and disappear. Even if Kaid could not be there with them, Donnan would hide in the forest or a nearby town, whatever it took to be close.

The coach clattered into the courtyard, and his people parted to make room for its arrival. Kaid took advantage of the distraction to stare at Delilah once more.

As if sensing him, she glanced over her shoulder and met his gaze. Her stare lingered a second too long before she dropped her attention demurely to the ground.

Something Elizabeth would do, but certainly not his Delilah. Nay, his Delilah would have stared boldly back at him.

The clan's murmuring blended into a hum of conversation he could discern bits of. None suspected Delilah to be anyone other than Lady Elizabeth. They all turned out to see her exchanged to her betrothed for their freedom.

They did not know the sacrifice she was making, how very strong she was, how brave. Nor the sacrifice he was making in letting her go.

The crowd quieted and regarded him.

He approached Delilah and bowed before her in reverent gratitude. "Lady Elizabeth, we thank ye for the help ye've given us and wish ye safe journey in returning to yer betrothed."

He straightened. Her face was as impassive as he hoped his was. "Ye give our people a freedom we havena known for many years."

The people gave a great cheer and Delilah inclined her head graciously.

Her hand was close to his. So close he could brush it and have it appear an accident.

The man in him wanted to catch her hand and press it over his heart, which ached with a fresh, stinging hurt.

The laird in him forced him to keep his distance.

"No!" A shrill cry rose up behind Kaid, and something knocked against his thigh.

A little girl with blonde hair ran past him and threw her arms around Delilah's heavy blue velvet skirt.

Claire's small fists grasped at the fabric and she looked up toward Delilah with tears streaming down her face. "Please don't go. Please. I love ye."

Delilah dropped toward the girl and scooped her up into her arms, foregoing all pretense of regal decorum. She hugged the child fiercely to her.

"I love you too." Delilah spoke so softly, Kaid would not have heard it were he not so close. "But I must do this, and you must be brave."

The girl's face was pressed into the crook of Delilah's neck. "I dinna want to be brave anymore. I canna lose ye too." The words were muffled, but still audible enough to slice into Kaid's heart.

He reached for Claire and Delilah reluctantly passed the girl to him. Tears shone bright in Delilah's eyes.

The girl struggled against Kaid's hold.

"I must go," Delilah choked out.

Claire twisted in Kaid's arms to see Delilah.

"It's time," Donnan said in a deep voice.

"I'm so sorry," Delilah whispered. Tears ran down her cheeks, and Kaid knew how badly she must want to tell Claire why she was doing this, that she'd be back soon.

But Claire couldn't know. No one could. No matter how much it weighed on his soul.

Claire sobbed with the same raw hurt he felt.

The man in him wanted to stop Delilah from entering the coach and bring her back to his chamber, where they could make love all day. He wanted her in his life, in his heart, at his side.

It was the laird who held the sobbing child as Delilah closed the door of the cabin and settled into the seat, disappearing from view.

Kaid watched the coach rattle away with the dawning realization that both the man and the laird loved the woman within.

And might have lost her forever.

• • •

Delilah's tears dried within the hour, but the ache never left. Not once in the entire two and a half days it took to arrive at Edirdovar Castle.

The skies had wept through the entire journey, as if they too could not stand the force of her suffering.

Leasa straightened in the seat opposite her. "There it is."

Delilah followed the direction of Leasa's gaze toward the castle in the distance. The red stone stood dusky against the gray sky, its walls high and imposing.

She turned to Leasa and took the maid's cold hand in her own. "We'll be fine." She had reassured Leasa many times, and knew it would not be the last.

Truth be told, the redundancy helped to assuage Delilah's own trepidation. They'd been over all the different strategies, until both women had memorized how alternate scenarios could be handled.

"I do not want to go," Leasa confessed in a voice laden with misery.

"Donnan will be near." Delilah gave Leasa an encouraging nod. "Everything will be fine."

Leasa's head bobbed in a mirrored nod and the coach rolled to an ominous stop.

Delilah sighed slowly before meeting Leasa's gaze. "It's time."

The other woman nodded again and swiped at her tears.

Delilah exited the coach first, her steps light and careful to keep the boxy cabin from rocking. A dark-haired man stood in the large entryway with a thick, black mantle draped about his squared shoulders.

He was handsome from what she could tell, with high cheekbones and a strong jaw. At least Elizabeth's father had intended to give her a husband near to her own age, which was far more than some fathers did.

The red stonework of the castle did not appear any brighter up close than it had far away, but the sheer size of the castle was significant. Delilah had to crane her neck to see its pointed top.

Laird MacKenzie approached her in a confident stride, and the mantle at his back fluttered like the folded black wings of a giant bird. "Welcome to Edirdovar Castle, Lady Elizabeth." He bowed low in front of her like a courtier and rose with a charming grin.

He was even more handsome up close, with straight, white teeth and a refined, aquiline nose.

Delilah gave the grand curtsy she'd perfected while at King James's court. "It is good to finally have arrived, my lord. Thank you for having procured my release so expediently."

His pristine smile glinted with an edge. "It's a good thing ye're bonny enough to appear to have warranted so great a price."

He crooked a finger back toward the castle and a servant emerged with a large sword held between his outstretched hands. The servant carried the sword to the coach and passed it to the driver.

Donnan had left their coach an hour prior to their arrival to secure a location where he could watch over them unhindered. Only the coachman remained.

A gust of wind ruffled Laird MacKenzie's hair. "We should head inside. It's far too cold for such beauty to stand idle." He turned away to enter the castle before she could. "Wouldn't want ye to get sick after all ye cost me." He didn't bother to temper the final words or shield them from her ears.

The entryway was large and lacking comfort and warmth. Much

like the rest of his welcome. Several sconces flickered on the walls, but they did little to chase away the darkness of the overcast day.

Laird MacKenzie motioned to a woman standing in the shadows. "Have yer maid go with her to unpack yer things. I'll have ye speak privately with me in my solar."

Leasa cast a hesitant glance at Delilah and did not move to follow his orders.

MacKenzie took an intimidating step toward Leasa. "Surely ye dinna mean to protect her from the man who will be her husband." The cold thread of condescension in his tone made Delilah want to land a very unladylike punch on his perfect nose.

Leasa's cheeks went bright red, and she dissolved backward into the shadows with the other servant. MacKenzie turned from Delilah and strode down a long hall, leaving her to follow him.

He led her into a solar which seemed almost as empty as the one in Kindrochit, the dilapidated castle where she usually lived with Sylvi and the rest of the women.

No books showed on the dark shelves, and only a few tapestries lined the wall—all simple and without gilded adornment.

MacKenzie walked around her in a slow circle, the way a wolf inspects its prey before attacking. The hairs at the back of her neck prickled. "I must say, ye look a bit different than I remember, but ye have grown into a comely lass."

An icy trail of dread trickled down her spine. He'd met Elizabeth before?

Delilah hadn't considered that. Elizabeth had never mentioned it.

But then, why would she have? Delilah was never supposed to have actually arrived at Edirdovar Castle. She had deviated from the original plan.

MacKenzie stopped in front of her and blatantly stared at her breasts so long, she had to fight the urge to fold her arms over them.

Finally he lifted his dark gaze to her face. "Ye please me."

He spoke as if he offered her a compliment, as if she were put there solely to bring him pleasure. And by his demeanor, surely he truly believed such.

His eyes narrowed. "I dinna remember ye having that before." He pressed a cool finger against the freckle at her jaw.

Delilah ducked her head in a shy gesture, one becoming of a lady. "I hope it does not displease you."

"We'll just ensure ye dinna go in the sun as much so ye dinna get more." When she lifted her gaze, she found him smiling at her, seemingly ignorant to the rudeness of his comment.

Delilah pursed her lips to keep them from letting them curl back with disgust. She wished she truly was Elizabeth and could wrangle him toward some decent manners.

He stared at her as if awaiting a response. She remained intentionally silent. It was a lesser rebellion, but the most she could offer. She would not do anything to make things worse for Elizabeth. For surely it would be bad enough for Elizabeth once she arrived. Delilah deeply regretted the trouble she would leave behind.

And she would be gone by then. Both she and Kaid had agreed the prior night that if Torra MacKenzie could not be located in three days' time, Delilah would return to Ardvreck Castle.

Laird MacKenzie cleared his throat. "In any manner, we'll ensure it's concealed tomorrow. In time for the wedding."

Delilah stiffened before she could stop the blatant reaction.

He smirked. "The banns have already been read long ago and everything has been awaiting your very prolonged arrival." He stroked her cheek. The chill of his clammy touch seeped into her bones, and it was all Delilah could do to suppress a shiver. "Tomorrow morning, my sweet Elizabeth, we will be wed."

Chapter Twenty-One

Delilah had been gone three days.

Kaid stalked the length of his solar like a caged animal. Pacing. And thinking too damn much.

He wished he could get a report from Donnan, but even if there'd been a way for him to send word to Kaid, there wouldn't have been enough time for the news to travel back to Ardvreck Castle.

Surely she'd be at Edirdovar Castle now.

Had MacKenzie accepted her? Did he suspect?

If he did not, what would he do to her?

Kaid proceeded down the other side of the room, trying to ignore the tension knotting in his shoulders and pounding in his head. His skin seemed like it was too tight on his body, and time stretched to eternal lengths.

Everything was different without Delilah.

A knock sounded at his door, making every muscle in his body flinch in agitation.

He glanced toward the chair by the fire where Claire was curled into a ball and fast asleep. The girl hadn't left his side since Delilah's departure. He was not sure which of them missed Delilah more.

"Enter." He didn't bother to walk toward the door to open it.

Rhona entered, the expression on her wizened face was withered and hesitant. "Forgive the interruption, laird. I wanted to ensure ye were well."

Kaid ran a hand through his hair and almost waved off the question when Rhona spoke again. "Actually, we know ye're no' well, laird. It looks as if ye've no' slept in days."

She let the door slip closed behind her. Her customary basket was slung around the crook of her elbow and her purple cloak thrown over her shoulders.

She stepped closer to him and the basket bounced against her long white hair.

"Ye know me too well, Rhona." He gave a hollow, mirthless chuckle.

The salty scent of roasting meat caught his attention and reminded him supper would be soon. He'd barely touched his midday meal and found he had no appetite. Claire would need to eat, though.

The girl hadn't moved from where she lay, wrapped in one of Delilah's shawls she'd left behind.

Rhona followed Kaid's gaze without any expression before looking back toward him. "The lady is where she needs to be." Her voice was lowered out of respect for the sleeping child, but her gaze sharpened. "With the man to whom she belongs."

Kaid's skin prickled at her words. He wanted to slam his fist into the wall and declare Delilah belonged to him, not MacKenzie.

But Rhona was old, and kind, and knew nothing of the swap between Delilah and Elizabeth. "I only hope it will be enough to placate MacKenzie." The man's name left an awful taste in Kaid's mouth.

"Perhaps he's far more of a rational man than ye think," she offered.

Kaid stared hard at her for a moment, at a loss for words. Was the old woman mad?

"I'm sure it was that rationality which led him to slaughter helpless men, women, and children in the village." Kaid couldn't help the gruffness in his voice when he spoke.

Claire shifted in the chair.

Rhona's crooked back straightened a little more at his words and her cheeks went pink. "Aye, well, I canna speak to that. But I ken ye most likely have need of more of yer sleeping draught. I hadna given ye more than a few days' worth, and ye havena asked me for more."

Kaid's mouth went dry.

Valerian root.

He wished he could admit to having not let it intrude on his thoughts. But he had. It'd been on his mind while he lay awake at night in a bed still smelling of Delilah, and while trudging through the torment of eternally long days

Thinking of the reprieve the valerian root offered was an escape from what he would think of otherwise—the constant worry over Delilah's safety, and the fear he might not ever see her again.

Sometime yesterday he'd finally allowed himself to consider the possibility that Delilah could die. MacKenzie's wrath would be great if he found out he'd been lied to.

Coming to terms with the thought had not brought Kaid any peace. No, it'd made the idea circle in his head like a predator.

Rhona gave her kind smile and handed him a slim vial. "Here ye go. I've more if ye have need of it."

Kaid accepted the vial. For being so small, it lay heavy in his palm. Cool and slick and tempting.

"Get some sleep, lad." She patted his cheek the way his grandmother had done when he was a boy. The grassy scent of herbs followed the touch of her dry palm.

Without another word, she walked from the room and let the door click closed behind her.

But it wasn't the actual effects of the valerian root he thought of when he stared down at the stoppered glass. It was Delilah, and how she'd pleaded with him not to take it, and the crackling hiss the emptied contents had made when they hit the flames.

He pulled the stopper out, strode to the fire, and let the clear liquid stream out. The glowing red logs flickered for a second before all trace of the sleeping draught was gone.

He let the container and stopper roll from his fingers, where they landed in the hot ash gathered around the embers.

Claire shifted behind him and gave him a bleary-eyed look. "Elizabeth?"

Kaid rubbed a hand over her tousled blonde hair. Her skin was warm from sleep beneath the silky strands. "Nay, lass. But I believe supper is ready. Go get yerself some food, and I'll see ye in the morning, aye?"

She nodded slowly and unfolded herself from the chair while wrapping Delilah's shawl more tightly around her shoulders. Her shoes clopped against the hard floor, but she stopped before she exited the room and turned back to him.

"Do ye think MacKenzie will be kind to her?" Claire asked, her face pinched with worry.

Kaid forced a smooth expression on his face. "Aye, of course he will."

Even as he said the words, they hung heavy around his heart, for he knew if MacKenzie were to discover Delilah's lie, he would be anything but kind.

• • •

Night hung darker in Edirdovar Castle than it did at Ardvreck.

Delilah lay in a great bed and stared at the underside of the canopy. She knew there were boards and beams crossing up there, but it was so high up, and the room so black, she could not make them out.

It left her with a dizzying rush of disorientation. No matter how much she tried to focus, or force herself into thinking she might actually see it, she could not.

No matter how much she wished to be at Ardvreck with Kaid, she was not.

And tomorrow she would need to find some sort of a distraction to keep from having to marry MacKenzie.

Her hands fisted in the thick sheets beneath her. The poor quality fabric was stiff and scratching where it touched her skin.

She rolled over in an attempt to find a more comfortable

position. Again. At this point, she was unable to determine if her restless sleep stemmed from a mattress filled with bumps or a mind filled with thoughts.

"Do you need anything, my lady?" Leasa whispered from her trundle bed beside Delilah's. Her voice was thick with the effects of sleep.

Guilt nipped at Delilah. She hadn't meant to wake Leasa. The journey had been taxing on the other woman and she needed the rest.

"I'm fine," Delilah lied.

Silence answered her, and Delilah assumed the maid had fallen asleep.

"Is it because of the wedding?" Leasa's voice had lost the heaviness of slumber.

Delilah flinched. "You know?"

"They want me to prepare you first thing in the morning."

The darkness pressed around Delilah, and suddenly the large bedchamber seemed like a tight box around her. "We have to do something to get out of it."

There was a long pause. "We have to find a woman here, correct?" Leasa asked.

This time Delilah had divulged the plan to Leasa en route to Edirdovar. It was a risk, in case Leasa accidentally said something she should not, but it was worth it to find Torra more quickly.

The creak of bed ropes indicated Leasa had risen from her bed. "If we look now, we might find her. And if so, could we not leave now?"

Delilah grinned. "That we could."

There was an erratic thumping clatter from the other side of the room before a beam of moonlight shot into the chamber where Leasa had obviously opened a window. The contrast of such brilliance to the darkness made the room seem as if it were lit as brightly as day.

Delilah slipped out of bed, grateful to no longer be locked in a battle of sleeplessness. "We should go separately. You explore the lower floors. If anyone asks where you are going, tell them you went to the kitchens to fetch me some bread and got lost."

A believable tale when they were not offered so much as a bannock on their arrival. A ball of hunger gnawed in the pit of Delilah's stomach.

Leasa pulled a heavy dressing gown over Delilah's night clothes. "And if I'm caught," Delilah said, "I'll say I went looking for you."

Delilah turned and found Leasa pale, either with fear or perhaps even from the white glow of the moon. Either way, she placed her hands on the maid's narrow shoulders and gave a reassuring smile. "If we find her tonight, we may leave. And if we do not, we'll…" Delilah's own confidence faltered. "We'll figure out something to keep the wedding at bay."

Leasa nodded, a gesture sharp with determination.

Together, they slipped into the darkened hall without the luxury of candles to light their paths, lest they call unwanted attention to themselves.

They knew little of Torra MacKenzie, only that she was several years older than Delilah and her hair was a mass of brilliant red curls. Surely her hair would make her easy to find, though neither Delilah nor Leasa saw a woman fitting her description upon their arrival the prior night.

One of the important lessons Delilah had learned with her training was the ability to move silently and blend into shadows. The skill was imperative on a night such as this.

While Leasa was tasked with searching near the kitchens, Delilah made quick work of the upper floors. She avoided the topmost floor, where the servants slept, and the bed chamber above her own in the squared tower, which she assumed to be MacKenzie's.

Not a single door was locked and every room but hers was empty. Not only without a person within, but also without any furnishings.

The haste with which MacKenzie intended to wed Elizabeth was suddenly becoming clear. Certainly it was not out of affection for the woman, but out of need to fill his surprisingly empty coffers.

It was obvious MacKenzie had no wealth.

No wealth, and no hidden sister.

Delilah's heart crumpled in her chest when she reached the last empty chamber. Perhaps there was something she hadn't checked, a room she had might have missed. Would he have hidden Torra away?

Delilah stared out of the empty castle from the stairs on the first floor to where a light rain pattered over the garden outside. Everything was slick and shadowed, but a stone chapel was visible a short distance away.

A chapel.

Consecrated ground.

If Torra was dead, would she not be buried there?

Delilah cleared the rest of the stairs and found a door leading outside. She slid the bar bolting it shut and pushed. The aged hinges gave a squealing groan.

She froze for a moment, and waited an endless second to see if someone would approach her.

Though she'd not seen any guards in the night, she knew them to be present. She'd seen many on her arrival, even if none appeared to be sleeping within the upper floors of the castle. Now that she thought of it, where did all the guards sleep? And why had she not run into a single one?

When no one showed themselves, she slipped outside and left the door slightly cracked. After all, she would be but a moment.

The earth was spongy under her slippered feet, loosened by the rain. The powerful scent of wet soil blended with the sweet perfume of summer flowers blooming. Vines and thick roots crowded the ground underfoot and made picking her way through the overgrown garden more time consuming than anticipated. Delilah kept her steps light yet focused, her concentration fixed on keeping her balance.

Fat blooms hanging from narrow stems bobbed haphazardly in her path and splattered rainwater against her night clothes when she slipped past them.

Though the rain did not come hard, it was substantial enough to soak through Delilah's overdress and the thin night rail, settling deep into her skin.

She was only just beginning to reconcile the true awfulness of her idea when the church loomed before her. Rainwater gathered at the eaves and trailed like tears down the broken stained glass windows which had once, no doubt, been fine.

Perhaps she ought to turn around. But she was *so* close.

A quick glance at the lawn behind the sad building revealed several stone markers set deep into the earth and one large jagged rock at the center of the graves. The overgrown plants had not confined their vengeance to the garden, and ran over the large rock in jagged black lines.

A flash of lightning lit the area in a wash of blue white.

The name on the rock was still carved deep despite the weather wear.

T— MacKenzie

Delilah's heart slid into her stomach. Was that Torra?

A groan of despair tore from her throat. If Torra was dead, there would be no helping the MacLeods.

"Elizabeth!" The irritation in the male voice bit through her concentration.

Delilah darted toward the rock, reaching for the tangle of vines over the name.

She had to see.

She had to know.

Her fingernails raked over the cold, rough stone. Despite the strength of her desperation, only part of the obscuring fauna gave way.

Enough to reveal TOR-

Arms caught her around the waist, pinning her arms to her sides, and pulled her back in a rough gesture. "Have ye lost yer mind?"

Had Delilah not already felt as though she'd been punched in the stomach, she might have fought back.

But there, seeing the grave marker in front of her, was an overwhelming shock. One she truly had not anticipated.

The man who held her whirled her around, revealing the very handsome, very angry face of Laird MacKenzie.

Chapter Twenty-Two

It was five days since Delilah's departure before the dark shape of a distant horse rider was visible on the thin trail over the hills. The early afternoon sun bathed the path in hues of red and orange, leaving the rider's shadow long across the landscape.

Kaid's pulse jumped to attention. He glanced at Claire, but did not share what he'd seen. Not yet.

He'd decided to occupy the girl's time with education, and the little girl had a square of parchment in front of her with several rows of numbers running down the topmost portion.

She held the quill pinched between her fingers, her tongue pushed out between her lips, and carved a number onto the page. The tip of the quill had long since bent, but Claire had not seemed to notice.

Kaid knew if he told her about the rider now, she might never finish. Certainly, she would be too eager for word of Delilah.

No, it would be better to wait for the rider to come to him.

Kaid would spare her the wait he must endure.

He bent over Claire's work and praised her. Happiness lit her face.

"My da was good with numbers." Claire proudly squared her shoulders in the same manner as Delilah.

It was hard to concentrate on the story that followed when all Kaid could think of was news of Delilah.

A knock came at the door and Kaid's heart hammered in his chest.

Lachlan entered the room, something long and awkwardly

bundled in plaid in his arms. "Laird, I have yer father's sword, as promised."

Kaid thanked the warrior and hefted the sword's proffered bulk. Claire looked up at him with her lips pursed. Kaid set the sword on the desk, away from Claire's work.

He ruffled her hair. "Ye may ask after Lady Elizabeth, and then I want ye to go to the kitchens for a bit while I speak with Lachlan, aye?"

Claire slid obediently from the large chair and went to stand in front of the other man. The size difference between the massive warrior and the fragile child was like comparing a bear to a kitten.

"Lachlan, can ye tell me how Lady Elizabeth fares?" she asked in her fragile voice. The look on her face was so openly hopeful, it near tore into Kaid's chest. "Does she miss me?"

Lachlan knelt in front of the girl and offered a kind smile. "She's doing verra well and misses ye terribly."

Claire beamed up at him with wide, unsuppressed joy and threw her arms around Lachlan's neck. "Thank ye."

Lachlan waited until she released him before he rose. Reassured "Elizabeth" was well, Claire strode toward the door, gave them both a shy wave, and slipped out.

Having the child leave the room was like walking from a beam of sunlight into the shadows. Lachlan's smile melted from his face and was replaced by his more common stern expression.

The time for placating niceties was done.

Lachlan nodded to where the sword was wrapped still on the table. "It looked like yer da's sword, but I wasna certain."

Kaid carefully unwound the plaid from the sword to reveal the wide pommel lined with twisted leather and the ornate image of a bull's head glaring stubbornly at him. The tension in his body washed away. "Aye, it's my da's blade."

He stared down at it for a long moment and saw in his mind the countless times his father had brandished the blade. Something in Kaid's chest flinched with a deep, unacknowledged hurt.

Kaid had stepped so quickly into the role of laird, and had been so overwhelmed by the loss of so many innocent villagers, he hadn't allowed himself to truly grieve his father's death.

The sorrow settled now across his shoulders, heavy and stifling. He pressed the heels of his palms on either side of the desk's surface. "And Lady Elizabeth?"

"I delivered her safely to MacKenzie who took her inside," Lachlan answered. "I heard the servants talking. He intended to wed her the day after she arrived."

A chill descended over Kaid's entire body, like he'd been plunged into a loch midwinter. "Today," he said.

Lachlan nodded. Exhaustion lined his young face, evidence he'd ridden most likely all day and night to arrive with the news. "Aye. It would appear he readily accepted yer offer of peace and is going along with everything as promised."

Kaid pushed himself off the desk and clapped Lachlan on the shoulder. "Go get yerself some food and rest. Ye've done well."

Without another word, Lachlan turned from the room and left Kaid plunged in a heavy press of silence.

Married.

The word echoed in Kaid's head until it made his temples throb.

To refrain from marrying would alert MacKenzie to something amiss. Kaid knew Delilah's determination to do what was necessary to ensure the success of their plan.

There would be nothing Donnan could do to stop it, nor Leasa—nor even Delilah herself.

There was nothing Kaid could do, but stand in agitated helplessness and wait.

He found his gaze wandering toward the open window. The sun had eased higher between the hills.

It would be noon soon.

And perhaps by then, Delilah would be married.

He realized his mistake then. Being two days away from her left time crushing against him. He'd been so damn worried about ruining the fragile thread of peace between himself and MacKenzie, he'd remained home.

He never should have tasked Donnan to go with the ladies. It should have been Kaid. He charged out the door and called to Lachlan. The weary man swayed back to regard him with bloodshot eyes.

Kaid caught up to him and clapped him on the back. "I'll be gone several days and need ye to mind things here in my absence."

Lachlan, ever the willing servant who had minded things not only in Kaid's previous absence, but in his father's as well, gave a dutiful nod. "But after I've slept, aye?"

Relief eased the churning tightness inside Kaid and he laughed. "Aye, after ye've slept."

Then he made his way down to the kitchens to where he'd sent Claire, to tell her he'd be gone a few days—and that he'd be home soon. He couldn't tell her he intended to bring back Delilah, but by God, he would not return without her.

· · ·

There was only so long one could continue to feign sleep.

The anxious pucker of Leasa's brow told Delilah she'd already pushed far beyond the limit.

Leasa knelt by the bed. "My lady, Laird MacKenzie wishes to see you. He's…not happy." Her hair was down and twisted over her right shoulder.

While becoming, the hairstyle was not one she'd ever seen Leasa wear before.

"Your hair looks lovely," Delilah offered.

Leasa's cheeks went red, but rather than meet Delilah's face with her bright, cheerful gaze, the maid glanced away and murmured her thanks.

Delilah's stomach twisted. Something was amiss.

"Are you ill?" Delilah searched the woman's face. She did not appear pale. In fact, she was rather flushed.

True, Delilah was faking to avoid the precipitous wedding, but perhaps Leasa actually was sick after the time she'd spent wandering the dark, chilly floor of the castle.

Leasa shook her head with her jaw tucked against the length of her hair.

A tremor rippled down Delilah's back. "Leasa—" Before the maid could stop her, Delilah reached out and pulled Leasa's hair back from her face.

Leasa gasped and tried to pull away, but not quickly enough.

Delilah saw the flash of bruised skin, the line of Leasa's jaw reddened across her cheek and already darkening at the center.

Outrage flashed through Delilah and she flew from the bed. "Did he hit you?" she demanded.

Leasa stumbled in her haste to pull herself back. "He…was just angry." She crossed her arms over her chest, suddenly looking miserable. "It happens."

"No." Delilah shoved her arms into the stiff sleeves of a dressing gown. "It does not happen."

"No," Leasa gasped. "My lady—don't."

But Delilah was already storming her way to where she knew MacKenzie's solar to be. Without bothering to knock, she let the force of her rage and anger slam through the door.

MacKenzie stood beside his desk where a tall, thin man with gray hair was bent over a book. Both men jerked their heads up, like two puppets whose cords had been tugged in unison.

MacKenzie glared at Delilah and closed the book the other man had been studying. "Leave me, Duncan."

The old man nodded once and quit the room with all the decorum of a skulking alley cat.

"I'm glad to see ye're recovered." MacKenzie gave her a grin so hard and so collected, it made her want to slap it off his face. "Though I dinna think yer dressing clothes will be a sufficient wedding gown."

Delilah didn't dare to step closer to him. Not when everything in her had to fight the urge to strike him, to show him how a woman could hit.

"You struck my maid," she bit out.

"She was being insolent." He took three purposeful strides toward her, halving the distance between them. "And now ye're being insolent." He considered her a moment. "Perhaps I should strike ye."

"And perhaps I should strike you." Delilah spat the words and had to imagine physically pushing down her anger in order to keep a handle on her temper.

MacKenzie laughed—a cold, brittle sound. "I know ye haven't the strength to hit a man like me."

He walked the last few steps toward her and the floorboards beneath him gave a long, tired groan. "Why were ye in the garden last night?"

Delilah's body was alight with the flood of energy and the thrumming pound of her heartbeat, the kind of surge a body gives before a good, ugly fight. It might have been due to him questioning her about the night before, which she'd known would come, or it might have been due to how badly she truly wanted to hit him.

"I sent my maid for food, as I went to bed hungry." She left the implication of his rudeness hanging in the air.

He gave an indifferent shrug. "Ye could use without an extra meal or two, but that doesna explain why ye were in the garden."

Delilah cheeks flamed, and she hated the obviousness of her reaction. "My maid did not come back quickly, and I feared she may have gotten turned around, as we're in a new place. I went to find her."

His brow rose with exaggerated impatience. "In the garden."

"I thought I saw something." It was a flimsy excuse, but it was all she had.

"And did ye?"

There was a large crack running up through the center of the hearth and Delilah's gaze continued to seek it out the way one's tongue wanders toward a split lip.

"Did ye see something?" he asked again.

"Did you kill Torra?" Delilah hurled the question at him. It was not diplomatic in the least, but perhaps it would offset his dogged determination to get a clear answer from her when she had none to give.

She did not expect his icy smile to widen, though perhaps she ought to have.

"Torra." MacKenzie nodded as one does when recalling a fond memory. "I've no' heard her name in years."

The last word left Delilah's skin prickling with fear.

"Did you kill her?" she whispered.

He took one more step toward her and stood so close she could punch him. "Ye could say that." There was an exotic scent to him, some foreign perfume. An expensive one.

All the hope pushing her through the awfulness of the ordeal at Edirdovar Castle, and the difficulty of being away from Kaid and Claire—it all crumbled into dust.

"Go to yer room." MacKenzie's gaze scraped over her, abrasive with scrutiny. "Get some sleep and get yerself cleaned up. I'll no' wed ye looking like a beggar."

Delilah turned to go when he reached out and grabbed her arm in a hard grip. She spun toward him and suppressed the urge to drive her elbow into his perfect nose.

He grinned. "I'm going to break ye, Elizabeth. And I'm going to enjoy it."

Delilah jerked her arm free and left the room before she gave in to the temptation to kill him.

• • •

Delilah regretted having not killed MacKenzie.

She paced her large chamber while Leasa assembled a meager bag of their most precious belongings.

It had been Leasa who had kept Delilah from killing MacKenzie. The guards, who seemed more plentiful by day than they had been by night, would have retaliated for their master's murder by seeing both Delilah and Leasa dead.

And while the sacrifice would have rid the world of MacKenzie's cruelty and freed the MacLeod clan to live in peace, Delilah could not allow herself to so endanger Leasa. Not after all the maid had been through.

But without Leasa there, Delilah would be free to kill MacKenzie.

It would be a worthy sacrifice, and she knew she could get another chance.

Her heartbeat quickened with the possibility.

Leasa could leave once the household quieted, something that wouldn't happen any time soon given the amount of bustling activity echoing from below. But soon all would quiet, and Delilah could pick the flimsy lock and let her maid escape to Donnan.

Delilah would stay, feigning ignorance at her maid's disappearance. Then, when MacKenzie demanded answers…Her fingers slid over the metal of her blade before letting the edge carefully scrape along her fingertips. Yes, she could still kill him.

And she would.

Footsteps sounded in the hall, near her door.

Leasa slid Delilah a frightened look.

"Hide the bag," Delilah whispered.

Leasa quickly complied and shoved the bundle into a corner behind the large bed. No sooner had she done so, the clatter of a key seeking purchase in the lock sounded and the great wooden door flew open.

MacKenzie strode in, followed by several guards.

Ten. There were ten guards.

Too many for Delilah to take on herself without risking Leasa.

"It would appear ye've lied to me." MacKenzie motioned toward them, and the guards rushed forward.

Large hands clamped around Delilah's shoulders. "What is the meaning of this?" she demanded with all the outrage of an offended noble.

"Ye've deceived me—and I know this because Lady Elizabeth Seymour just arrived an hour ago."

Chapter Twenty-Three

Delilah had expected the dungeon.

The guards were not kind in their act of half carrying, half walking her down the length of the hall. A quiet whimpering sound behind Delilah told her Leasa was sobbing.

They stopped before a door, but it was no dungeon—it was MacKenzie's solar.

Delilah was shoved inside and Leasa was pushed into the room after her. She landed on the hard ground with a cry of pain. Delilah immediately bent to help her, but several men held her back.

"She can rise on her own, the clumsy wretch."

Only after Leasa struggled to her feet did Delilah notice there were more in the room than the soldiers and MacKenzie.

There, standing beside his desk, were two women she recognized with such suddenness, she had no idea how she'd missed them in the first place—Liv and Elizabeth.

A part of Delilah wanted to run forward and embrace Liv, to bask in the affection of a familiar face when the last few weeks had held so much chaos.

The little gray cat, Fianna, peered at her from Liv's lap. It was all she could do to keep from stretching an arm out to pet Fianna's thick, silky fur.

Liv and Elizabeth both kept their faces impassive, but Delilah knew with stomach-clenching certainty what they must both be thinking of her betrayal. They sat perfectly still, Elizabeth regal in a burgundy gown with her honey-blonde hair piled beneath gold netting and Liv equally as beautiful in a plain blue dress, her red hair plaited in a simple braid.

She wished they were alone so she could explain. Instead they were separated by a heavy wall of silence and unspoken accusation. MacKenzie turned toward Elizabeth. "Well? Do ye know them?"

Delilah's heart scampered into an erratic beat. Elizabeth could condemn them with a single word. Then again, doing so would condemn herself as well.

Lady Elizabeth looked Delilah and Leasa over and shook her head. "I've not ever seen them before."

MacKenzie's eyes narrowed for a moment in consideration. "A MacLeod sympathizer, then," he muttered in Gaelic. He nodded toward his guards and spoke with clenched teeth. "To the dungeon."

The rough hands were on her once more, clamped at her shoulders and partially dragging her. This time the journey was a greater distance and down several flights of stairs. The final descent plunged them into near darkness where the air was wet, and the odor of metal and damp earth nearly choked her.

A dungeon.

It was a far cry better than the gallows. Though Delilah would have fought then. Most likely she would have died trying, but she would have regardless.

Their chances of escaping were far higher in the dungeon than facing certain death.

MacKenzie opened a large barred door despite its scream of protest. "Since ye were so concerned, I figured I'd ease yer mind before yer death."

With that, the women were shoved hard into the room and the door immediately slammed shut behind them. Delilah turned to find MacKenzie twisting the key. He gave her one more hard look before slinking back into the darkness, away from their cell.

A single, narrow window framed the moon and allowed a square of its fair light to fall onto the floor before them. Something shuffled in the darkness beyond where they could see.

That something was in the cell with them.

A low moan sounded in the darkness, and shivers raked down Delilah's spine.

Leasa pressed her hands to her mouth, but it was not enough to squelch the sound of her cry.

A shape emerged from the shadows, ragged and large.

Delilah slipped her fingers into her pocket where the lining had been cut away to make the dagger at her thigh more accessible. She crouched low, her muscles coiled to strike, to fight.

The beast moved forward and gave a hoarse swallowing sound.

Delilah edged backward, encouraging it into the light so she could see what she might need to kill.

The moonlight hit the thing and revealed it to be not a thing at all, but a young woman. She was slender and dressed in a ridiculously extravagant gown for the sorrowful pit of despair where they'd been left.

The woman pointed toward Delilah. Bits of ruined lace hung from her sleeve like clumped cobwebs. Dark hair fell around her face in lank waves and cast her face in shadows. Still, Delilah could make out her mouth working, as if she intended to speak.

The woman gave a mewling sound and shook her head in irritation.

Leasa stepped backward to put herself behind Delilah. The maid's fear was as thick in the air as the pungent odor of the woman's unwashed body.

"Who?" The woman's mouth formed an exaggeration of the word and she stabbed the air with her bony finger.

Delilah stepped to the left, forcing the woman into the light in order to keep eye contact. The pale light fell on her face, and Delilah realized the woman was not as young as she first thought. Strained lines creased her brow and rimmed her mouth. Nor was her hair dark as it had been in the shadows, but a streaked and dirty red.

"This is Leasa." Delilah indicated Leasa, hesitating for a moment over her own name. But what did sharing her name matter? No one knew her surname, not that her surname held much traction in Scotland. "And I'm Delilah."

The woman's gaze lowered to the ground and searched the darkness before she suddenly dropped into a very stiff curtsy.

When she rose, she looked up at Delilah with the wide, wounded gaze of an animal often beaten. She licked her lips and swallowed.

"I..." The sound came out in a long croak. The woman grimaced and shook her head again, as if chastising herself. "I..."

She gave a feral growling noise and pressed her hand to her bony chest. "Torrrr."

Her features relaxed into a look of accomplished victory.

Delilah pointed at her. "Tor?"

The woman shook her head vehemently and hit her chest hard enough that the thump echoed off the wet walls. "Torra." She nodded in obvious encouragement for Delilah to understand. "I'm Torra."

• • •

Donnan always was good at hiding. It was why Kaid had sent him to Edirdovar in the first place.

If only he wasn't so hard to find. Even in the light of a new day, it was impossible to locate him.

Kaid skimmed the treetops for anything amiss. Staying aloft was one of Donnan's best hiding tricks. Kaid had left his horse at a paid stable in the village and walked the remainder of the way to the castle.

He'd had to duck away from several guards. Thus far, his labors had rendered him unseen.

Now he was entirely visible in the forest, scanning the trees like a fool. He itched for a good cleaning after the hard travel and his mind fogged with exhaustion.

"Anything interesting up there?" a voice asked nearby.

Kaid smirked and stared into a thick patch of bushes where the question came from. A white smile flashed at him.

He strode toward the bush and ducked beneath the cover of it to sit beside Donnan. "I dinna know if I should hit ye for being an arse or hug ye for helping me find ye."

Donnan had dirt smeared on his face and his plaid pulled around his body. He shrugged. "I prefer hugs."

Kaid pulled his plaid around his body and over his head to ensure his own optimal cover. "I heard MacKenzie intended to marry Elizabeth." He searched his friend's dark gaze. "Is that true?"

"I heard similar, but it's no' happened yet." He jerked his head toward a stone building near the castle garden. "If the priest is as ruined as the chapel, I wish him luck."

Donnan was right. The building was in sore disrepair, its windows gaping and jagged like broken teeth and embedded in a tangle of weeds.

"There could be one inside the castle," Kaid offered.

Again, Donnan shrugged. "I canna imagine the inside is much more grand. From what I see in the windows, the halls are empty. No' just of the clan, but of furnishings." He nodded toward several figures standing near the entrance of the castle. "Even the guards. They're mostly paid men, no' MacKenzies. Mercenaries who work by day, and all but a few leave at night."

"So, MacKenzie agreed to this so readily because he needed the coin of Elizabeth's dowry?" Kaid surmised.

Donnan grinned. "Exactly. Which explains why we've no' had any more raids."

Kaid nodded to himself and braced his chin on his folded hands. "If his clan is not around him, they dinna support him. But if Torra can be found…"

A door opened and a woman with honey-colored hair walked out into the sunshine.

Kaid's heart stuttered to a stop.

Delilah.

How he wanted to call out to her, to capture her in his arms and kiss the lushness of her mouth, revel in the sweetness of her voice, bask in the beauty of her joy.

He'd drawn her almost as soon as she'd left Ardvreck Castle, but it wasn't the same.

How he'd longed to let his hands skim over the luxurious softness of her skin.

But now, her posture was stiff, her gait uncertain.

Something was wrong.

"What's happened?" Kaid asked.

"There was a coach last night." Donnan shook his head. "I dinna know what that meant then."

"I mean with Delilah." Kaid indicated Delilah.

Donnan gave him a hard look. "That's no' Delilah."

Kaid's gaze snapped to the proud back facing him from far away. How could Donnan be so sure?

Before he could ask the question, Donnan spoke again. "Because that's no' Leasa."

Kaid noticed, for the first time, the woman at Delilah's side. No, not Delilah. His heart clenched around the realization.

The woman's maid had auburn hair that shone like copper in the sunshine. Donnan was right—she was not Leasa.

And the woman...

As if in compliance with the demand of Kaid's thoughts, she turned toward him and his heart plummeted to the ground.

She was not Delilah.

His skin prickled with the cold fear of his realization.

She had to be Elizabeth.

Then what the hell had become of Delilah?

• • •

The rising sun had cast light into the dismal cell of Delilah's existence.

Torra lay in slumber on a narrow bed in the corner. The meager mattress she slept upon hung down in clumps and threads from the bed ropes. Her gown was smeared with grime and so torn, it looked more like rags than anything once considered fine.

Her filthy thumb was properly lodged in her mouth, and she sucked at it like a child.

Leasa stared down at her with a slight frown. "How long do you think she's been down here?" she whispered.

Delilah looked around the room. There was a crooked desk with a dirty, curved mirror and a stool missing a leg, as well as a table which appeared as well-worn as everything else.

"I'd say for several years," Delilah replied quietly.

Heavy footsteps strode in a slow rhythm toward their cell. A guard peeked through the bars, his brows lifted with purpose, before turning away. Delilah followed his departure as far as she was able to see. There were more guards around the cell, which was why she hadn't at least freed Leasa by now.

MacKenzie would realize too quickly if the maid had escaped, and then Torra and Delilah would never stand a chance to flee.

And of all of them, Torra was the most important.

The woman's red hair fell down her back in dark, greasy waves. She'd combed it repeatedly with the brush now sitting on the scarred surface of the desk. She'd then tied a ribbon of mostly fraying silk at the back of her head.

Though Delilah and Leasa had tried, Torra could not be persuaded to speak any more than her name before finally falling into an exhausted sleep.

It would be a long journey to recovery for the heiress of the MacKenzie clan.

Something gray darted through the bars of the prison and Delilah jerked away. She'd never had the nightmare encounters some had with rats, and had no wish to start now.

But it was no rat threading between Delilah's ankles.

A gray and white cat peered up at her with beautiful blue eyes.

Delilah stroked the familiar smooth gray fur. Fianna purred and rubbed her fuzzy head against Delilah's palm.

It was then she noticed the harness on Fianna's back. The one Percy had fashioned for the small cat to use when passing messages between the women.

Delilah slid her hands into the seam of the harness. Her fingertips met the crackle of folded parchment.

Her stomach dropped. She knew what the correspondence would say before she even read it.

Delilah turned her back to the cell door in case a guard happened past, and unfolded the note. A slim bit of charcoal rolled out onto her palm.

The means to reply.

A quick skimming of Liv's missive revealed exactly one word which sucked Delilah's heart into her stomach.

Explain.

To the point and without judgement until detail had been provided. Perfectly Liv.

Delilah balanced herself on the stool and wrote out the admission of her betrayal, all the while hoping she would not lose the only allies who might truly see Kaid's people safe.

Chapter Twenty-Four

It was long past noon when Kaid finally woke. He hadn't thought sleep would be possible with all the worry thumping around in his mind. In fact, his eyes were heavy with want of more.

Donnan was crouched beside him, staring at the castle.

Something skittered past Kaid several feet away from where he slept. He cut a questioning look at Donnan who nodded for him to rise.

Kaid sat upright and turned toward the castle as another stone skipped through the forest, missing them by far.

Lady Elizabeth's maid, the woman with bright copper hair, stood near the fence, her gaze intent on the foliage around them. She shot a reassuring glance behind her before hurling another stone in their direction.

It was obvious she knew of their presence in the forest, but not their exact location.

Perhaps she had seen them before and wanted to lure them out. But why?

The woman stepped toward the fence where several slats were missing. After another cursory glance at the garden behind her, she spoke in a low voice: "I know Delilah."

Hearing Delilah's name was all the confirmation Kaid needed. He and Donnan rushed to the edge of the fence and crouched at the perimeter, hiding as best they could.

"Where is Delilah? How is she?" Kaid couldn't stop the questions from tumbling from his mouth.

The woman knelt on the ground before several flowers and

pulled a pair of large shears from a basket at her side. Her gray gaze settled on him, her expression shrewd. "There was supposed to be only one of you."

"I'm Donnan," Donnan offered in introduction. "This is Laird MacLeod. He came out of worry for the lasses."

The woman looked between the two of them before finally nodding. "Very well. I'm Liv and have been working with Delilah for years." She glanced over her shoulder once more. "She's been found out. They don't know she was working with Elizabeth's father and assume she was working with you." She pinched the delicate stem of a large yellow flower and snipped its base. "Not that she should be working with you in the first place."

Kaid ignored the comment. "Where is she now?"

"In the dungeon." She snipped another flower. "With Torra."

Kaid's heartbeat pounded harder in his chest.

Torra was still alive, and Delilah had found her.

"We have to use any means necessary to get them free," Kaid said.

Liv selected another flower and nodded without looking at him. "I'm already coordinating with Delilah to get them out. When that happens, she will need to see a woman in Killearnan."

"What can I do to help ye get them out?" Kaid asked.

She slid him an icy glare. "I think you've done enough already. She wouldn't be here if it weren't for you."

Her words hit him like a slap.

"You've put every one of us in danger." She snatched up the basket and rose so abruptly one of the flowers fell to the ground. "Tonight. Wait for them to be freed a little past midnight."

Without another word, she turned and left. The abandoned yellow bloom lay on its side, the fragile petals cradled in the long grass.

She was right, of course. He had put everyone in danger. But he'd also seen no other way.

"Well, she seems nice." Donnan gave a wide smile.

The familiar gesture couldn't even draw a smirk from Kaid's lips.

"I'll make this right." Kaid spoke with vehemence.

Donnan's expression didn't fade. "Ye've no' done anything wrong. The lasses made their own decision, and we'll get them to safety tonight."

The most treacherous part would be getting them from the dungeon to the forest. Then again, getting them through the forest wouldn't be easy either. While there weren't as many guards at night as Kaid had initially assumed there might be, it only took one seeing them to ruin everything.

Kaid's palms prickled with sweat, and he had to focus on his breathing to keep it steady.

This was not Ardvreck.

This was not that day in the village where everyone had been slaughtered.

There would not be so much blood.

The forest seemed to blur in front of him.

Kaid closed his eyes, and when he reopened them, the world had stopped whirling.

His breath came easier, and his mind was clearer.

"No matter what, we'll get them free," Kaid promised.

And he meant every damn word.

• • •

It's time.

Delilah's heart leapt at the words gracefully curling over the slip of parchment. She bent and stroked Fianna's glossy back. The cat arched her body and curled her tail toward Delilah's fingers.

An emphatic purr filled the air and made Torra clasp her hands in delight. While Torra refused to pet Fianna, she took great pleasure in the cat's recurring visits.

Delilah sat beside Torra on the sad little bed. "Torra," she said. "We're going to be leaving."

The woman's eyes went wide.

"You're going to be free," Delilah whispered. Her skin prickled with the eagerness to liberate Torra from her confined hell.

But it was not gratitude so plainly visible on Torra's face—it was fear.

She shook her head emphatically. "No. No. No. No. No. No."

Delilah glanced toward the cell door to ensure no guards were nearby. "Shh, Torra. It's a secret."

"I can't leave." Torra's voice pitched in a wail. "I'm no' allowed to."

"It's only for a bit of time," Delilah said in what she hoped was an encouraging tone.

Leasa knelt at the woman's side. "I'm scared too, but if we stay together, it'll make us braver."

Torra pursed her lips and grasped Leasa's hand with both of hers. Black showed around Torra's nails, but Leasa did not appear to care.

Footsteps sounded on the stairs, and Delilah's body tensed, every muscle tight.

It was time.

Delilah watched the door to their cell and removed her daggers. The one from her bodice, she gave to Leasa. The one hidden in the hollow sole of her shoe, she twisted free and passed to Torra. "To make you feel safer," Delilah offered. Torra finally removed one of her hands from Leasa's and took the blade with a tentative nod.

Delilah recovered the final dagger, the largest and most wicked of the three, from where it was strapped to her thigh.

Torra watched her with large eyes. "Where else have ye got those things stashed?"

Delilah winked at her. "Just know I'll not let anything happen to you."

The tension in Torra's shoulders seemed to relax, and she shared a trusting nod with Leasa.

A quiet rustle sounded outside their cell, like a sack of flour falling to the floor.

Or a body.

Delilah slipped the pin from her hair and made her way to the cell door. She unfolded the lock pick from where it lay against the hairpin and made quick work of the lock. The door creaked open to freedom.

The hallway was silent and dark.

Delilah motioned to the other two ladies to remain in place before she crept out into the hallway.

Liv was crouched beside the body of an unconscious man, holding a length of rope. Fianna hopped gracefully atop the man's slumped back before bounding toward Delilah.

"Is anyone there?" Delilah whispered.

Liv shook her head.

Delilah motioned for the other two women to come forward. They moved as one, their hands each clasping one another as well as a dagger.

If nothing else, they would be able to defend themselves. Though Delilah truly hoped it would not come to that.

They stalked up the dungeon stairs in a silent group. All four guards who had been stationed there lay unconscious on the ground, bound with a secure rope.

Their sleep was too deep, and Delilah knew Liv must have given them the sleeping draught Percy had concocted. It left the person hazy when they awoke and uncertain about the minutes leading up to their unconsciousness.

It allowed the women to remain anonymous without having to take lives.

Liv led them to the right rather than the left when they reached the next floor. Escape was so close, Delilah could almost smell the wet, sweet air of the overgrown garden.

They were halfway down the hallway when the baritone of multiple voices and the heavy tread of boots echoed around them. One of the women behind Delilah sucked in a gasp.

Delilah turned to them and indicated they remain quiet. The two nodded in unison.

"Go on ahead," Liv whispered. "I'll distract them." She didn't wait for a reply before slipping down the hallway toward the sound of the men.

All the women who worked together under Sylvi were experienced and confident enough that they could each handle her own.

Liv would be fine.

Delilah motioned for the other two to slip into the shadows of an alcove.

"I can't find where the kitchen is." Liv's smooth Gaelic sounded in the distance. "Could you help?"

Someone said something indiscernible and Liv gave a giggle.

They were sufficiently distracted.

Delilah led the women to the door leading out to the garden. Her heart tripped a frantic beat.

Had Liv not been there to distract the men, they might have been caught. Even now, they still could be.

They were so close to freedom that it made her skin prickle with the prospect.

She pushed against the door and found it open, Liv having already picked the lock in anticipation of their escape.

Delilah charged into the garden and held the door for the other two, whose movements were more hesitant.

Torra stopped and stared up at the sky where the moon shone bright upon them. She drew a shaky gasp and pulled Leasa closer to her. "It's beautiful," she said in a choked whisper.

Delilah let the door slip closed with great care to ensure it remained silent.

Something hard gripped the back of her neck and squeezed.

Delilah's body acted on instinct, grasping blindly for her assailant while she ducked her body forward and sent him sprawling over her.

One of the women gave a sharp squeak while another shushed.

The man looked up at Delilah in shock before her elbow came down hard on his temple. She didn't have any rope to tie him with, but the draught tucked in her waistband would work nonetheless.

After quickly dumping the contents into his mouth, she gathered the other two women against her with Leasa at her left and Torra at her right. Together, the three of them ran toward the fence at the forest.

Donnan would be waiting for them. Freedom would be waiting for them.

But it was not just Donnan's face which emerged from the shadows of the trees. Another man stood beside him, his skin had been darkened like Donnan's to aid in making him invisible within the forest.

Perhaps that was why it took her a moment before she recognized the man in one pulse-pounding second.

Kaid.

Chapter Twenty-Five

The moonlight became brighter when she appeared.

Delilah.

Kaid's soul was awash in her light, flooded with the relief of her safety. And damn proud of how she'd put down her attacker without a moment's hesitation.

The lass could fight.

She ran toward the forest with two women huddled against her, but her gaze was fastened on Kaid. There was a fierceness there, something protective and determined, and he locked the image in his mind to capture in his book later.

She would be with him soon.

But not soon enough.

He was moving forward before he realized what he was doing, eager to scale the fence to get to her faster. Something hard and solid pushed against his chest.

"Nay, laird." Donnan's voice. "More movement will only draw attention."

Kaid gritted his teeth against the logic of his friend's words, but held his place.

An eternity passed, and finally the women were clambering over the fence. First Leasa, and then a red-haired woman with a look of wild fright about her. Torra.

She allowed herself to be pulled over by Donnan long enough to have her feet set on the ground before lurching back from them all. The odor of greasy hair and unwashed body hung thick in the air around her.

Delilah came next, deftly hurtling over the fence.

Kaid caught her in her midair leap and let her topple them to the ground together so their breathless laugh tangled into a breathless kiss.

The passion of their kiss was explosive, stoked into a fevered longing with the threat of danger swelling around them. She sighed into his mouth, and her body arched against him.

Donnan cleared his throat.

Kaid pulled back from Delilah, and they shared a laughing look before getting to their feet. Torra watched them from the veil of her thick hair, her eyes wide where they flicked back and forth between him and Delilah.

Donnan grinned. "Dinna mind us, we're just waiting to no' be caught."

Kaid slid him a dark look, but couldn't help the smile creeping over his lips. He nodded toward Torra. "Lady Torra?"

Torra spread the tatters of her gown and gave a bow fit for a formal gathering. Her gaze remained fixed on him, as if she did not quite yet know what to make of him.

Delilah's face shone with pride at her success.

"Ye've done well, my love," Kaid said.

"I'd never let you down." She glanced toward the castle where all appeared still. "But Donnan is right. We mustn't tarry."

Donnan put a hand on Leasa's lower back. "Follow me, and mind ye stay quiet."

Together they moved through the forest, backs hunched, footsteps careful. All of them but Torra. The woman clattered through bushes and tripped over roots with such regularity, it was as if she were aiming for them.

Delilah, ever the pragmatic lass, gave Kaid an apologetic smile and squeezed his hand before falling back to aid the other woman through the brush with meticulous patience.

They were more than halfway through the forest when something rustled several feet away from Kaid. He held up a hand and everyone stopped.

Except Torra.

She shoved through a tree, her steps cracking on the dry leaves underfoot while her slender arm snapped a twig.

It was all the enemy needed.

The world exploded into shouts and war cries. Men leapt at them from all angles. The movement was apparent but a moment before a man was on Kaid with a blade flashing the light of the moon.

Kaid reacted without thinking and shoved his sword into the man's gullet. A savage scream behind Kaid turned his blood to ice.

He turned and found Torra being held by the throat. Delilah lunged at the attacker, but the man's blade was too fast.

The world dragged to the hideously slow pace of a nightmare.

But this was no nightmare.

Kaid was awake, watching from two paces too far away to help. The attacker drew his arm back with the intent to strike at Torra. Delilah ran between the woman and death with nothing more than a dagger clutched in her fist.

The man's blade moved downward. Faster than Kaid's feet, which seemed to slide in the layers of leaves beneath his boots.

Down the blade came, slicing through air, and then slicing into Delilah.

She fell back, her face alight with surprise.

The dagger fell from her fingers.

A cry wrenched from Kaid. The world sped forward, and he moved like a madman, without thought, without care, without anything funneling through him but the hatred of the man who had cut down the woman he loved.

Delilah.

It was her name which her attacker last heard before his life was brutally ended.

Everything had fallen quiet. The fighting had stopped. All the guards were dead.

Kaid jerked to where Delilah lay on the ground, immobile. A shadow covered her torso, hiding the gore of her wound from him. He didn't want to see.

But he had to.

"Delilah." He fell to his knees beside her and clutched at her shoulders. The woman he loved.

A moan eased from her throat and his heart wrenched.

Her hand fluttered over her stomach where she'd been struck, obstructing his view. "Help." The word came out between gritted teeth.

She struggled against his grasp.

"Dinna move." He wasn't sure what he could do to help, but was certain her wriggling around with a stomach wound was not going to improve matters.

"I need help sitting." She reached up toward him for assistance. "I can't get up in this blasted corset."

The moonlight glinted at her stomach, but not against blood. No, something metallic gleamed beneath the split fabric.

"I forgot I'd worn my steel corset." She grasped his palm, and he moved to help her, his gaze still fixed on her torso.

"Ye dinna—" The words died on his tongue, absorbed by the relief flooding through him.

"Percy made us all steel corsets." She glanced down at a seam of blood that had appeared against the narrow slits of visible skin. Little more than a scratch. "They're a beast to wear, but this one just saved my life. I put it on when I readied myself to flee, when I thought Torra was—"

The wonder left Delilah's face. "Where's Torra?"

Kaid kept his hand still clasped on Delilah. Not that he assumed she needed his protection—she'd already proven herself capable enough—but somehow touching her reassured him she was there.

She was alive.

She was safe.

His throat drew tight with happiness, and he said it again in his mind twice more just for the sheer joy of it.

Delilah was alive.

Torra was easily found, crouched like a frightened child beneath a fallen tree. Scratches showed on her cheeks, but she was otherwise unharmed.

As Kaid watched Delilah reassure the woman, a realization slammed into him. He'd not hesitated once in battle.

His vision had not blurred, his heart had only pounded steadily and confidently, as it had done before the massacre. Even his palms had remained dry against the hilt of his sword.

He didn't know when, or why, or how, but through loving a woman so brave and sacrificing as Delilah, he found himself restored to the man he'd once been.

• • •

Torra lay slumped between the brace of Delilah and Kaid's shoulders.

The poor woman had been so frightened, Delilah had no choice but to offer the woman one of Percy's draughts. She'd only been given half so she could still walk, but was terribly disoriented regardless.

"Where am I?" Torra slurred. "Why?"

"We're taking you to a ball," Leasa said in a soothing tone.

Delilah looked at Leasa who offered a helpless shrug. It was a ridiculous answer, but seemed to placate Torra.

While Delilah felt a stab of guilt over Torra's drugged confusion, it was perhaps best the woman forgot everything that had happened prior to her taking the dose.

For now, they were heading toward Killearnan, where Delilah would have to face Sylvi. Already the city line was in view, and Delilah's heartbeat pounded faster with each step closer.

"I'm going with ye into Killearnan," Kaid declared.

Tension throbbed at Delilah's temples. "You can't." The time for being quiet about the other women was over. "It wasn't just me who was hired by Lady Elizabeth's father."

A knot of guilt lodged itself in her heart. She hated having to involve the other women. If going against her mission weren't already betrayal enough, this was the twist of the dagger.

She shifted Torra's arm on her shoulders to ensure the woman would not slip free.

"Who else is there, aside from Elizabeth's maid?" Kaid asked.

"Elizabeth's maid isn't a maid at all," Delilah replied. "Her name is Liv. But it isn't just the two of us who do work for hire. There are several of us. I'm to meet with the woman in charge of us all. Kaid, if you come with me, she'll try to have you hanged in order to see my assignment fulfilled."

Kaid was quiet a moment too long. "I'll no' leave ye to go without me." There was a determined edge to his tone, one she was sure he was used to seeing obeyed.

But she was not one of his men, so easily commanded. "It's too dangerous. She wants to see you—"

"She doesna know anything about me," Kaid said abruptly.

He was right, of course. Even Lady Elizabeth's father did not know who might seek to abduct Elizabeth. It was only known MacKenzie had many enemies and so the possibility was great.

Elizabeth had been delivered to MacKenzie safely, which made their mission successful.

A protest readied itself on Delilah's tongue when Kaid's look stilled her words. His expression was not hard or insistent, but desperate with pleading.

"I lost ye when ye left for Edirdovar. I thought I lost ye forever in the forest when ye were struck." He swallowed. "I canna lose ye again, Delilah."

Her heart squeezed around his words and the depth of meaning behind them.

The inn came into view on the edge of town, nondescript and unnamed from the missing sign outside. Exactly where Sylvi had told Delilah to meet her.

Delilah gave a resigned nod to Kaid against her better judgment. But she knew from his determined stare toward the building, he would not be dissuaded.

Within minutes, Leasa, Donnan, and Torra were all secreted into a room through an unseen entrance near the rear of the inn, thanks to a well-placed coin. Kaid and Delilah remained in the main area of the inn.

A woman with a sapphire blue scarf over her head sauntered down the stairs with such an air of seduction, Delilah could not help but stare. The woman's dress was a vibrant blue, and tiny charms jingled at her wrists and throat.

It wasn't until she stopped before their table and regarded them with sky blue eyes beneath a layer of slanted kohl that Delilah recognized her.

Isabel.

The excited flutter of recognition quelled when Delilah's fellow spy fixed her focus on Kaid.

"Who is this?" Isabel spoke in an accent as exotic and foreign as the gem glittering between her brows and the heavy spicy scent hovering around her.

Delilah rose to embrace Isabel, who refused to take her gaze from Kaid.

"I'll explain when I speak to Sylvi," Delilah said.

Isabel walked around them like a cat eyeing her prey. "She'll not let you take him with you."

Kaid rose to protest when a door opened and Sylvi appeared, wearing her customary men's trews and loose leine along with a hard expression. She flicked a gaze toward Kaid and grinned, obviously assuming Delilah victorious.

Delilah's heart went heavy and slid into her stomach. Though she'd tried many times to come up with a way to tell Sylvi, it all sounded so insufficient in her head. And it all resonated with the exact words Delilah had so dreaded to say.

She had failed.

"It's not what you think." Delilah spoke as soon as the door sealed her inside the room alone with Sylvi.

Sylvi raised a brow.

"I didn't bring him to be punished. I—" The words stuck in Delilah's throat.

The enormity of what she'd done slammed into her. She'd

gone against her orders. She put Elizabeth, Liv, and Leasa at risk and destroyed the discretion of their entire assignment.

Delilah suddenly wished to be anywhere but there.

"Delilah." Sylvi's voice was sharp enough to cut through the fog of self-pity, something Delilah desperately needed.

"I went to Edirdovar," Delilah said.

The skin around Sylvi's eyes tightened. The cramped room had one lone window, which let in a slant of morning sun. It sliced into the dingy chamber and glowed against the blonde braids twisted back on Sylvi's head. "Why did you go there?"

"I had to help the MacLeod clan achieve peace to ensure there would be no more massacre—"

"That was not what you'd been told to do." Sylvi's tone was tipped with an ice so cold, it frosted down Delilah's spine.

She steeled herself against the disappointment resonating in Sylvi's hard stare. "I know. I deviated from the plan, but I don't think I've ruined—"

"Is Elizabeth at Edirdovar?" Sylvi asked.

Delilah nodded.

"And what did Laird MacKenzie say to you when Elizabeth arrived? Or was it you who came after her?" Sylvi's mouth thinned.

"She arrived after me. I was thrown in the dungeon." Delilah winced against her next admission. "Along with Leasa."

Sylvi's brows rose. "And how, pray tell, did you escape that? How many of his men did you kill? Did he find out why you were there?"

"He didn't know why I was there. I swear it." There was a note of desperation in Delilah's voice. She hated how it sounded in her own ears.

Sylvi strode to one side of the room. The heavy boots she wore thudded against the uneven floorboards. "Delilah, do you know what you've done?" She stopped and stared with a look of such stark disappointment, Delilah actually felt the force of it strike deep in her heart. "You haven't just failed your mission, you've failed me, and you've failed your sisters." Spots of color showed on Sylvi's pale cheeks. "You've put all of us in terrible danger."

There was a clatter outside the door before it burst open and Kaid strode into the room with Isabel staggering after him.

"I willna have ye talk to Delilah in such a way." He planted himself in front of Delilah with a wide-legged stance. "If ye've rage to spew, direct it at me, but no' at her."

Delilah was stunned into silence. Part of her was outraged at the intrusion, at how clearly helpless he thought her. But there was another part of her, a wounded, sad part, which had never been defended before, and reveled in this masculine show of protectiveness.

Everything he'd said and done up to this point proved something rewarding enough to make all the hurt of this meeting worthwhile. He cared.

About her.

"Shut the door, Isabel." Sylvi turned slowly and let her cold gaze slide down Kaid. "Who the hell are you?"

Chapter Twenty-Six

Kaid stared at the woman dressed in men's clothes and knew she would not be easily handled.

Her clothing was all black, and her hair was braided back from her face and twisted into a wild mass of blonde hair. She looked more Scottish and wild than English. Even a subtle underlying lilt to her words suggested as much.

Hostility shone bright in her pale eyes. The openness of her dislike made the black bow tied at her neck appear nothing short of ridiculous.

"I'm Kaid MacLeod of Sutherland, laird of the Clan MacLeod." He squared his shoulders. "It is my people Delilah sought to help."

"It is you who caused Delilah to abandon her mission?" The woman named Sylvi tilted her head and regarded him. "If I'm correct, I am assuming you're the very man she was supposed to bring in to kill. And now you're here. How very convenient."

The tall, slender lass was obviously trying to intimidate him. It would have been funny were he not so concerned for Delilah.

"Nay, she aided my people because she has a good heart." He glanced back at Delilah. Her face was flushed bright red. His explanation faltered into silence.

"Do not talk about me as if I'm not in the room." She clenched her fist. "I helped your people because seeing the cruelty they've endured broke my heart." Her shoulders sagged. "Sylvi, if you saw them…"

A wash of uncomfortable warmth spread over Kaid. He didn't want his clan to be pitied, but wasn't that the perspective he'd forced upon her when she arrived? It had gotten her to help him, which he had desperately needed.

Sylvi stood in front of the one window to peer out before speaking. The morning sunlight left her hair a glow of white around her shoulders and face. "Your heart has always gotten you into trouble, Delilah." The words were said with more kindness than their previous conversation. "I know how much you wanted this mission." A hard set returned to Sylvi's jaw. "This meant everything to all of us."

"I know." Delilah spoke so quietly, it made Kaid want to stand in front of her once more.

"I dinna know what her success with ye would afford her," Kaid said. "But what she's done for my people will save lives."

Sylvi looked between Kaid and Delilah. "You didn't disclose the details of our mission?"

Delilah's cheeks went red. "I told him it was Elizabeth's father who ordered we bring any potential attackers to justice."

The chilly touch of Sylvi's gaze settled first on Kaid, then back on Delilah, and her expression relaxed. Somewhat. "I'd like to see your castle."

"Ardvreck," Kaid provided.

"Yes. Ardvreck," Sylvi amended. "I'd like to see it."

"Ye'd be a welcome guest." Kaid gave her a bow. Probably an awkward one, most likely stiff. Hell, he didn't know what he was doing, but he thought it might help his cause.

Delilah's cause.

"You should know we travel with a woman who is very ill," Delilah said and quickly explained Torra's situation. "Our travel may be slow, but we can plan as we ride. I would also like to get Elizabeth and Liv out of there as quickly as possible."

Sylvi hesitated. "If it weren't for Elizabeth, I'd say we could just kill MacKenzie now."

Kaid felt himself suddenly liking the blonde woman more. "We need Torra to take back the land with the support of her people. If MacKenzie dies without an heir, who knows who will take his place."

Sylvi's sigh was almost inaudible in the silent room. "So many complications. Very well. We'll bring Percy and discuss our options on the road. Let's not waste another moment."

A rush of victory swelled through Kaid. Not only had he been able to defend Delilah's choice, but he had enlisted the aid of what appeared to be a very capable woman.

This would all be over soon, so long as they could get Torra to cooperate.

• • •

They'd snuck back into Ardvreck Castle with their hoods up against the moist chill of the night air, creeping in the dark like thieves.

The journey had taken over four days.

Delilah helped ease Torra into the large bed of the chamber she'd shared with Leasa when they were last at Ardvreck. The woman immediately curled into a ball and pulled the covers over her head.

A sense of urgency nipped at Delilah, tempting her to leave Torra as she was.

Kaid waited for Delilah in his room. He'd slipped the words into her ear with a velvety voice and a look of such longing her body still hummed with the effects.

How she wanted to lose herself in his touch, his kiss. She suppressed a sigh lest it come across as impatient.

Torra had been nothing if not uncooperative, not that Delilah could blame her. After the good part of a lifetime confined to a prison cell, it made sense that she felt impossibly small in the wide openness of the world.

"Is she still frightened?" Percy asked from beside Delilah.

Concern puckered Percy's brow, but even with the delicate lines, Percy was still the most beautiful woman Delilah had ever seen, with her long golden hair and deep blue eyes rimmed with long dark lashes.

A rhythmic sucking sound came from under the covers and Delilah knew Torra had her thumb in her mouth.

"It's all been too much," Delilah said gently.

Percy nodded with her characteristic kind patience. "I understand."

Delilah knew she did. After years of keeping herself hidden behind Kindrochit Castle's walls, it was unexpected to see Percy outside.

"I'll stay with her," Percy said. "I don't want her locked in here alone, and I have a tea I think can help."

Delilah offered a grateful smile to her friend. Leasa was still in Killearnan with Donnan and Isabel, gathering the remaining MacKenzies to garner support for Torra's lairdship. Percy's help was necessary in their absence.

Kaid was waiting.

Though Delilah tamped down the thought, her pulse quickened.

"Thank you." She caught Percy's hand and squeezed it.

Percy smiled in return. "Of course. Go get rest now."

Delilah obeyed and headed toward the door, but it was not rest she planned to have.

It was Kaid.

She opened the door and found Sylvi standing with her feet braced wide. "I'll stay with them tonight, but I wanted to talk to you first."

Delilah pulled in a breath and nodded. In truth, she was surprised Sylvi had not approached her during their travel. While she'd expected the conversation, Delilah was still not looking forward to it.

Especially if it might take long.

Impatience scrabbled over Delilah's nerves.

The four days of being near Kaid, but not touching, not allowing herself to be with him, had been torturous. She'd endured it well enough, but now that minutes separated them, eagerness nearly tore her apart at the seams.

"You don't have to hide it."

"Hide what?" Even as she asked the question, heat spread over Delilah's cheeks.

Sylvi didn't break her gaze from the two women in the chamber. "That you're in love with him."

Delilah tensed. Though she ought to deny the claim, she knew in her heart she could not.

Sylvi was right. Delilah was in love with Kaid.

Who was waiting for her.

Impatience raked over her once more, hot and annoying.

"You've a soft heart, Delilah, as I said before," Sylvi said. "It leads you to bad decisions."

"This is not a bad decision."

Sylvi cast her a sidelong glance. "So if he were not part of it, you would still sacrifice everything to save these people?"

"Yes," Delilah answered without hesitation. "Yes, I absolutely would."

Sylvi gave a thoughtful nod. "And what will you do after all this is over, if he decides he doesn't want you anymore?"

The question was so unexpected, Delilah's heart tripped over the stark prospect before she staggered out a reply. "I hadn't—that is, I didn't expect—"

"No, you didn't expect, of course. But you hoped." Sylvi turned toward Delilah now, her face unreadable. "Hope is far more fragile than expectation."

Delilah didn't reply. She could not. The walls around her, once familiar, suddenly seemed cold and pressing as foreign surroundings do.

She would be unwanted.

Sylvi leaned back against the doorframe and regarded Delilah with consideration. "I will never forget how you looked when I first met you. You were the embodiment of misery, as though you thought your life had ended." She fingered the black bow tied around her neck. "I'd never seen such a pitiful creature."

A knot formed in Delilah's throat. She wanted to jerk away from the conversation and run down the hall.

To Kaid's room.

Thoughts of the king tangled with thoughts of Kaid. She hated having them in such near association with one another in her mind.

The burn of the humiliated rejection she'd faced with the king slammed into her heart. "We needn't have this conversation," Delilah said against the hurt aching in her throat.

Her anticipation to see Kaid muddied into something embarrassing, almost shameful.

"But we do." Sylvi's expression eased. "Because you're not that girl anymore, Delilah. You're strong, and you're confident, and you're beautiful. And I don't ever want to see you reduced to that pitiful creature again." She put her hands on Delilah's shoulders. "You will always have a home with us. We will always love you."

The ache in Delilah's throat tightened.

"But if he does ever wrong you in any way…" Sylvi pulled her dagger from her waist and scraped the point along the underside of her fingernail. "I'll slice off his cock."

She flashed Delilah a smile, slipped into the chamber, and let the door click closed behind her.

Delilah stared at the wood grain on the closed door for a moment before turning to walk down the hall, her cheeks aflame. All this time she'd thought herself unloved. Unwanted by the large family who'd raised her, forced into the group of women she fought beside. She'd never considered they might truly love her.

Her steps down the hall were not as quick as they might have been only minutes before.

Kaid was not the king, she reminded herself. There was more between them, and their affair had been different.

And yet that place in her which had been once shattered, the one crisscrossed with thick and ropey scars, flinched at the idea of loving him.

She opened the door to his chamber and he stood there before her. Hungry desperation lit his expressive blue eyes. Firelight gleamed off his naked torso, teasing the pulsing arousal back to life.

And as she ran to him, her poor heart squeezed against the impossible truth.

Even if he would someday hurt her, she could not help loving him.

Chapter Twenty-Seven

It was too good to be true.

The floral perfume pulled at Kaid, but he couldn't tell if it came from a dream or reality. If it was a dream, he didn't want to wake.

He pulled in a deep breath of Delilah and reveled in the scent of her.

Delilah.

A low groan slipped from his throat and was answered with a feminine sigh.

The warmth of a body wriggled against him. "I see you're awake." Delilah's voice was low and throaty from sleep.

He opened his eyes and found her staring at him, her hair pouring over the pillow like a fountain of sunlit honey. "I have something worth waking up to," he said.

Her lazy smile made his heart stir. "Are you glad to be home?" she asked.

"Aye." He pulled her closer to him. "And I'm glad to have ye home with me."

She arched her curvy body against him. Her skin was hot silk beneath his palms, and his cock went thick with desire. He kissed the smoothness of her naked shoulder before slowly easing his mouth to her nipple.

One day he would sketch her in his bed like this, beautiful and flushed with sweet longing. If he could ever stop himself from loving her long enough to pull out his book and charcoal.

A knock came at the door.

Delilah tensed slightly beneath him, but he spread both hands across her narrow waist to still her before letting his tongue deliver a slow and careful swipe over her breast. Someone was at his door, but he had no intention of—

The knock came again. Harder this time.

Kaid eased away from Delilah and ground his teeth in irritation.

"If you'd like my continued help…" Sylvi's voice came from the other side of the door. "It would be in your best interest to assist us in calming down your newest guest."

She was sly, that one.

She knew Delilah was with him, she had to—and yet she did not state as much. Sylvi also did not mention Torra by name.

If nothing else, the hard-faced lass knew discretion.

Kaid bowed his head over Delilah and pressed a kiss to her stomach. "Aye," he said in a voice loud enough to pierce the wooden door. "I'll be along shortly."

The sound of her heavy boots thumped away from the door. Kaid gave a regretful sigh before he and Delilah rose from the bed to quickly wash and dress.

It was not easy to avoid the servants as they made their way to Torra's chamber, but they were able to keep Delilah's presence a secret.

His people could know of his arrival and Sylvi's since she'd been invited to meet his people as an old friend of Kaid's. But Delilah and Torra must remain a secret, as well as Percy, who insisted on staying hidden.

Later he would tell his people about Delilah and their deception against MacKenzie, of course, but not until he was ready. And it would be Torra who would determine as much.

When he and Delilah slipped into Torra's chamber, they found Percy kneeling beside the bed and stroking Torra's hair. The mad-woman sat in the large bed with her legs tucked against her torso and her arms crossed tightly over her shins.

Percy gave Delilah a worried glance and moved away from Torra for Kaid to approach.

The MacKenzie heir did not react when Kaid stopped beside

the bed. She continued to shake her head repeatedly. "Shouldn't be here, shouldn't be here, shouldn't be here, shouldn't be here," she mumbled over and over again.

"Lady MacKenzie." Kaid said her name in the same voice he used for his men while training.

The muttering stopped and she looked up sharply. The skin under her eyes was bruised from exhaustion, and the wrinkles on her brow and around her lips were more pronounced.

"I'm Kaid MacLeod of Sutherland, laird of the Clan MacLeod. Do ye remember me?"

She nodded.

He knelt beside the mattress. "I'm the rightful laird here, just as ye're rightful laird of the MacKenzies."

She swallowed and shook her head. "Ye canna say that. I canna be here." A tear tracked down her face, leaving a wet trail in its wake. "I dinna belong here."

"Where do ye belong?" he asked.

She squeezed her arms more tightly against herself. "In the dungeon," she whispered. "Where no one can see me."

"Ye're a laird," Kaid said. "Ye dinna belong in a dungeon. Ye belong on the seat of authority and leading the MacKenzies."

Torra looked down at the tangled bedsheets and shook her head. "I canna."

"Why?" Kaid asked.

"Because they'll kill me." She was staring off at something she couldn't see.

The tinkling of bottles clinking against one another sounded behind him, followed by the moist grassy scent of steeping herbs.

"Ye have protection, Torra," he said.

She looked up at him, and again he was struck by how much older she appeared than himself when it was rumored they were the same age. Thick threads of white shone in her red hair.

"Ye have me and all of the MacLeod clan," he said. "Yer brother has been tormenting my people and yer people for years. They all will gladly protect ye and stand against him."

She shook her head. "Not my brother. His mother was here when she died, before she could marry Father."

"So yer half brother." Kaid's heart thumped faster with her confirmation of the rumors. "And a bastard."

"If ye call him that, they'll beat ye. Kill ye." She shook her head vigorously. "Beat ye and kill ye. Beat ye and kill ye."

Kaid put a hand up to stop her. "Is that what happened to most of yer clan? Did he kill all his own people?"

Torra stopped chanting, lowered her face to her knees where her legs were tucked against her and loosed a low sob. Kaid's stomach dropped. Surely MacKenzie did not kill off his own people? What would be the point of being a laird with no one to rule?

"Help me," Kaid said. "Take back yer people. Be their laird. They need ye even more than my people need an alliance with ye."

Torra shook her head and her hair fell around her like a red curtain, blocking her from his view. "I canna help ye." She curled her hand in a fist. "I canna help ye," she repeated with finality.

Kaid stared down at her, incredulous. Surely she could understand the logic of what he said and realize she would be protected. She was his only chance at peace with the MacKenzies.

"Lady MacKenzie," he said.

She did not look at him.

"Torra." He spoke in a firmer tone this time.

She was unresponsive.

Not crying, not speaking—only staring into the space of nothing in front of her, all while Kaid's chance for peace slipped away with the shreds of the woman's remaining sanity.

• • •

Kaid had lost his patience.

Delilah watched him carefully and could almost pinpoint the exact moment when it slipped away.

Torra was difficult to manage, she would give him that.

"Torra, what did you think of the dungeon?" Delilah asked.

She slowly walked toward the other woman and sat on the bed beside her.

Kaid regarded them for a moment before standing and pacing the room.

Torra pursed her lips.

"It was very cold in there," Delilah said, small bumps prickling her flesh. The memory of the dank dungeon was far too fresh in her own mind.

"Aye," Torra said. "And dirty."

"Yes," Delilah agreed. "Very dirty. But you aren't cold here, nor are you dirty."

She took Torra's hand. Torra did not jerk her arm free, but instead kept her gaze fastened to where Delilah examined her clean fingers.

"You were treated like a prisoner in your own home when you were little more than a lass. They say you were down there for almost fifteen years. Is that true?" Delilah said in a quiet voice. Something caught in her throat.

Torra seemed to consider this a moment before finally nodding. "I was sixteen. Father had just died."

"But you're not in the dungeon now, Torra." Delilah folded her hand around the other woman's. Her palms were clammy and cold. "You're free."

"I'm in another room," Torra said. "Not a dungeon, but not free."

Delilah's stomach clenched. The woman was right. "Then you can leave whenever you like."

Perhaps Delilah imagined it, but she swore she actually felt the weight of Kaid's gaze against her back. True, what she said was risky, but making Torra feel as though she'd gone from one prison to another would not do.

"I can leave?" The hope in Torra's voice shot deep into Delilah's heart.

She nodded anyway.

Torra looked around the large chamber, her eyes bright with the prospect, and then she seemed to shrink into herself like a flower withering. But Delilah understood. Torra had nowhere to go.

"Or you could stay here, as a guest," Delilah offered. She knew she was speaking for Kaid and hoped he would not mind. Because truly there was more to this than convincing Torra. This was also about helping to heal another of those who MacKenzie had broken. "Whether you decide to take back your inheritance or not, we are your friends."

Torra watched her with a large, sorrowful expression, and again Delilah was reminded of a dog who had suffered a hard life from a cruel master. Torra wanted to trust. She wanted to be loved.

And the desperate ferocity of her look made Delilah's heart squeeze with the evidence of such sad hope.

She rose and pulled gently at Torra's hand, which had grown warmer against her own. "Please, come with me."

Torra hesitated before unfolding herself from her balled-up position and allowing herself to be led to the window. Delilah unclasped the shutters and pulled them open.

The summer air pushed in, fresh and cool, and brought with it the sweet scent of pastries from the market below.

Torra closed her eyes and leaned her face toward the crisp breeze. Her chest expanded with the force of her inhale and she smiled.

"Let me show you freedom." Delilah motioned to the window, encouraging Torra toward it. She complied in slow, shuffling footsteps, her eyes still closed in appreciation.

Delilah glanced toward the rear of the room where Percy was adding drops to a steaming mug. Kaid was facing Delilah, watching her with a light expression on his face. There was something about the casual half-grin, the way he had made himself comfortable leaning against the wall, which made her heart swell with what she saw there.

He was proud of her.

Heat fluttered low in her stomach and blossomed over her chest and cheeks. But she was not yet done.

"Open your eyes," she said.

Torra obeyed and looked at the castle and its many guards below, with the village beyond and all the people who bustled at the thriving market. Even further were the swells of craggy hills, all velvety grass with jagged gray stone peeking through.

"This is freedom," Delilah said.

Torra's gaze moved slowly as she regarded the scene below, taking it all in—the beauty, the vivacity of it all. Her eyes went glassy with unshed tears and the tip of her nose reddened.

"This is freedom," she repeated in a voice thick with emotion.

"This is how Edirdovar should be too," Delilah said gently. "You can bring this back to your people if you desire."

Torra did not turn from the scene. "It's dangerous."

"We would be at your side." Delilah squeezed the woman's hand. "You need only think about it. You are free regardless of what you choose. And you have our friendship and protection always."

A tear crawled down Torra's cheek, but she did not swipe it away.

Delilah backed away from Torra, leaving the other woman to witness the extent of her freedom. When Delilah crossed the room and slipped from the door with Kaid, Torra still had not moved from her place at the window.

No servants appeared in the hall near Delilah, but she eased herself against the wall and in the shadows at the same time Kaid shifted to stand protectively in front of her.

She knew she couldn't be seen, not before Kaid was ready to announce the plan. And first they'd need Torra's compliance. Hopefully it would come soon, not only through their efforts to convince Torra of her rightful place, but also through the tea Percy concocted.

Based on what Percy stated, she'd found a combination of extracts and herbs to aid in bringing Torra's wits together. It sounded an impossible task, to be sure. But then, Percy was a woman who made miracles happen on a daily basis.

Footsteps sounded nearby and Kaid nudged Delilah back into

one of the darkened alcoves. While Delilah didn't want to be caught, she was very much enjoying the press of Kaid's body against hers. Their eyes met and they shared a secret smile.

"Ye were amazing in there, Delilah." The quiet intimacy of his voice sent warm ripples of desire through her. "I dinna know how ye do it, how ye're so patient and ye know exactly the right thing to say. I dinna know what I'd do without ye."

She flushed at his praise.

Sylvi was wrong to offer such a silly warning against Kaid. The more he touched Delilah, and kissed her, and loved her, the more she knew his affection to be true.

"We shouldn't linger," Delilah whispered.

"We should go somewhere no one will find ye." He grinned. "Like my chamber."

The blatant suggestion in his voice turned those delicious ripples of pleasure into excited prickles of anticipation.

The footsteps turned the opposite direction, away from them. He caught her hand and pulled her out of the alcove. Together they made their way down the hall, and were almost to Kaid's chamber when a little voice stopped them mid-step.

"Elizabeth?" it whispered in wonder. "Elizabeth!" This time the shout was high-pitched and desperate.

Delilah swung toward the cry, and her heart nearly burst from her chest with delight at the girl running toward her with arms outstretched.

Claire.

Chapter Twenty-Eight

"Claire." The child's name clogged in Delilah's throat, and she dropped to her knees to embrace the girl.

Claire wrapped her arms around Delilah and clung to her with impossible strength.

The little girl whispered in Delilah's ear, which was really more breath than words. "I missed ye so much, Lady Elizabeth."

Lady Elizabeth.

Delilah winced against the reminder. She had so much to explain. She only hoped sweet Claire would understand.

"Let's go to the solar." Kaid's voice abruptly interrupted the reunion.

Delilah caught the repetitive padding of leather-soled shoes heading for them. She moved in the opposite direction, toward his solar.

Claire curled her arms around Delilah's neck and allowed herself to be carried without complaint. The girl's slight heft was comforting against Delilah's hip and brought to light the realization of how much she'd missed Claire. An odd thought. She'd never desired to be a mother, and now this child made her heart swell with something light and beautiful.

Kaid motioned them both into the solar and let the door lock behind them.

Delilah lowered Claire to the ground. The girl was wearing a lovely blue dress with a ring of lace stitched onto the edge of each sleeve.

Delilah remembered the girl mentioning the dress when they'd spoken before. It had been resewn, but there'd only been enough lace for the sleeves. "Was this your mother's dress you told me about?" she asked.

Claire nodded emphatically. "Do ye like it?"

"It's the most beautiful dress I've ever seen." Delilah placed a kiss on the girl's silky blonde crown.

Before she could straighten, Claire's hand found hers and clasped it tight.

"Thank ye for bringing her back, laird," Claire said. "And I'm so glad ye love her too." She grinned and looked between the two of them.

Kaid slid a glance toward Delilah. "And how do ye know I love her?"

Delilah's heart tripped over itself in spite of her own flimsy warning.

Claire grabbed Kaid's large fingers. "I know ye love her because ye brought her back to us. That, and ye were holding her hand, and ye're always staring at her. I canna imagine ye'd look at someone for so long without loving them. Especially—"

Claire lifted her shoulder in a shy gesture, as if she meant to hide her face beneath them, and turned red to the tips of her ears.

"Especially when she's so bonny?" Kaid offered.

Claire gave a wide smile and nodded vigorously.

"I couldna agree more." Kaid moved closer, embracing Claire and Delilah together, and pressed an endearing kiss to Delilah's lips. "I do love my bonny lasses."

Claire beamed up at Kaid.

It was then Delilah knew with certainty in her heart that this was where she belonged. This was what families were supposed to be, what love was supposed to be.

Kaid loved her.

Hadn't he just said so?

The giddy thought tickled through her and she suddenly wished Sylvi could be there to witness the heartfelt embrace, the bond of their mismatched, yet perfect, family.

Shouts came from below and pulled Kaid from their embrace. He strode toward the window, looked once, and then ran to the door. "I need to be in the courtyard. Stay in here, Delilah—we canna have anyone seeing ye. No' yet." He winked at Claire and gave Delilah a look which lasted long enough to demonstrate the depth of his affection.

"Delilah?" Claire asked, her confusion evident in the furrow of her brow.

Delilah's heart flinched. The time had come to tell Claire about who she was.

"My name is Delilah," she said, kneeling so she was level with the girl. "I was only pretending to be Lady Elizabeth."

Claire's face was smooth and without accusation. "Why?"

"To try to protect you and the rest of the MacLeods from MacKenzie." Delilah tilted her head toward the window, but heard no more shouts below. Whatever the issue was had clearly been resolved.

"Ye pretended to be MacKenzie's bride. To save us," Claire surmised.

Delilah stared for a moment at the clever girl with sunshine hair and her heart in her eyes. "Aren't you a smart one? Yes, I pretended to be his bride."

"Ye're a hero, Delilah." Claire darted forward and bestowed another squeezing hug.

Delilah had been many shameful things in her life—a mistress, a deceiver, a thief when necessary—but never had she been considered a hero. The idea of such innocence thinking so highly of her brought a fresh embrace of affection to her already enamored heart.

While she'd done as much as she could thus far, Delilah would never confess the truth to the child—that there was still considerable danger.

Her stomach gave a savage snarl of hunger.

She put a hand to her bodice and laughed. "It would appear I forgot to break my fast this morning."

"I can get ye something from the kitchens if ye like."

"You don't have to. I—" Delilah almost said she would go down herself. But that wasn't possible, was it?

"The laird told ye to stay here. Besides, the cook likes me, and I always get a bit of sugar." Claire winked, the same as Kaid had done earlier—a slight head cock and a half-smile to accompany the action. "I'll be back quick. I swear it."

Delilah nodded slowly, finally conceding. "Very well, but come straight back. I can't wait to hear what you've done while I've been away."

Claire released her and darted from the room with purpose. Only when the girl was gone did Delilah realize they had not told her to keep what she'd seen secret.

Before Delilah's heart could even descend into her stomach, a knock sounded at the solar door.

Delilah relaxed, assuming Claire had changed her mind and she could tell her to keep Delilah's appearance a secret. But when she pulled open the door, her lowered gaze met only the waist of a well-made dress and slid up to find Percy's face, her skin pale and her blue eyes wide with shock.

"Percy?" Delilah gasped.

"Oh, thank God you were in here. I'd hoped it was where you'd be when I realized you weren't in Kaid's room. It's Torra." Percy shook her head. "You must come. I need help."

• • •

A scream from one of the rooms above pulled Kaid from his interference with the courtyard tiff. He didn't have to guess from which chamber the high-pitched shriek emerged.

The two merchants who had decided to settle a price war with their fists gaped up toward the open window as well. Kaid shot them both a stern warning look in the hopes that the issue was resolved and hurried up the stairs.

He was greeted with a scene of chaos.

The table in Torra's room was overturned, and all the chairs lay pitched on their sides. Several of Percy's books lay strewn across one side of the room as if they'd been swept to the ground.

Torra charged around like a bull with Percy and Delilah fluttering nervously around her. Both were entirely capable of stopping her physically, but he was sure neither would do so at the risk of jeopardizing the rapport they'd worked so hard to establish. And from a corner, Sylvi watched the entire scene with her arms folded over her chest and amusement quirking at her lips.

"It's her," Torra howled. "It's her! She's coming for me." She gripped her hair in her fists and spun around toward Kaid. Her eyes were wild and at some point, she'd torn the fabric of her sleeve.

"Enough," Kaid commanded in a hard tone.

Everyone in the room stopped.

"I told them they should have squeezed her neck until she slept." Sylvi shrugged.

Kaid gave her a sharp look. "I'm sure ye'll remember, Lady MacKenzie is a guest at Ardvreck. We dinna treat guests in such a manner."

He righted a chair and set it to the floor with a hollow clack. "Have a seat, Lady MacKenzie."

Torra's body trembled, but she managed to stagger to the seat and collapse into it. Delilah slid him a look of gratitude. Even her patient demeanor seemed ruffled from the ordeal.

He regarded Percy. "Please go get some ale for Lady MacKenzie from the kitchen."

"Um…" Percy's face went red and she twisted her long, slender fingers.

"Percy is to stay here." Sylvi pushed herself off the wall. "I'll go."

Percy settled a touched Torra's shoulder. "I'll make you a tea to calm you."

The nod Torra gave was one of cultured politeness, the sort one would expect from a laird's daughter. For all the time the woman had been in the dungeon, a part of her still had not been broken.

"I saw her. The white-haired woman." Torra squeezed her

hands together and placed them over her heart. "I saw her. She's going to kill me."

"The white-haired woman is going to kill you?" Delilah asked, her voice patient as ever.

Torra nodded and began to cry in snuffling sobs. "She's here. She's going to kill me."

"We willna let anyone kill ye," Kaid reassured her. "Describe this woman to me."

Delilah put her hand on Kaid's. "I need to get back to the solar. Claire went to get me food, and I fear she'll worry since I've been gone so long."

He nodded and was hit with the urge to let his lips brush over hers before she left. But now was not the time, nor the place. Instead he watched her as she gracefully strode from the room.

Percy appeared beside them and passed Torra a cup. The wet spicy scent of steeped herbs filled the room, and a curl of steam rose from the concoction.

"Drink this to calm yourself," Percy said. "It tastes like flowers, and I've added some honey for good measure."

Torra immediately sipped the tea.

Kaid's patience began to ebb. "Who was the white-haired woman?"

"Her." Torra turned to him. "She locked me up. She told me not to tell anyone he's a bastard. She told me she'd kill me." Her voice was thick with emotion.

Kaid shook his head. "I willna let her kill ye, but I need to know who she is."

Torra nodded. "The one who locked me up, the one who told me she'd ki—"

Kaid put up a hand and the rambling ceased. "Who is she to have done this to ye?"

"Seumas's grandmother," she said.

"Seumas MacKenzie, ye mean—yer bastard brother?" Kaid asked.

Torra looked down at the tea. "Yes. She locked me up," she said miserably. "She said she'd kill me."

"And ye saw her here?" he asked.

Torra nodded toward the open window. "In the courtyard."

Alarm spiked through Kaid. MacKenzie's grandmother was at Ardvreck Castle.

Percy settled a hand on Torra's shoulder again, the gesture soothing. "No one will hurt you now." Her easy reassurance sent fresh tears rolling down Torra's cheeks.

"I was just down in the courtyard. I dinna see anyone out of the ordinary." He combed through his memory and shook his head.

Percy motioned to the tea and Torra obediently took a sip. "She left," she said after she'd swallowed. "Through the other side of the courtyard from where ye were."

Behind his damn back. "Who?" He had to fight to keep his demand from being too hard with his desperation. "What did she look like?"

"The same as she always has." Torra shuddered. "Long white hair and a purple cloak."

A chill went through Kaid's veins. There was only one person who fit that description perfectly.

Rhona.

Chapter Twenty-Nine

Rhona was nowhere to be found.

The hairs on the back of Kaid's neck prickled with unease.

He pushed his first and middle fingers against his temples to stave off the building pressure and entered Torra's chamber once more.

She stood where she always did now, staring out the window overlooking the village in the distance.

Percy glanced up from her book and kept her finger on the page where she'd stopped reading.

"Ye canna find her, can ye?" Torra asked without looking at him. "Nathaira."

"Nathaira?" he repeated. "Ye mean Rhona?"

"If that's what she goes by here, then yes—Rhona. It has been some time since I've seen her at Edirdovar." Torra turned from the window. The late afternoon sun glowed against her face and lit her red hair like a flame.

There was very little anxiety on her face now. She was regal in the deep blue gown of velvet with split sleeves and full skirts. Her hair hung loose around her shoulders in silver and red, and her back was straight and proud.

Percy's teas had worked wonders.

"I knew she'd left with how she walked," Torra said. "Too fast, desperate almost. She kept looking toward ye."

"Do ye know where she's going?" He figured he already knew the answer, but wondered if she might have better insight.

"To my half brother." She spoke calmly, but a line of concern creased over her forehead. "If she knows I've escaped—if she tells him where I am and they find me—"

"We will protect ye no matter what." Kaid hoped she would hear evidence of his genuine promise in every word he said.

She flicked a glance out the window before returning her haunted gaze toward him. "And if I do not feel safe, I can leave?"

It had been a generous offer Delilah had extended, a wild gamble. Though Kaid would never have been so daring as to propose freedom, he understood why she'd done it and still held tight to the hope it would pay off.

He nodded. "If that is what ye wish."

Torra considered this a moment and drank another sip of tea before speaking again. "He will bring a powerful force to see me dead." She stared out the window and shuddered, as if she could already see the men coming over the hills.

"I'd rather bring a powerful force to see him dead—with you and I at the lead together," Kaid said. His pulse raced with the danger of moving too quickly and frightening her. It was like reaching out the first time to stroke a skittish horse's neck.

Torra swallowed and swung her gaze back toward him. "You truly want an alliance with me."

Kaid gave a nod. "Ye're the rightful laird to the MacKenzie clan."

One of Torra's fingernails dug against the edge of her thumb. "And ye're just as serious about helping me reclaim my rightful place?"

Kaid's heart swelled with a hope so great, it almost stole his breath. "Aye."

"My father wanted this." She spoke more to herself than to him and lifted her chin with a tilt of defiance. "Then gather yer men and tell yer clan. Ye will have an alliance with the MacKenzies, and I will take back my rightful place."

Kaid bowed low. "Aye, Laird MacKenzie."

She beamed and extended her arm to him, which he grasped as he would any man he respected.

"Percy, we will have a clan meeting at sunset with her. Will ye be able to have her prepared in time?" Kaid asked as he made his way toward the door. He would need to act quickly to gather everyone, and did not wish to put off the announcement until the following day.

Percy looked to Torra for confirmation, received it and nodded to Kaid. "That will not be a problem."

It was all he needed. He pushed through the door from Torra's chamber, victorious, and all but ran into Delilah.

Elation glowed through him and a smile pulled at his lips. The only thing better than having accomplished so wonderful a goal was having Delilah there to celebrate with him.

He caught her by the waist and spun her around. "She agreed."

The happy confusion on Delilah's face gave way to joy. "Oh, Kaid, that's wonderful."

He set her down and gently pressed her back against the wall, capturing her mouth in a kiss. Desire surged through his body, demanding to be sated.

If only he had more time.

"I need to gather the men," he said between kisses. "For a clan meeting."

It was more a reminder to himself. He pulled back and found a worried expression on her face.

His elation waned. "What is it?"

"Claire is missing."

Kaid cupped Delilah's face. Her skin was like warm silk against his palm. "She's a lass who has gotten used to roaming the castle of her own accord. I'm sure she's fine." He swept his thumb over her lips to smooth away her frown.

It remained. "I sent Sylvi to find her since I cannot be seen around the castle yet." Her gaze surveyed the empty hall.

"She's fine," Kaid said reassuringly.

"I know how much she had missed me. I don't think—"

Kaid pressed another kiss to her mouth. "She'll turn up, Delilah."

Delilah did not kiss him back. "Kaid—"

"I must get the word spread about the clan meeting," he said. "Once we announce to them all ye're no' Elizabeth, ye will be free to roam the castle. Everyone will know who ye are and everyone will know Torra to be the rightful laird of the MacKenzies." He caught her by the arms and looked deep into her worried gaze. "This will all be over soon. Finally. And because of ye."

The concern did not leave her brow, but she nodded.

He released her reluctantly. "I'll look for Claire while I'm assembling the clan."

Her shoulders relaxed somewhat and again she nodded.

Kaid took her hand in his and raised it to his lips like a grand courtier. Surely he felt like one, almost giddy.

His people were going to be safe. This would all finally be over.

And with that, he left to gather his men for the most important clan meeting of his life, where finally he was going to be the laird they all wished him to be. The kind of laird who would have made his father proud.

• • •

Claire was still missing.

Delilah gathered in the main courtyard with the rest of the MacLeods, though she stood at the front near Kaid's side, waiting to be introduced to the clan for who she truly was. The position afforded her the opportunity to search the sea of faces for one sweet, blonde child in a blue gown.

Kaid spoke in a voice loud enough for all to hear, and the clan listened with rapt attention. Perhaps she ought to be listening as well, and focusing on him. Certainly enough faces had turned to look upon her. Had he said her name? People smiled with appreciation and clapped.

She returned their warm expressions in what she hoped appeared genuine, for all she could focus on at present was Claire.

This was the moment Kaid had wanted for so long, what he'd sacrificed and risked death to achieve. Though he'd never said it, she knew he felt as though he'd let his people down before. And now he would be their savior.

Her gaze swept over the crowd once more, and the pull on her heart dipped even lower. Still no Claire.

Something brushed Delilah's fingers, warm and soft. She jerked her attention to the touch of a hand, but it was Torra.

"Ye look more nervous than I feel," Torra whispered. Her fingers trembled against Delilah's.

"I'm looking for someone." Delilah let her gaze roam over the crowd once more. "And not finding her."

The clan cheered and clapped, and many faces turned toward her. She smiled at them. Kaid must have been unveiling her participation in the ruse to free Torra.

"Rhona?" Torra asked.

Delilah shook her head and almost replied with Claire's name, but then it occurred to her Torra had not ever met her. "A young girl with blonde hair."

Torra drew a shaky inhale. "There are so many people here." Her voice was a thread of a whisper.

Delilah turned her attention from the crowd and found Torra's face white and glistening with sweat. "Torra?"

"Too many people." She gave a long, slow blink.

Delilah grasped her hand and found Torra's palm wet and her fingers like ice.

"Take a deep breath," Delilah whispered. "You can do this. You're a laird in your own right. You're doing this for your people, to liberate them from your half brother, to give them a good life."

Torra's chest swelled in compliance and she nodded.

Kaid indicated Torra and she met the curious gazes with a look of such confidence, it left Delilah's skin prickled with pride.

"Who will come?" Kaid asked his people. "Who will come with me to aid Laird MacKenzie in taking her land back and fostering a peaceful allegiance with her and her clan?"

Man after man shouted their intentions to join with a sharp jab of their fists in the air.

Delilah almost sagged with relief. They had found Torra, helped pull her from the darkness she'd been buried in for too long, and gotten her to agree to claim her inheritance, and now Kaid had the full support of his clan.

It was all coming together, just as Kaid had intended from the beginning.

Regardless, unease nipped at Delilah's conscience.

Claire.

The very thought of the girl's name caught Delilah's heart in a heavy grip and dragged it to her stomach.

Delilah scanned the crowd once more, stopping at each waist-high face, and each blonde-topped head. A hand clasped Delilah's forearm.

"Ye did it," Torra said. "Ye and Kaid, ye did it. We're marching out the morning after next."

A small blonde girl darted between two men. Delilah straightened with hope and leaned to the right to follow the girl's path. But the child was wearing a green dress. Not blue. And without the lace bits on the sleeves.

"Ye still canna find her?" Torra asked. "The little girl with blonde hair?"

Delilah nodded. "I haven't seen her since this morning."

Kaid finished his speech, and the crowd roared with noise. Torra turned her gaze to the ground.

When the swell of cries dwindled, Torra finally lifted her gaze. "I saw a blonde girl with Nathaira—Rhona, as ye know her. She dinna look as though she wanted to go, but Nathaira was pulling her by the arm. Rough."

Delilah's heart pounded in her chest. If the clan continued to roar behind her, she no longer heard them. "Could you see what she was wearing?"

"She wore a blue dress."

The air sucked from Delilah's lungs.

"Was there anything else about the dress? Anything special?" she asked.

Torra tilted her head in thought and nodded. "Aye, she had a bit of lace trimmed on the sleeves. No' the hem, just the sleeves."

Delilah's body tingled with dread and the breath, the life, whooshed out of her body. "No."

Torra reached out for her. This time it was Torra keeping Delilah up and not vice versa.

"Do ye think it was her?" Torra asked.

"Yes." The word came out in a whimper.

Claire—abducted by Rhona. To be taken to the man who had brutally murdered so many. Delilah swallowed the thick emotion welling in her throat.

Kaid. She needed to speak with Kaid.

They needed to leave immediately.

They had to rescue Claire.

Chapter Thirty

Preparations for the clan's attack were underway.

Kaid strode into his solar and rummaged through several sheets of parchment. Neat rows of numbers reflected the stores of food they would have to bring, the number of weapons for his men, the assignment of each horse to those who didn't already have their own.

There was much to do in one short day prior to their departure. They would need to purchase many items while they traveled.

Now that Torra had agreed to take back the ownership of her people and ally with him, he did not want to risk her changing her mind. The longer this took, the greater the likelihood that Torra would go back on their agreement.

He checked the doorway for Lachlan, but found it empty. Impatience set Kaid's feet stalking across the room in a restless pace. He needed to speak to Lachlan, to finalize some of the finer details about the men who would be coming.

Kaid glanced out the window where the heavy cloak of night blanketed the quiet village. The festivities had finally quieted. The evening had slipped from him like water through a sieve. There was still so damn much to do.

Not that it mattered. This was what he'd been born to do. This was why he was laird of his people. After having left his clan starving for vengeance, he would finally deliver.

The light of a flickering candle hovered outside the door, pausing a moment before entering. But his visitor wasn't Lachlan.

"Delilah." He couldn't help but smile as he spoke her name.

She was a refreshing change to the all-consuming details of the impending attack.

She was a dream with her long honey-brown hair falling in gentle waves around her face and her dark eyes gazing at him imploringly.

A tear slipped down her cheek.

He straightened in surprise and caught her in his arms. "Delilah, what is it?"

"I haven't been able to find you." She clung to him, her fingers strapped around his arms like bands of iron.

Truth be told, he'd been so busy, he had only thought of coordinating his men and this attack. But then, Delilah wasn't a woman who needed coddling.

"I was speaking to the men who will join us." He carefully wiped the tear from her cheek and was relieved to find there weren't more. "What's wrong?"

"It's Claire." Delilah's voice broke. "She's with Rhona."

Kaid shook his head. "I dinna understand. How do ye know? And why would the lass go with Rhona?"

"Rhona took her." Another tear ran down Delilah's cheek. "I promised Claire I'd never let anything happen to her again. I let her be taken, Kaid. I wasn't there to save her."

Delilah, Kaid's strong, beautiful Delilah, broke down then into a fit of sobs. Kaid held her and let her cry against his chest. Beneath his tear-soaked leine, his own heart crushed against his throat.

Claire, with Rhona.

On their way to MacKenzie, that bastard.

His stomach twisted. What would they do with Claire?

Lachlan appeared in the doorway and cast them a wary glance.

"A moment," Kaid said to Lachlan, who nodded and slipped from view in an obvious show of offering privacy. He wouldn't go far, Kaid knew, not when they had so many important details to finalize.

Delilah lifted her head and looked toward the empty doorway.

"Go to the room," Kaid said softly. "I'll be in later this evening. We can discuss it more then."

"No," she gasped. "We have to leave now."

"It's no' possible. No' with so many men—"

"Kaid, they'll kill her." Tears brimmed in her eyes. "So many men cannot travel quickly." She spoke fast, as if doing so might possibly change his mind. "We could catch them. Stop Rhona before she gets any further."

"They're already too far, and we dinna know the path they took." He tried to keep his tone gentle, but her wounded expression hardened.

"You could have men go after them," she said.

"My men are needed to prepare for the march on Edirdovar. We'll save Claire when we get there." Kaid reached for her, but she jerked from his grasp.

"By then she might be dead. I thought you loved her," Delilah whispered. "I thought you loved us both."

If she'd meant those words to be a dagger in his heart, she'd hit her mark perfectly. He almost staggered beneath the pain of the blow.

Lachlan's dark head peered around the doorway, a reminder of the limited time and the growing list of important details to discuss.

Kaid staunched the ache emanating from deep within. He couldn't think of the way Claire smiled with such tenderness, nor how she held such trust when she regarded him with her large blue eyes, or the sweet warmth of her skinny-armed hugs.

Kaid swallowed the tightening sensation in his throat. "We can't always make decisions with our hearts, Delilah." It was said harshly, more as a reminder to himself than to her.

She lifted her head and regarded him with cold calculation. He felt as much a monster as MacKenzie. "Because a soft heart leads to poor decisions?" The words were like a splash of acid.

Lachlan crossed his arms and studied the hearth with such intensity, his discomfort was palpable.

Kaid caught Delilah's arms and met her gaze. "Go to the room, Delilah. We will speak of this no more tonight and will leave in the morning as planned."

In truth, he could not allow himself to focus on the topic anymore. He couldn't let his mind be clouded with the hurt of Claire's loss when he had so many lives at stake.

Delilah turned from the room without another word and stalked past Lachlan, who nodded in greeting. He glanced behind him and regarded Kaid. "Is something amiss, laird?"

Kaid shook his head. "No' anything we can do much about now." Then he tried as best he could to shove out the racing thoughts about Claire and Delilah. Being distracted would help no one.

He had a war to plan.

• • •

Delilah's throat burned with the swell of a rising scream. She wanted to let it loose until her throat bled. Maybe the searing cry would staunch the direct flow of damage to her heart.

Kaid had told her to go his chamber.

Kaid had clearly forgotten who she was.

She was no damn guard to be ordered about. The soles of her shoes clacked hard against the flagstones, the sound echoing against the cold walls and then fading into the open night air as she stepped outside.

A flash of a blade reflected a glint of moonlight in a shadowed corner of the courtyard.

Sylvi—always finding a place to practice. It was exactly what Delilah had hoped for. Her body flared with energy. She wanted to let her anger explode out of her, unleashed on an opponent.

Soundless, she hurried over the uneven cobblestones to where only the subtle swish of a blade cutting through the air could be heard.

"What are you doing here?" Sylvi's hard voice sounded from the shadows.

Delilah stepped into the darkness, and her eyes immediately adjusted to the absence of the moon's wide-faced glow. Without a word, she picked up a discarded staff from where it lay on the ground. Sylvi never trained without several weapons at her disposal.

Delilah lifted the staff and whipped it behind her back before stopping it directly in front of her in a silent challenge. Her body braced for impact, her knees bent and her muscles tensed to strike.

Sylvi's mouth curled into a smirk. "I haven't had a good spar since I arrived at Killearnan."

Instead of replying, Delilah pushed the force of her frustration and rage into the hearty swing of the staff, directly toward Sylvi's legs. Sylvi leapt a scant second before the knobby wood head would have connected with her knees. She landed silent as a cat and swept the blade toward Delilah.

The attack was slow and easily avoided. Sylvi no doubt did this on purpose.

"Don't go easy on me," Delilah said through clenched teeth. "Not tonight." She whipped her staff toward Sylvi's head, but only succeeded in catching the end of one pale blonde braid.

Sylvi rolled on the ground and popped up in front of Delilah with a grin. "I take it someone made you angry."

Delilah held her staff with both hands and shoved it so hard against Sylvi's chest, the other woman grunted.

Sylvi held fast to the staff and pulled it from Delilah's grasp. "It would appear as much," Sylvi answered her own question and tossed her sword to the cobblestones with a metallic clatter. "Switch weapons with me and talk before you kill us both."

Delilah snatched up the blade and adjusted her hold on the hilt. The wound leather there was still warm from Sylvi's grip.

"Is this about the little girl?" she asked. "Claire?"

Delilah swung the blade, and a growl snarled from between her clenched teeth. Sylvi snapped the staff up in time to keep the blunted edge from connecting with her skull.

"How do you know about her?" Delilah demanded. Her body was alight with the burn of anger and vengeance. Each attack, each block, each flex of her muscles gave way to the comfort only spent energy could provide.

"I see more than you realize." Sylvi thrust the staff toward her, but Delilah knocked it away. "And I know she's been taken."

Delilah thought back to the hallway where she first saw Claire. Sylvi must have been lurking in the shadows. How very like Sylvi to witness such an intimate moment and not reveal herself.

"Did you see what happened when I asked Kaid if we could leave now to save her?" A fresh wave of molten fury rushed through Delilah's veins. She waited for Sylvi's slight pull back on the weapon in preparation to attack before Delilah lunged into her.

Delilah braced Sylvi's legs with her own then shoved hard at Sylvi's torso. The blonde woman went down with whuff of air.

"He said no, didn't he?" Sylvi stuck her arm up in silent request for friendly aid.

Delilah gripped the proffered forearm and hauled Sylvi to her feet in a smooth heft. "Did you see that too?" Delilah couldn't keep the irritation from her voice.

"No." Sylvi smirked. "But he's a leader on the cusp of war, Delilah. Even if Claire were his own daughter and he had no one else left in the world, he would not sacrifice the lives of his people by departing prematurely."

Delilah's cheeks went hot with the certainty in Sylvi's tone. "Even if there's a child in danger?"

Sylvi stepped back and eyed Delilah. "Do you know which path she took? Which towns she'll stop through?"

"No," Delilah said. "But we know where they'll end up."

"At a highly defended castle over two days' journey from here?" Sylvi shook her head as if explaining common sense to someone daft. "With either no army or an ill-prepared one?"

Sylvi swept the staff toward Delilah's legs. Delilah stumbled backward. "Yes," she admitted sheepishly.

When she caught her footing, she kept her knees slightly bent, ducked the blow of Sylvi's thrust and rose with the blade pressed to Sylvi's throat. "And what would you do if you knew someone you loved were to be harmed?" she panted.

The blade of the sword pressed to the black silk ribbon tied to

Sylvi's throat, so close it brought the thin silk down just enough to reveal the ragged pink skin of a raw scar.

It wasn't until she saw the reminder of what Sylvi had been through that Delilah realized what she'd said, what she'd done. The pulse at Sylvi's throat leapt hard and fast.

Delilah lowered the blade.

Sylvi took a long, slow breath in and then carefully hissed it free. Sweat shone at her brow. Delilah knew it was not from their exertion.

Three years ago, Sylvi would have had Delilah on the ground and bleeding for having touched her neck. After being the sole survivor of her family's massacre, Sylvi was tender about the reminder. The scar along her neck where someone tried to have her join them in death wasn't without its own level of sensitivity.

Sylvi regarded Delilah with her cold, pale stare. "I would do anything to save them. Even if it meant leaving on my own." She threw down the staff. It landed silently on a cloth bag lying against the side of the castle wall.

Delilah staggered back. She'd been so upset over Kaid declining to leave early, she hadn't even considered the option of going alone. Perhaps because she didn't want to leave without Kaid.

Not again.

And yet, if it would save Claire...

Sylvi looked beyond Delilah's shoulder. "But before you decide to go out on your own, you may want to see what he says about that." With a smirk, Sylvi strolled out of the shadows, toward the castle.

Delilah winced inwardly. She knew who was behind her before she turned. Yet still she allowed herself to spin on her heel and peer into the darkness for the familiarity of his face.

True to her suspicions, it was Kaid.

And she couldn't help but wonder exactly how much of their conversation he'd overheard.

Chapter Thirty-One

"Were ye considering leaving without me?" Kaid asked.

Delilah stared at him for a moment and took in how the moonlight fell behind him, leaving a white glow surrounding his broad shoulders. He was strong, powerful, handsome.

She was still angry with him.

"How long have you been standing there?" The demanding tone might have sounded a bit petulant, but at that point, she was so frustrated, so wounded, she didn't care.

"Long enough to hear Sylvi's suggestion and familiar enough with ye to recognize the expression on yer face." He strode forward, confident as always.

A cold breeze blew off Loch Assynt and carried his scent toward her. She wanted to close her eyes and remember all the caresses, all the love.

Instead she kept her eyes open and her wits about her.

He bent and grabbed the staff Sylvi had dropped. "Will ye spar with me?" he asked.

Delilah lifted her brows.

He knocked the tip of the staff against the sword, which she'd let dip to the ground. The weapons connected with a hollow clunk.

"I won't go easy on you," she warned.

Kaid watched her earnestly with his vivid blue gaze. "I wouldna expect anything less."

Delilah put space between them. "Which weapon do you want?" She indicated Sylvi's impressive stash.

Kaid considered the staff in his hands before releasing it and letting it whack onto the hard ground. "No weapons."

Delilah tossed her sword to the pile of weapons. "Very well."

"I canna have ye killing me out of anger." His jest came out flat.

Delilah crouched low. "I don't need a weapon to kill you."

Before he could reply, she leapt toward him and punched with her left fist.

Blocked.

Then her right.

Blocked.

And threw up her left arm to stop a blow he attempted to land.

Kaid reached forward and caught her around the waist. "I understand ye're angry with me." He spoke into her ear, and the delicate hairs at the back of her neck stirred.

Delilah suppressed the urge to give in to a delicious shiver. "I am." Her elbow came back and caught him in the ribs.

He released her, and she spun around. Her skirt swirled about her legs before twisting back the other direction and swinging against her ankles.

"Angry enough to leave for Edirdovar?" He moved to grab her waist once more.

This time she ducked low and met him halfway into his attack. She gripped his hips and tried to sweep his feet from under him. To no avail. The man stayed stubbornly upright.

She rose and met his gaze. "Angry enough to leave without you."

He took advantage of her moment of self-righteousness by grabbing her shoulders and knocking her knees forward so they gave. He'd done to her exactly what she'd intended to do to him.

No sooner had Delilah's back hit the ground than Kaid was on top of her, his arms braced on either side of her head. Though she was already warm from their sparring, she found the additional heat he provided rather pleasant.

Even if she didn't want to.

"Ye think I dinna love Claire." The solemn way he searched her gaze told her how much of what she'd said wounded him.

"She could die, Kaid." Tears pricked Delilah's eyes again, threatening a new wash of tears. "I'll never forgive myself if she dies, alone and with no one to comfort her."

The image rose in her mind of Claire in that massive castle, in the dungeon, cold and alone and waiting for death. No, waiting for Delilah to save her from an awful fate.

Waiting as Delilah did not come. As Delilah failed her.

Kaid eased off her and pulled her to a sitting position. He did not resume their battle. Instead, he wrapped his arms around her and held her.

"She has no one to comfort her," Delilah said against the solid strength of his chest.

"They have her for a reason, lass." Kaid spoke against the top of her head and pressed a kiss to her hair. "They willna kill her. They wouldna take a child just to kill her. Rhona knows we love the lass and means to use her to their advantage."

Delilah shook her head. His words were little comfort.

Kaid eased Delilah away and captured her chin between his thumb and forefinger. "I love that lass as if she were our own flesh and blood," he said. "And I love ye as if ye were my wife."

Delilah drank deep a long inhale of air. The coolness of it eased some of the fire burning within her.

"When we return from Edirdovar with Claire safely with us once more, I want us to take her on as our own." He rubbed her shoulders. The firm touch of his palms skimming her skin was reassuring. "And I want ye to be my wife."

"Your wife?" she asked dumbly.

He gave her the warm, affectionate smile she loved. "Aye, my wife. I love ye, Delilah. Ye helped bring the MacLeods to safety. I want ye to be there with me to enjoy it."

His words were the most beautiful ones she'd ever heard in all her life. She'd found someone who made her feel special, important, so much more than just another mouth to feed. Joy lit through her, and she wondered how she could have been so angry only moments ago.

"I would love to be your wife," she said softly. "And nothing would bring me greater joy than having Claire as our own child."

"Then when this is done, both shall come to be." Kaid caressed her cheek. "I love ye, my beautiful Delilah."

"And I love you, Kaid." Delilah's soul nearly burst at the pleasure of voicing the words she'd locked for too long in her heart.

Sylvi had been wrong about Kaid. He was a good man, an honest one who would not lie about matters of the heart.

And yet something still niggled at the border of her conscience. Their life together would begin when the war ended.

But what if the war did not end in their favor?

• • •

While the preparation for their departure made Kaid's night a long one, his clan had managed to leave the following morning and travel an uneventful two and a half days to Killearnan.

With every warrior they could spare, the party was too large to travel with haste. They'd stopped far enough on the outskirts of the town so as not to not draw any unwanted attention.

Together Kaid and Delilah began the trek toward an unnamed inn in the village. Donnan and Leasa were supposed to meet them there. Kaid's heart thumped a little harder at the prospect of their discovery.

"Do you think they found many of the MacKenzies?" Delilah asked.

Kaid kept his gaze fixed on the inn. "I was wondering as much myself."

Delilah leaned forward in her saddle. "Do you see their horses tied somewhere else?"

Kaid looked toward the same open stable as she. No horses but Sylvi's and Percy's. He glanced around the surrounding area to no avail. "I don't."

Delilah settled back in her saddle with the same resigned silence she'd maintained for most of the trip. She smiled when she caught him staring at her and tried to pretend all was well. Kaid knew better.

The silence pressed in on them the closer they drew to the inn.

"Torra seems to be traveling better." Kaid was as desperate to break the quiet as he was to not think of what the empty inn meant.

Delilah nodded in agreement. "She's not hugging her body to her horse as she did leaving here last."

"Has she been well?" Kaid asked.

There was a pause before Delilah answered. "She's scared."

Kaid nodded. "Will she still be able to continue on?"

They stopped their horses and swung down from them. "She will." There was enough confidence in her tone to ease Kaid's worry.

At least until she cast him an anxious look before they pushed through the wooden door of the inn. Sylvi and Percy were waiting for them along with the strange woman he'd met before, the one with the diamond winking between her brows. Isabel, he believed her name was. Several bags lay packed and ready at their sides.

"Where are Donnan and Leasa?" he asked.

"They came only once." Isabel gave him an apologetic shrug. "They were thus far unsuccessful."

Kaid tried to quash the rising swell of disappointment.

Attacking a defensible castle. Without a massive army behind him, it would be all the more difficult.

"Are we to wait for them?" Delilah asked.

"No." Kaid replied at the same time Sylvi shook her head. "MacKenzie already knows we're coming. The longer we wait, the more time he has to prepare."

"Do you have enough men?" Isabel asked Kaid.

He wished he could give them an answer which would set their mind at ease, but he could not.

"Without the additional men we assumed we'd have," he confessed, "we dinna have as many as MacKenzie. But his are paid men, and paid men are easy to drive from battle. There is only so much coin one is willing to stake their lives on."

Delilah stepped to his side, her back proud and straight. "Even without the MacKenzies, I will still fight."

Sylvi secured a sword belt around her hips. "Liv is still within the walls of the keep. I will no more let her remain in the hell you endured than I will allow you to go into battle without me at your side."

She took her place beside Delilah and put a hand on her shoulder.

Isabel gave a grin that could only be described as feral, with sharp white teeth behind the brilliant red of her lips. "I cannot stand the thought of a man like MacKenzie having control of a woman like Elizabeth. I will fight."

Percy remained with her head bowed beneath the hood of her cloak. She never took it off except when she was in the room with Torra, Kaid noticed.

"I will go, but will remain in the back." She slowly hefted a bag and a curious clacking sounded from its depths. "I have already risked being seen by so many."

They were a curious lot of women, but a brave one—he'd give them that.

After buying the innkeeper's silence with considerable coin, the five of them headed once more to where the MacLeods were camped.

Kaid was quiet on the short ride there, his mood depressed. While his men were only slightly more numerous than what he estimated MacKenzie had, they were not nearly enough to take a castle. His heart hammered with the threat of the familiar fear he thought he'd finally left behind.

The MacLeods had lost so much. So many had been killed.

So many more would be killed.

And it would be at his lead again.

He'd failed them once before.

Would he fail them again?

Something brushed his leg. He glanced up and found Delilah at his side.

"We will win," she said quietly. "And we will save Claire."

He nodded. They would need to win. They would not let Claire down.

He could not let anyone down.

Those words repeated in his mind until the beat of his heart steadied to match the rhythm of his chant.

"What is that?" Sylvi pointed in the distance to where Kaid had left his people camped.

Before Kaid could reply, he saw she was not indicating the MacLeods, but a mass of men on horseback racing toward the camp at incredible speed.

Was MacKenzie ambushing them before they could even get to Edirdovar?

As if sensing the urgency, Kaid's horse charged forward. "Go," he bellowed into the rush of wind.

The women quickened their pace. Though they rode with enough speed to give the wind chase, still they were not quick enough.

The large riding party met his people before he could arrive to do anything to prevent it.

Chapter Thirty-Two

It was not a battle waiting for Kaid, and for that he was thankful.

The men, all dressed in the earthy green tartan of the MacKenzie and surrounding clans, were off their horses by the time Kaid and the women arrived.

"Is this the MacLeod clan?" a tall man with red hair asked.

Kaid stood at the head of his people, his body tense. "It is."

"And ye have our rightful laird?" the man asked.

Kaid turned over his shoulder to find Torra watching. "Aye," Kaid answered. "We do. And we mean to help her into her rightful place. Is it yer intention to offer yer allegiance?"

The man bowed his head. "Aye, all of us mean to see her take her proper place as laird once more."

Kaid beckoned Torra toward him with a subtle nod. She drew a deep breath and approached with measured steps until she stood before the man.

He immediately dropped to his knees in the lush grass, as did the hundreds of men behind him.

It was a sight to behold, so many highlanders bent on reverent knee before the laird too long denied to them. Kaid's heart swelled for Torra, and for the people she would lead.

But there was more than just pride in his chest.

There was hope.

He looked down beside him, where Delilah watched with tears shimmering in her eyes.

And there was love.

He held her waist and together they watched the red-haired man lift his head.

"Yer father, the former laird of the MacKenzies, was a good man," the man said. "He raised ye with a good heart. When he died and ye disappeared, we thought ye'd been killed."

"I'm sorry." Torra placed a hand under his chin.

"I'm only sorry for the ten years we spent without ye." The man's voice carried with the force of his passion, and Kaid knew he spoke for all to hear. "The ten years of murder, rape, and theft brought on by a man no' deserving of the title of laird. I, Callum MacKenzie, will fight until my final breath to see ye restored as the rightful laird of the MacKenzies."

He took her hand in his and pressed a fierce kiss to her knuckles.

The MacLeods' applause behind Kaid thundered through his soul. They too felt hope and victory singing through their veins.

Though the process took time, Kaid waited until every man had sworn fealty to Torra. By the time they were done, the sun had begun to sink into the jagged distant hills behind them and left the afternoon light rich with red and golden orange.

It glinted behind Torra, framing her in the same gilded light as the painted figures he'd seen of the Virgin Mary, as if God himself ordained her as laird to her people.

"I think it best we battle at night," Delilah said. "The longer we stay here, the more likely Seumas MacKenzie will find us. After all, they did."

She nodded toward the MacKenzie clan.

Callum looked in their direction, having obviously overheard them. "Aye, we heard from other travelers which way ye'd passed. If the bastard has any spies about, they most likely know already."

Kaid nodded. "They willna expect us during the night." His chest swelled with pride at Delilah being his. Not just his lover now, but soon to be his wife. Surely there was no finer wife to be had. No woman more talented, more intelligent, more exquisitely beautiful.

Two riders appeared in the distance, coming from the direction of the inn.

"The man and woman who found ye," Kaid said to Callum. "Where are they?"

"They were going to the inn to meet ye," Callum replied. "Have ye gone by already?"

"Aye, but they werena there." Kaid pointed toward the riders. "But it looks as though they're still arriving in time for the fun."

Within several minutes the two riders arrived together. The first slipped from his horse easily and managed to catch the second when she tumbled from hers.

Aye, definitely Donnan and Leasa.

"Start preparing yer men for battle," Kaid said to Callum. "We ride out within the hour, before we lose the last of the light."

"Ready?" Delilah asked.

"Aye," Kaid replied. "It's time to put Torra back in power." He caught her hands in his. "And we'll save our Claire."

• • •

Many lives were at stake, but it was the image of a child which sent energy flaring through Delilah, powerful enough to guarantee victory no matter the foe.

She would save Claire, even if she did so at the expense of her own life.

Their large group moved through the forest toward Edirdovar. The red stonework could be seen above the treetops, growing larger and larger as they closed in on their target.

While Sylvi led the other female spies, Delilah stayed by Kaid's side per his insistence.

She knew if it were up to him, she would not have come.

She also knew he realized she would never allow herself to remain behind.

The shush of an arrow being shot was as loud in the silence as a musket ball being fired. Another arrow cut through the air and thunked into the tree beside Torra's head. One arrow pinned the other into the thick bark by its middle.

An impossible shot.

A shot only one woman would be able to make.

Delilah turned to find Percy's hooded form sliding another arrow from her back and crouching low in the brush.

A hand caught Delilah's, warm and strong—Kaid.

"It's beginning," he muttered. He searched her face with his determined gaze. "Be safe, my love." He caught her face in his large hands and pressed a hard kiss to her lips, so fierce the scratch of his whiskers ground against her chin.

"I love you," she whispered against his lips.

"And I ye," he growled.

Then he turned from her and loosed his war cry.

Both MacKenzie and MacLeod warriors roared their own cries, the shouts blending together.

Delilah slipped from Kaid's side to join Sylvi and the other women, who continued onward in stealthy silence with only the hiss of Percy's arrows. They moved quickly and easily in their black leines and men's trews. While the women could fight in gowns, battle required more liberating garments.

The guards surrounding the castle grounds were quickly and easily dispatched. There weren't many.

But MacKenzie knew they were coming. No doubt almost all of his guards were stationed within the walls of Edirdovar, ready to defend the castle.

Little did they know how easy their walls could be breached.

The edge of the forest met them, and beyond it stood their prize. The redstone castle of Edirdovar.

Kaid stepped forward, into the line of sight.

Figures along the top of the castle drew back their bows and Delilah's chest tightened.

"Torra MacKenzie is the rightful ruler of this castle." Kaid's voice rang clear and confident in the thin night air. "If ye willna relinquish Edirdovar to her, we will take it by force to seat her in her rightful place."

A tall figure appeared at the high edge of the castle, his arms folded behind his back with an arrogance only Seumas MacKenzie could wield. "I welcome ye to try."

He turned to a man on his right, who held an arrow nocked. "Attack."

The archer hesitated. Negotiations prior to battle were sacred, even among paid men.

"Attack." The word came louder, and this time the archer did not hesitate. But Kaid had already melted back into the shadows of the forest with the rest of the force. The arrow shot through the air and landed soundly into the rich soil, the head sunk almost midway to the shaft in the wet earth.

The MacLeod and MacKenzie archers took aim and fired along with Percy. Her confirmed hits were easier to spot. The men she shot did not pitch over the castle, dead or soon to be—they were merely hit in the arm, the hand, disabling them from attacking further without being lethal.

Delilah adjusted her grip on the hilt of her sword, more out of anxious anticipation than necessity. Once they breached the castle walls, she could find Claire.

A glow of light flared to Delilah's left, and her heartbeat quickened.

It was time.

The pungent odor of sulfur tainted the air, followed by the hiss of a flame catching. Delilah looked to the left, where Isabel's exotically painted face was lit in a brilliant wash of fire.

Cupped in her palm was the thick round pot filled with gunpowder and plugged with wax. The string jutting from the milky center fizzled and smoked. Isabel grinned and rolled the pot over the cobblestone walkway to the massive wooden door barring their entrance into the castle.

The flame swirled and danced during the pot's path toward its destination while the gritty warbling sound of clay on stone captured everyone's attention. The pot bumped harmlessly into the door and remained there for a moment before the flame met the wax.

The flame went out.

A disappointing fraction of a second sucked at Delilah's spirit before the pot exploded and left fine dust raining down where it had once been.

While the door still stood, a majority of the bottom portion was gone and a large crack had appeared at its center.

One more would do it.

And it was already rolling toward its destination. This one exploded with more expediency than the first, and with far greater impact. Fragments of the door flew into the air and landed on the stone ground with hearty clunks.

Kaid's men cried out once more and together they rushed toward the open entrance while the MacLeod and MacKenzie archers covered their attack. Delilah let herself be taken with the rush of bodies along with Sylvi.

Everyone caught at the entrance for the briefest of moments, bodies all tangled against one another in haste to get in, until one person pushed free and made room for the next.

The excitement and energy crackled amid the chaos and left Delilah's pulse thrumming in her ears until all she could hear was the pounding of her heart and the shouts of men.

She shouldered her way into the castle. The barren hall greeted her with memories she did not welcome.

She was finally inside the castle.

Chapter Thirty-Three

Delilah ran down the first hallway where she knew the doorway to the dungeon would be. Despite her haste, she was aware of every sound, every movement, her body on high alert for any kind of danger.

She didn't want to descend to the dungeon any more than she wanted to be in the castle. But if Claire was down there...

Delilah shuddered at the thought of the girl huddled in the dark, frightened and alone. Delilah's arms ached for the sweet weight of the child in her arms where she could be safe.

Delilah pushed on the door to the dungeon. A hearty clack met her ears.

Locked.

She dropped to her knees and pulled the pick from her hair. Her fingers trembled.

She drew in a deep breath and slowly let it out in an attempt to calm herself. The shaking stilled enough to allow her to slip the pick into the gaping lock.

Footsteps sounded to her right, heavy and rapid. She turned to the sound to find one of the MacKenzie's paid mercenaries charging toward her. She leapt to her feet and swept her sword free.

She'd battled men many times, but usually she had a pill to slip them once they were unconscious, to keep them sleeping for a while. But none of the women had any this time.

This was no mission of discretion—this was battle. There would be death.

It was information they all knew going into it, and yet now Delilah's conviction faltered.

"I don't want to kill you," Delilah said. "If you leave now, you can do so with your life."

The man smirked. "And what if I want to kill ye?"

He didn't give her a chance to reply, but swung out at her with the huge war axe he clutched between his meaty fists.

Delilah ducked and lunged toward him. Not only did she fail to knock him down, but running into him was like hitting a solid tree trunk. The breath whooshed out of her, and she was knocked backward, momentarily stunned. He swiped at her, but she dropped into a ball and rolled between his spread legs.

Before he could lumber around, she shoved her sword forward with a grunt of exertion. It pushed through his body with far more ease than she could ever have imagined.

He roared, and the axe slipped from his grip, landing with a metallic clunk before he sagged to his knees and pitched forward.

All the strength sapped suddenly from Delilah's body. She stared down at the large man who had meant to kill her.

The man she had killed.

Footsteps sounded behind her, and her body launched into action before her mind could catch up with what she was doing. She pulled at her sword to free it, but found the blade stuck.

The hairs on the back of her neck stood on end, and she turned quickly to face her new opponent. A fist punched the side of her arm with enough force to leave it numb for a brief moment.

The man was dark-haired and short, his face set in a grimace of concentration. Energy roared through Delilah and her blade pulled free with a sickening wet sound. She did not hesitate this time.

The man swept his dagger at her, the blade still red with the blood of his previous victim. Delilah bent low to evade the hit and came up with her sword aimed at his heart. Which was exactly where the blade pierced.

Everything went still save the frenzied hammering of her heart. She pulled her blade free, this time with learned strength, and sagged against the stone wall. It was cold against the heat of her back. Her hard breathing filled the narrow hall, panting and wild.

She was wasting time.

She knelt at the door once more and squeezed her fingers around the pick where it still jutted from the lock. This time she could not still her fingers from shaking.

Her arm was tired where it'd been hit. It was an exhausted, bone-deep ache, and the limb didn't seem to work properly as a result. The man had punched her harder than she thought.

The lock popped free, and she pushed the door open. The wet, dank air slammed into her, bringing back memories of fear and uncertainty.

It was dark below. Too dark to see.

Her skin prickled, and she rubbed the sore spot on her arm. Something wet met her fingertips.

She pulled her hand back in horror and stared down at the brilliant smear of blood on her fingers. Confusion rocked her brain. Had the men bled on her? When had they had a chance to?

Pain penetrated her muddled thoughts, a deep, burning hurt spiraling out from her arm where she'd been hit and out through her whole body. With great trepidation she looked down at her arm and found a gaping slash there.

Her sword arm.

Damn.

Keeping her ears pricked for the sound of any more men heading toward her, she ripped free a section of her shirt and tied it over the wound, as she'd seen Percy do. It was an awkward bandage, and she had to use her teeth to secure the binding, but it was done.

Fortunately, Sylvi had insisted they all learn to train with both arms. While Delilah's left had never been as strong as her right, she was at least still capable.

She lifted the weight of her sword into her left hand and tried to ignore how unwieldy and foreign it seemed. Then she plunged into the uncertain darkness in search of Claire.

• • •

Kaid stopped and strained to listen for the sound which had stopped him dead in his tracks.

It sounded again: a high-pitched cry.

A child.

Kaid's heartbeat sped. He turned in the direction of the sound, where a long hallway led to a large closed door banded with metal.

Without hesitation, he sped toward it and kicked it open. It hadn't been locked and flew open so hard it slammed against the stone wall with a reverberating smack.

Rhona stood toward the rear of the room with Claire pinned into place in front of her by the shoulders and a woman beside her who looked like a rumpled version of Delilah whose hands were bound by rope. A woman he'd seen before.

Elizabeth—the *real* Elizabeth.

Claire's reddened eyes lit up when she saw him. His throat grew tight. She tried to run toward him, but Rhona kept her hands clutched at Claire's slender shoulders.

The girl's blonde hair fell in messy tangles around a dirty face, but aside from that, she looked well enough.

"Well, if it isn't the failing laird of the MacLeods," Rhona said with a sneer. "How are yer nightmares?"

Kaid steeled himself against her words. He'd worried too often about how he'd failed his people. He wasn't failing them now, though. With Delilah's help, he'd saved Torra and banded together the MacKenzies and the MacLeods for peace.

He had not failed.

"I dinna have them anymore once I found out ye were poisoning me." He didn't attack, but he didn't lower his blade either.

"It was that woman." She spit out the word "woman" as if it were bitter. "The one ye used to trick Seumas, along with this one." She jerked her head toward Elizabeth.

"Ye were poisoning me." Kaid's hand tightened around the hilt of his blade. "We took ye in when ye needed the help of a clan."

Rhona shook her head and rolled her eyes heavenward. "Ye daft fool. I came to spy on ye to see if we could take Ardvreck. Ye've more coin than ye need and Seumas needed some to secure his marriage."

Kaid let his disgust show. "I suppose yer foolish grandson spent everything on men paid to fight?"

"An investment," Rhona said. "And a means of seeking revenge from ye killing his ma. My *daughter*." She leaned forward, and Claire gave a whimper, ducking low as if she could free her shoulders from Rhona's clutch.

"Leave the girl out of this, Rhona," he snarled. "We tried to help yer daughter—"

"Ye let her die." The accusation rasped from Rhona's throat. "It's because of ye she never wed Seumas's da before Seumas was born. It's yer fault he was a bastard."

"She was ill." Kaid still remembered when the woman had been brought to Ardvreck Castle, pale and soaked in sweat. She remained that way for two weeks after giving birth before she finally died. The healer at the time had only just been able to save the baby. "We couldna help her, but were at least able to save Seumas. We told Laird MacKenzie several times of her condition, but he never came."

"Lies," Rhona hissed. She pulled a blade from her waist and held it to Claire's throat before the girl could wriggle away. "I wanted to wait for that woman to be here before I did this. So ye'd both ken the pain of loss as I did."

Kaid tensed and weighed her words for a bluff. If she were being honest, he could lose Claire. If she were lying, he would be killing an old woman.

"Ye couldna protect yer father or yer people," she said. "No' when ye mysteriously had the sense knocked from ye." She gave him a cruel grin, one which told him exactly who had struck him on the head that day. "And ye canna save the girl."

"I'll kill ye." Kaid stepped closer.

Aye, she was an old woman. But she'd been responsible for the deaths of too many of his men. He'd be damned if he let her cause Claire's also.

"It doesna matter." She gripped Claire's hair and jerked her head back so the translucent skin of her fragile neck was exposed.

A scream strangled from the girl, and Kaid flew forward. Before he could reach her, Elizabeth lunged at the old woman, grabbed her blade, and jerked it upward into Rhona's narrow chest. She blinked in surprise as red seeped in a glistening pool on her purple cloak.

Claire bowed her head free of the clutched hand and met Kaid's gaze with wide eyes. "Laird!"

A warning rang out in the back of Kaid's mind, but it was too late. Fire split through him and the bloody point of a blade sprouted from his chest.

As soon as the sword was in him, it pulled free. Kaid stared down at the gash, disbelief churning in his head before his legs failed to support him. He staggered to the floor, and the wash of his own blood spread hot and wet beneath his body.

A scream filled Kaid's ears and raked over his brain until his nerves were raw from it.

MacKenzie stepped over him, and the screaming pitched to a wild frenzy, something no longer human, but an animalistic, primal fear.

He grabbed Elizabeth by the throat.

Kaid pushed with all his might and lifted himself onto one arm. Despite his efforts, his hand slipped in the blood, and he crashed to the floor in another spray of agony so powerful it left spots of white pulsing in his vision.

Claire grasped MacKenzie's arm, but he knocked her out of his way. She flew across the room and landed with a hard smack of her head against the edge of a table.

She fell still.

Kaid gave a wounded groan and tried to rise once more. Daggers of pain shot through him, and his chest felt as though a boulder sat atop it.

The scream cut short.

Kaid jerked his attention to where MacKenzie had held Elizabeth, where she now lay crumpled on the floor in a pool of blood large enough to rival Kaid's.

MacKenzie turned from Elizabeth and strode to the other side of the room.

Toward Claire.

Kaid's heart pumped harder. He gritted his teeth against the ache and rose a foot, two feet. The pressure on the wound eased.

"No," he ground out.

MacKenzie stopped midstride and turned to Kaid. "Still alive?" Two short steps brought him in front of Kaid. "Then I'll let ye watch, and kill ye later after I've caught yer woman."

He pulled his leg back and slammed it into Kaid's back.

The impact was indescribably excruciating, a ball of white-hot blistering pain curling in on itself until it robbed him of breath and thought. Kaid collapsed onto the floor, helpless as a babe.

MacKenzie turned back to where Claire lay still on the ground.

"You will die a thousand deaths before you touch that girl." The threat was spoken with the vehemence of a mother protecting her child.

Kaid's heart rose in his throat in a mix of relief and indescribable fear.

Delilah had arrived.

And he could not help.

Chapter Thirty-Four

Delilah's footsteps were quiet on the floor, but Kaid sensed her nearing. Her sharp gasp told him she'd seen him.

"Have you killed him?" she asked in a hollow tone.

Kaid tried to speak, but only a low groan sounded in his throat.

"Kaid." Her voice caught.

He strained to look up. She stood over Claire with her sword held in her left hand. Her right arm shone with fresh blood.

She was injured.

Kaid tried to rise, but his body was still frozen with the stunning agony of MacKenzie's kick to his wound.

"Save...Claire." He croaked out the two words with all the concentration he could muster.

The difficult struggle had been worthwhile. A look of determination settled over Delilah's face, and she lowered into a tensed fighting position.

Move, damn it.

Sweat prickled at his brow with the attempt to rise. His body trembled. To no avail.

Kaid watched helplessly as MacKenzie swung his sword toward Delilah and she blocked it.

If Kaid could move, just several feet, he could attack MacKenzie from behind. He could kill the bastard.

Delilah blocked the next blow and struck out with her own, her left attack not as powerful or fluid as her right.

MacKenzie easily evaded her.

She would need all the power she could get, or she wouldn't survive.

His beautiful, incredible Delilah. She would do anything to protect Claire. Sacrifice anything.

Even her life.

The idea of losing her made the ache of his wound seem nothing in comparison to the powerful hurt in his chest.

Move, damn it.

• • •

Delilah kept her gaze fixed on MacKenzie's cold, handsome face. His eyes were dark and empty. The eyes of a predator, completely oblivious to the blood soaking the room and the bodies strewn about.

Rhona with her chest glistening, Elizabeth bent over like a discarded doll thrown in a corner, Kaid…

Delilah's throat drew tight while Kaid struggled with injured movements to rise.

She wanted to tell him to be still, that she would be there soon.

But she looked into the dead, predator eyes fixed on her and knew this could very well be the last day she lived.

Seumas moved to her right, but she did not relinquish her position in front of Claire. He shifted left, and still she did not move.

In a smooth lunge, he jabbed his sword toward her. Delilah brought her blade down hard and swiped the dangerous tip of his weapon from where it'd been aimed at her heart. The muscles of her left arm burned with exertion.

She would be able to keep up the energy only so long. A shiver of anticipation squeezed down her spine.

She knew what would happen when she could hold it no longer.

A moan sounded behind Delilah. Claire was coming to.

"Close your eyes, Claire," Delilah said in as soothing a voice as she could.

After all the girl had been through, Delilah could not bear her to witness the carnage of the room.

MacKenzie smirked and swiped his blade in an arc toward Delilah's torso. It whistled in the air with its powerful speed, but she leapt back in time to avoid the strike.

She had to mind her feet when she landed to avoid stepping on Claire. Still, the girl flinched on the ground.

Delilah chanced a glance at the nearby open doorway. If Delilah could get Claire to leave, perhaps the girl could still live even if Delilah fell.

"Keep your eyes closed and crawl forward, Claire," Delilah said.

The girl started to cry. MacKenzie growled and swept his sword to the right.

Block.

He attacked from the left.

Block.

Delilah's left arm screamed in agony.

"Keep crawling." Delilah's throat ached with the threat of tears, but she kept her voice strong. For Claire's sake.

MacKenzie snarled his frustration and redoubled his energy, his slashing attacks so vicious, Delilah had no choice but to step backward with each strike. Her arm trembled, and she knew her strikes were lacking the power they'd possessed only moments before.

The rustle of fabric was the only indication she had that Claire obeyed. Surely she was close enough to the door now.

Delilah's blade drooped. It was only for a moment, but MacKenzie saw it and thrust his sword at her. She jerked her own weapon upward to defend herself and made it by only a hair of a second. Even as his knocked blade passed over her body, the tip raked against her waist and left a narrow line of red blooming beneath the torn fabric.

She would not be able to last much longer.

"Stand up and look only forward," Delilah said to Claire.

"But—"

"Do it," Delilah hissed. "And run!"

She lunged forward, throwing her body into MacKenzie and attacking with every last bit of energy she had. Her sword thrust until it was knocked from her limp grasp and clattered away, out of her reach.

She clawed and spat and bit, all in a blind fury of sheer desperation, lashing out like an animal caught in a trap.

Like a lioness protecting her cub.

Something cold and sharp bit into her hip. She shoved aside the discomfort and raked her nails over MacKenzie's face.

He howled in agony. His bleeding face went purple with rage. He grabbed her by the shoulders and threw her to the ground with such force, she could not catch herself.

She lay on the floor, exhausted and bleeding, thinking how very much like Elizabeth she must look.

Poor Elizabeth, whom she had not been able to save. The girl whose father had loved her only so far as to send someone in her stead to ensure the safety of his investment.

Had the girl ever known a good life?

MacKenzie loomed over Delilah.

She kicked hard at his shins with all her might and sent him crashing to the floor at her side. He sat up with a groan and rolled over onto her.

His hair stood up in all directions, and his eyes were wild and dark. "Ye stupid bitch. I'll kill ye for that."

He jerked something from his waist and a dagger glinted in the moonlight streaming in through the open shutters. Delilah wanted to put her arm up to block him, but her left one was too weak, and her right completely immobile.

She tried to turn away, but there was nowhere to go.

Nowhere but death.

MacKenzie's eyes widened and near bulged from his head. The breath hissed from him in a low groan and his body sagged forward on top of her.

Delilah blinked, her brain rattling with confusion for a split second before a heavy body collapsed beside her and a hand slid into hers.

Warm and tender, and wet with the blood of her attacker.

Her heart swelled into her throat. She could only lie there and cry while holding tight to Kaid's hand until they were both inevitably claimed by death.

Chapter Thirty-Five

"I taught you better than to lay around." The hard voice pulled Delilah from the fog of sleep. "You'd better not be dead."

Sylvi?

The heavy press of weight over Delilah's chest lifted and air flowed into her lungs so much easier and cleaner than before.

Delilah squinted.

Sylvi stared down at her without speaking for a long moment. "You're alive."

Emotion clogged Sylvi's voice and Delilah knew her friend was crying.

The hand in Delilah's was still warm. "Kaid?" she whispered.

A breeze swept over Delilah, scented sweetly of violets and herbs.

"He's alive," Percy said in her gentle voice. "But only barely. I need light so I can see his wounds."

Two large shadows entered the room. Kaid did not make a sound when they lifted him from her side, but his fingers remained clasped in hers.

Percy tried to pull Delilah's grip away. "You have to let him go."

"I can't." Delilah's throat was so tight, she could scarce breathe, let alone talk. "I love him."

"Then let me save him," Percy said.

Delilah pulled her hand from his and let the men take him. It wasn't until he was gone another sharp thought pricked her mind. "Claire." She tried to sit up, but Sylvi shushed her.

"She's fine," she said. "Liv found her. The girl was frightened, but unharmed. If it weren't for her, Percy would have still been in the forest and not summoned here as quickly as she was to help."

Delilah rose on her shaking left arm despite Sylvi's protests and sat upright. "Help me up. I want to see her."

"Like hell you will." Sylvi gave a throaty laugh. "Not until you're cleaned up. You'll scare the poor girl."

Only then did Delilah look down at herself, at the gashes of blood showing through her clothing. Not just on her hip and arm, but all over. Some of it hers, most of it likely Seumas's.

It all slammed into Delilah like a hammer. Kaid's stillness as he lay beside her with his hand locked on hers, Claire's fearful cries when Delilah was trying to get her to be strong, the way Elizabeth lay crumpled in death, unloved and forgotten.

Sobs choked from her chest and Sylvi held her in a comforting embrace Delilah hadn't known the woman was capable of offering. It was there, clinging onto the support of her friend, that Delilah finally succumbed to the darkness.

She didn't awaken again until many hours later, after the darkness of night had given way to the sharp light of late afternoon. It wasn't until after her eyes adjusted to the brilliance of the sun that she realized she was in a large chamber. Aside from the massive bed she lay upon, there was no additional furniture in the room or even tapestries on the wall.

Only then did she remember Edirdovar Castle.

And Claire.

And Kaid.

She turned to her side. A burning pain pulled tight at her skin, but the injury was worth it.

There, lying beside her, was Kaid. His face was pale still, but he was alive.

Her eyes stung with tears and blurred his sleeping form.

"Kaid." She reached out and touched his face. The two days' growth of his dark beard rasped against her fingertips and made her want to rub her cheek against it for the familiar, wonderful sensation.

His brow puckered and his eyes opened, as vividly blue and

beautiful as always, lit with intelligence and kindness and the emotion which only shows when a man really and truly loves a woman.

"Delilah." He said her name with the same wonder as she'd spoken his. "I thought—"

She shook her head. "I'm alive, thanks to you. Kaid, you saved me." Tears clogged her throat, but she continued. "You restored Torra to her land and you kept our Claire safe. You've saved your people, Kaid. You did it all."

"I couldna have done it without ye, lass. Ye were so brave defending our Claire—" He stopped short and jerked his gaze around the room.

"Claire?" He almost half shouted her name and sat up with a heavy grimace. "Claire!"

Delilah eased herself into a sitting position as well despite the searing discomfort which made the simple act difficult. "She's safe. She—"

The doors to the chamber flew open and Claire ran through with Liv chasing behind her.

"Delilah," Claire cried. "Laird." She scrambled onto the large bed and crawled into their arms, leaving an exasperated Liv staring after her.

"I've tried to keep her from coming in here all day." Liv twisted a thick mass of red hair back from her flushed face. "She has been very insistent."

Claire caught Delilah's face between her palms and stared at her so closely her eyes appeared crossed. "I missed ye." She kissed Delilah on the forehead, then promptly turned to Kaid and repeated the gesture.

Liv caught Delilah's gaze, and they shared a smile. Liv quietly quit the room and closed the door behind her, leaving the reunion to continue in private.

Claire grasped Kaid's arm and drew it over her like a blanket, then curled into Delilah's arms with her sweet, silky head resting just under Delilah's chin.

"This is how it should be," Kaid said. "Us together as a family."

He put an arm around Delilah and the girl. "Claire, we would be honored to raise ye as our daughter, if ye'll have us."

She sat up and stared at them both. Her mouth opened and closed, then opened once more, but nothing came out. Tears shimmered in her eyes, and she could only nod before she threw herself against them both.

Her slight body was uncomfortable against Delilah's injuries, but Delilah paid them no mind. Not when she had Claire safe in her arms and Kaid alive at her side.

"And ye, Delilah." Kaid touched her hand with his free arm. "Ye know I love ye. For yer heart, and yer beauty, and yer bravery, and for the amazing talent ye possess. I'd be honored to be yer husband, if ye'll have me."

Delilah swallowed the knot in her throat. How could she say no?

And it was all as he'd said it would be. He was truly making them, their small group of the orphaned and unwanted, a family.

"Yes," she answered in the exhale of a breath she didn't know she was holding. "A thousand times yes."

She leaned over and kissed the familiar warmth of his mouth. The rasp of his whiskers grazed her chin and left her smiling.

This was how life should be. She wrapped her free arm around Claire and settled back with her shoulders touching Kaid's.

Her risk had been worth it for the love of her beautiful new family.

• • •

Kaid looked out over the faces of his clan from where he waited with more impatience than was customary even for him. The pastor was a gangly lad with a thatch of thick dark hair atop his narrow head and a grin Kaid probably couldn't wipe off his face if he tried.

Finally the doors to the chapel opened and Delilah strode in wearing a gown of deep blue. The silver edge winked and danced along her hem and sleeves the way the stars sparkled in the heavens.

Kaid stared, awestruck. She caught his eye and beamed so wide, he knew her joy to be entirely genuine.

Claire eased around Delilah's long skirts and danced down the aisle toward him, scattering bits of herbs on the ground. Several chuckles rose from the audience at the sweet innocence of her excitement. Claire grabbed Kaid's hand and pulled him down to her.

He leaned lower, not taking his eyes off the woman who was about to become his wife.

"She looks like an angel," Claire whisper-shouted into his ear.

The congregation laughed aloud this time, and even Delilah laughed along with them.

When at last she joined him at his side, he could scarce take his gaze from her. The pastor gave him a phrase to repeat.

And repeat it, Kaid did—anything to secure Delilah as his wife. But he couldn't remember what he'd said, nor what she'd spoken in turn.

He was sure the pastor had grinned his goofy smile, and Claire had danced around like a happy flower bobbing in the sunshine, but he didn't truly notice any of it.

All he could remember was how Delilah's hair fell around her shoulders in waves of beautiful honey brown, and how her full lips curved into a smile of bliss when she spoke. And how the depths of her soul and all her love showed in her warm brown gaze.

At long last, the ceremony had ended, and he claimed his bride's beautiful mouth in a long, slow kiss to proudly proclaim to all that she was truly his.

The kiss elicited a few cheers, which he gladly encouraged.

Torra sat in the front row, watching with her hands folded over her heart and a whimsical grin on her lips. Donnan sat near her with a grin so wide it near split his face. Leasa was at his side, watching the exchange with tears shimmering on her cheeks.

The only thing which might have made the day mean more was if Delilah's friends had stayed. But after Percy was no longer needed for her assistance in healing, Sylvi had packed up Percy, Isabel, and Liv with her wee cat and set off for London.

Sylvi insisted they return Elizabeth's body to her father. MacKenzie had been such a greedy bastard, he'd already written to her father days prior asking for her dowry since they were already wed. The women would not be faulted for Elizabeth's death.

Deep down, Kaid was glad Delilah did not need to go with them for the task. She already carried enough guilt over the woman's death, even though Sylvi had assured her the fault was not hers.

Claire turned toward them and grasped both Kaid's and Delilah's hands in her small warm ones. "Are ye happy?" she asked.

Delilah gave him a beautiful look of joy which sent bliss straight into his heart. "Aye, lass." He glanced down at Claire. "Are ye happy?"

She loosed a long sigh. "Ach, aye, I've an angel and a da all in one day."

Kaid and Delilah laughed together, and both caught Claire in a shared hug.

Nothing could be more perfect.

He'd earned the trust of his clan, he had a beautiful, amazing woman at his side, there was peace in his land, and he had a family to love.

Kaid's life, as a laird and as a man, was truly and utterly complete.

Acknowledgments

I am so very fortunate to have so many supportive people in my life. Thank you to my agent, Laura Bradford, for always providing such wonderful guidance. Thank you to Jaime Levine and Eliza Kirby for their work in editing *Highland Ruse*, to Erin Mitchell for all her hard work in getting *Highland Ruse* out there for everyone to see, and to the rest of the staff at Diversion Books who have been integral in getting *Highland Ruse* out there for people to read.

Thank you so very much to my beta readers: Kacy Rozier, Karen Archer, Alli Preslar, Liette Bougie, and Carin Farrenholz for their help in making this book the best it can be.

Thank you to my Marvelous Ladies who are always there to help me come up with a good title, iron out plot details, promote my sales, and share in my exciting news. We are a close group of women who share a lot and have a ton of fun doing it. I feel so very fortunate to have all of you in my life.

Thank you to my wonderful family—to my dad who is always supportive and ready to tell people about his daughter who writes historical romance novels, to my mom who is always my biggest fan and my final proofreader, to my brother and sister-in-law who always support and love me. And a huge thank you to Mr. Awesome for all the times he's stepped up to help out with the minions so I can hit a deadline or attend a conference. Thank you to the minions for always being so eager to tell people their mom is an author and to try my books—thank you for your unending love and support.

And a mega huge thank you to all my readers, because you are the key that makes writing absolutely magical. I appreciate all the hours you've spent reading my books and the effort you've put into the reviews you've left for me. Thank you for giving my stories voice and purpose.

MADELINE MARTIN is a *USA Today* bestselling author of Scottish-set historical romance novels. She lives in Jacksonville, Florida with her two daughters (AKA OldestMinion and YoungestMinion) along with a man so wonderful, he can only be called Mr. Awesome. All shenanigans are detailed regularly on Twitter and on Facebook.

Her hobbies include rock climbing, running, doing crazy races (like Mud Runs and Color Runs), and just about anything exciting she can do without getting nauseous. She's also a history fan after having lived in Europe for over a decade, and enjoys traveling overseas whenever she can.

Madeline loves to hear from her readers. You may find various ways to connect with her and find more information on her at: **www.MadelineMartin.com**

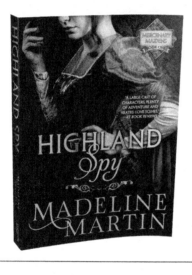

CPSIA information can be obtained
at www.ICGtesting.com
Printed in the USA
BVOW03s1917290917
496276BV00002B/2/P